Ordinary Time

Ordinary Time

CATHY RENTZENBRINK

PHOENIX

First published in Great Britain in 2024 by Phoenix Books,
an imprint of The Orion Publishing Group Ltd
Carmelite House, 50 Victoria Embankment
London EC4Y 0DZ

An Hachette UK Company

3 5 7 9 10 8 6 4 2

A CIP catalogue record for this book is
available from the British Library.

ISBN (Hardback) 978 1 4746 2117 5
ISBN (Export Trade Paperback) 978 1 4746 2118 2
ISBN (eBook) 978 1 4746 2120 5
ISBN (Audio) 978 1 4746 2121 2

Typeset by Input Data Services Ltd, Bridgwater, Somerset

Printed in Great Britain by Clays Ltd, Elcograf, S.p.A.

MIX
Paper | Supporting
responsible forestry
FSC® C104740

www.orionbooks.co.uk

Every heart has its own skeletons, as the English say.
Anna Karenina

Last night I dreamt I was watching a woman on a train. She had a book in her lap but was looking out of the window towards the sea. There was tension in her shoulders, a tight grip in the hand that held the book. I willed her to turn around. I wanted to see her face. Did I need to help her? And then the air between us dissolved, and I realised the woman was me.

I might have looked like I was staring out of the window, but I wasn't appreciating the blues of the sea and the sky, or watching the distant people on the beach. All I could think of was the moment when I'd arrive at the station and he'd be there waiting for me.

I'd breathe him in and get into his car, and we'd drive off together. And I needed time to slow down then, because I couldn't bear that there would come a point when he would take me back to the station, and I would get on another train and return to a life I no longer wanted to inhabit.

'How did you end up here?' he asked, before I had crossed any lines, back when I still hoped that the quickening I felt when I saw him could be put down to an innocent pleasure in making a new friend. We were sitting on a bench outside the church, the shadow of the monkey puzzle tree falling across his face.

'It's a long story,' I said.

He smiled down at me. 'We've got plenty of time.'

Cornwall, June 2019

One

I rinse the last plate, put it on the draining board and look out of the window. There are two enormous seagulls strutting down the garden path and a magpie sitting in the tree staring at me. *One for sorrow*, I think, and am immediately annoyed because I remind myself of my mother and I hate it when that happens.

Tim comes in. He is wearing his dog collar.

'Look,' I say, pointing at the magpie. 'All that black and white you're wearing. You could be the magpie's friend. Arrived in the nick of time.'

He looks confused.

'One for sorrow,' I say. 'Magpies are bad luck on their own. You need two for joy.'

'Oh,' Tim says, 'superstition.'

I wonder if I should try to explain that it was a joke but can't be bothered. The closer Tim gets to God, the less he has a sense of humour.

'I've got to get over to the hospital,' he says. 'Lillian Holt collapsed this morning. They think she's fractured her skull.'

'Poor Mrs Holt,' I say. 'Where was she?'

'In the garden. With her daughter. One minute she was talking about her salvias and the next she was on the ground. She's asking for me. Her daughter says she's got something on her mind.' He looks at his watch. 'Can I have some water?'

I turn on the tap, fill a glass. He takes it, and I see the movement in his throat as he swallows. His mind is already at the hospital with Mrs Holt. Tim likes a crisis. And who could turn down being spiritually necessary in the face of death? He hands me the empty glass.

'Will you be back for school pick-up?'

He looks at his watch again. 'Hard to leave a death-bed.'

'I can do it,' I say, 'don't worry.'

Not that Tim is worrying. It was his idea to collect Sam on Wednesdays so they could have some quality time together, but it rarely happens. Too many situations are hard to leave, and Tim's well-meant intention to spend time with his family collapses under the weight of the demands of his congregation. I need to get a job, really, as that is the only way he will respect my time, but if I mention it, he purses his lips and I can see he still thinks it is too soon. He doesn't want to lose access to my tap-turning-on abilities until he is more settled into this new parish.

He leaves without saying goodbye. I rinse the glass under the tap and put it on the draining board. Then I pick it up again and replay the moment when Tim asked for water and I gave it to him. What was the point of me in that interaction? A moving part, but less essential than either the tap or the glass. I could be replaced by a robot. Or Tim could just do it himself.

This is my life. All day, every day. Filling cups and plates, and then cleaning them so they are ready for when Tim and Sam need to be replenished. I look out of the window. The seagulls have gone. The magpie is still in the tree. How strange that the whole of the human race cannot tolerate its single status and wants it to couple up. *Don't do it*, I whisper. *Stay free*. It stares back at me. Then, almost a wink, or a grin, and there is a flash of iridescent blue as it flies off.

Two

Sometimes I think I could write an instruction manual on how to be a vicar's wife. Or a survival guide, because I couldn't tell you how to do it well, but I could share what I've learnt about how to keep just on the right side of the line between adequate and disappointing.

I was given some advice on my wedding day from Janet, the wife of the vicar who married us. She was a kindly woman whose father had also been a vicar. 'You could say I was born to it,' she said, and then, when I confessed to being a little apprehensive about how I would shape up: 'All you really need to do is be yourself.'

I had a go at that but I can't say it went well, and over time I constructed a more suitable persona. Now I couldn't be myself if I tried, because I no longer have much of an idea of who I am.

I often think of her, Janet. *Born to it*. Perhaps we could go as far as to say it was her destiny to exchange a father for a husband and continue on her path of service. Not like me. I am an accidental vicar's wife.

It all started on a cold but sunny January afternoon, the day after my thirtieth birthday. I had been running the book club at the homeless centre. Usually my friend and colleague Sarah came with me, but she cried off at the last minute. She was lying on the sofa in the staffroom at the library, with a tea towel pressed against her head. 'I'm fit for nothing today but alphabetising the romance section. Go on your own. You might get off with the sexy vicar.'

We'd seen Tim a few times. He was tall and good-looking in an earnest way. He was always being helpful, carrying boxes or moving furniture or dishing out soup. Sarah liked to tease that he had a crush on me. She'd poke me in the ribs and whisper, 'Palpable sexual chemistry,' when he walked by.

She was just having fun, I thought, but when I almost bumped into him as I was leaving, I did think there was a warmth in his manner.

'On your own?' he asked.

'Sarah's a bit hungover,' I said. 'She was enthusiastically celebrating my birthday last night.'

'Many happy returns.'

'I should give up trying to mark it,' I said. 'No one ever wants to go out in January.'

'I've never been much of a drinker,' he said.

'I suppose that's good. Keeps you off the communion wine. I went to a Catholic school and the altar boys were always squiffy.'

I was aware I was babbling.

'You're a Catholic?' he asked.

'No, it was just the nearest school. My dad was, but very lapsed. He hated religion, said that confession was an excuse for the priest to know everyone's business.' It occurred to me that might not be tactful. 'You're not Catholic, are you?'

'No,' he said. 'I don't take confession. For any motive.'

'I'm afraid I'm not anything, religion-wise. Do you get that a lot? Is it a professional hazard? People apologising to you personally because they don't have a faith?'

'If people are talking to me, it's often because they are a bit more interested than they think they are.'

'A subconscious yearning?' I said, thinking this was all a bit much.

'Maybe. Do you ever go to church?'

'I don't.' I remember that precisely. Can picture him standing there in the gateway in his dog collar, wearing a multi-coloured striped scarf that looked like it had been knitted by hand, but not very well. The sun was in my eyes as I squinted up at him. 'I did sometimes envy them, the Anglican girls in their christening bracelets and the Catholics with their confirmation dresses. And I was always jealous of my friend Kitty, who'd miss most of double maths when the priest came to hear confession.'

Tim took a card and a pencil from the inside pocket of his jacket and wrote on the back. 'Ten thirty,' he said, 'this Sunday. Why don't you give me a try?'

As he walked off, leaving me there holding the card, I wondered if I'd misheard him. Did he really say, 'give me a try' and not, 'give it a try'? Was I imagining the – not exactly flirtatious, that was to overstate it – but the undercurrent of attraction. Just a bat squeak, nothing inappropriate, but something?

I went back to work. I didn't tell Sarah. Perhaps he invited everyone he ever met to come to church. That was what they were supposed to do, wasn't it, vicars? They were supposed to grow their flocks.

It was ridiculous to even think about it, but he had all his own hair and teeth and was obviously committed to doing good in the world. That was what I kept saying I wanted; a respectable boyfriend who might turn into the father of my children. I had started to despair of meeting anyone. Attractive single men didn't come into the library, and I knew it wasn't a good idea to encourage the over-familiar dad who made eyes at me when he brought his little boy to Rhyme Time. I'd tried internet dating, but the best that could be said was that it provided material for anecdotes. Whether in real life or online, I attracted what my brother Stephen referred to as 'ageing crooks'. Which was a bit harsh but not hugely inaccurate. Stephen gave them all nicknames to his own template. TFC was That Flash Cunt. TMC was That Married Cunt. Because yes, to my great shame, I'd allowed myself to be what my mother would have called 'a bit on the side' to a man I occasionally met in a hotel room and who didn't turn the TV off when we had sex.

So, I needed a radical change. Sarah had been reading a self-help book that suggested we should do something new every day, and all I'd managed so far was to once get an almond rather than a chocolate croissant on my way to work. I decided to go for it. I paid some attention to my appearance. I washed my hair and put on make-up, just powder and blusher and a flick of mascara and a swoosh of tinted lip salve. And I thought how my mother would say, 'It's not a fashion parade,' as I chose a white blouse under a blue pinafore. Green beret, red scarf, black gloves. I nodded at myself in the mirror as I left.

On the bus to the church, I looked at his card, at the neat yet confident handwriting. Next to the time he had added 'Do come!' and there was something about the exclamation mark that I found endearing. I was too early and walked up and down outside to the sound of church bells, questioning why I was there at all. I nearly ran away, but when other people started to arrive I sneaked in and sat at the back, because I didn't know when to stand and when to sit so would have to copy everyone else.

I liked the atmosphere, the smell, and the hush sitting beneath the bells. And Tim looked different. I was used to the dog collar but surprised by his robes. Did he look silly? A little, but I admired his presence and liked the way he scanned the church and almost jumped when he saw me. And when it was time for communion, he explained – as though it were for me – that you had to be confirmed to take communion, but that you could come forward for a blessing; 'just keep your hands down'.

I didn't move. I stayed at the back as all the other people shuffled out of the pews and went to the front to kneel by the rail. Tim walked along giving them the body of Christ, and I watched his face, and their faces as they walked back, and there was something beautiful about it, happening in the glow of the light coming in through the stained-glass windows throwing patterns onto the stone floor. I regretted the mascara, but how could I have guessed that I would cry? And at the end, when he told us all to go in peace to love and serve the Lord, and I walked out of the huge church doors, he said, 'I'm glad you came,' and, 'Do you have to rush off?'

We went to a cafe around the corner. He'd swapped the robes for a jacket and was wearing the stripy scarf. We took our large cups of tea to a table in the corner with a red-and-white checked cloth.

'Nice scarf,' I said, as he hung it over the edge of his chair.

'A present,' he said, proudly. 'One of my recently widowed parishioners has taken up knitting to help her pass the time. This was the first thing she made.'

I waited for him to add that he knew it was a bit peculiar, but he didn't. He just looked pleased that this woman had given him the first fruits of her grief-knitting.

'Tell me about yourself,' he said.

I struck a pose, as if I was on a dating show. 'My name is Ann Barry. I'm thirty and I'm a librarian.'

Tim didn't laugh or reply in kind, just asked me to tell him more about what I did at the homeless shelter. 'You run a book club?'

'We're trying to go out into the community more. Not just wait behind the counter for readers to come to us.'

He nodded enthusiastically. 'A sense of mission.'

'It's a reverse book club. Rather than discuss something everyone has read, we talk about a book, and then they can go off and read it if they like.'

He was really listening to me. Such a change from all those men who glazed over whenever I said anything about myself. I explained how a conventional book club could be more challenging for people who might not have a lot of stability in their lives, and how satisfying I found it to empower reluctant readers to the point where they felt they belonged in the world of books. Yes, I had always loved reading, was the sort of kid whose favourite treat was a trip to the library.

Tim asked about my family.

'I've got a brother called Stephen,' I said. 'A year younger than me. Our mother lives in Somerset.' And then I hesitated. I traced the checks on the tablecloth with my finger. I'd never found a way to talk about my father that didn't make me want to throw up. I didn't find it easy with anyone, but it was especially horrible in any kind of dating situation. I loathed the way I couldn't help but pay attention to the reaction I'd get, the possibility that I might be pouring my heart out to someone who looked bored or like they were thinking I was a bit much. I didn't want Dad to become a story I had to tell in an appealing way, so I'd developed a strategy of dodging my way past any enquiries, trusting that the right person would forgive me if the relationship lasted long enough for us to get to the truth. I looked across at Tim's open face, glanced down at his dog collar. I didn't want to tell even a white lie.

'My father died when I was fifteen,' I said.

'I'm sorry.'

I did feel sick, but I ploughed on. 'He was walking home from the pub. There was this bridge over the railway line. He ended up on the track.' I could feel the tears spilling down my face. I shouldn't have tried to say it. I'd never been able to say it without losing control. 'Sorry. I still miss him.'

Tim reached over the table, put his hand on mine.

'You're not running away,' I said.

'Why would I run away?'

'People do,' I said. 'Men do. Men don't like an unhappy woman.'

'I don't mind you crying,' he said, and patted my hand some more.

Later, as we walked along the canal watching dufflecoated children feeding the swans, Tim told me he'd been on a course where they said that bereavement by suicide could feel like grief with the volume turned up. I nodded and said that over the years I hadn't in any way 'got over it' but that it had settled into a background hum; always there, sometimes faint, often loud. After reading an article about fathers who had just disappeared – one had gone out for a pack of cigarettes and never come back – I'd tried to be grateful that we did at least know Dad was dead. I might have screwed my life up even more if I'd been hoping that he might walk through the door. And I'd chosen to try to believe it was an accident, though Stephen thought he'd done it on purpose because he'd lost his money and couldn't cope with the shame.

'Another thing I learnt,' Tim said, kindly, 'is that it isn't always helpful to try to put a reason to the action. Only the person who died could know why they found it impossible to live.'

'I should pass that on to Stephen,' I said. 'Not that we talk about it. We are close, but when it comes to Dad or our childhood, it's like we're tiptoeing over a battlefield full of mines and traps.'

We walked in silence for a while and then crossed over a bridge. Tim stopped in the middle and leant against the railing, looking down at the canal. He said he was an only child, that he'd never been close to his parents, who had sent him away to school when he was eight. He'd been fifteen, too, when his mother died of cancer. 'My father remarried and moved to France. He's an atheist. He didn't come to my ordination. I haven't seen him for years.'

I hardly knew what to respond to first from the bleak list of facts. Tim was still looking down. I considered putting my hand on his arm, but that wasn't quite right.

'Look,' I said, and I pointed below to our reflections. 'There we are. See how the colours of your scarf wobble in the water.'

'There we are,' he repeated, with a note of surprise in his voice.

When it started to get dark, he said he must be getting back to take Evensong. As he walked me to the bus stop, he said, 'We carry the gifts and burdens of our upbringing. We must believe that we will do better when it is our turn.' I felt something unfamiliar and wondered if it might be hope.

The next day, at work, I did a keyword search on vicars and then spent my lunchtime reading Joanna Trollope. There was another book called *Married to the Ministry*. I flicked through; it was full of women complaining about their husbands not being at home enough.

On Friday, Sarah popped her head around the staffroom door. 'Your vicar is here.'

'He's not my vicar.'

'It's sweet. He's pretending to browse, but he's obviously looking for you. Go and put him out of his misery.'

'Should I?'

'What's the worst that can happen?'

Over the next few weeks, I remade myself in the image of the woman I thought Tim wanted. I stopped smoking, cut right down on drinking, stopped bothering with make-up. I went to church on Sundays, learning when to sit and stand. At work, I no longer walked straight by the religion section but would stop, pull a book off the shelf randomly, and open it, looking for guidance. One day I read Martin Luther's opinion that there is no more lovely, friendly or charming relationship than a good marriage.

'Are you sure about all this?' Sarah asked, after I refused a drink because I was going to bible study group. 'You're changing a lot about yourself. Is it a good idea?'

'I've been trying life another way,' I said. 'I never want to be a bit on the side again.'

The next time Stephen phoned, I told him I'd met someone.

'Not married, is he? Tell me he's rich. Or at least useful. Can he climb a ladder and hold a drill?'

'He's a vicar.'

'What am I going to call him. TVC? I'm not sure it really works.'

'Don't give him a nickname,' I said.

'It's like that, is it?'

'Yes, it is.'

It was a relief not to be hanging around with someone who was easy fodder for Stephen's ridicule, and the more Tim talked about his sense of purpose and his desire to be in service to others, the more I liked him. What a contrast, I thought, from feeling like a man was using me to tick things off a sexual to-do list, only biding his time before suggesting a threesome. How magnificent that I would no longer end up doing things I didn't want, or pretending to be a good sport to retain the interest of men I didn't even like. Wholesome is how it was, how I thought it would be in the future. That was what I wanted.

'So, do you believe in God now?' Sarah asked one day, as we were processing the reservations.

'I'm not sure,' I said. 'Tim says that's fine. Doubt is part of faith.'

'And have you actually shagged him?'

'Don't be vulgar.' I lifted a stack of large print Georgette Heyers out of the crate.

'So you haven't.'

'He doesn't believe in sex before marriage.'

'Bloody hell.'

'Nor did Georgette,' I said. 'None of these heroines were putting out before the wedding bells.'

On Easter Sunday, I sat near the front as Tim preached about the resurrection. He talked about how just when all seemed lost, hope could burst into the world, that whatever hurt or pain we'd been through, there was always the chance of starting again. 'With God,' he said, 'we can begin afresh, with a clean slate.'

Tim was radiant that day. The vocabulary was still unfamiliar – I didn't feel comfortable using words like 'God' or 'blessing' – but it did feel that Tim had come into my life to change it, and that everything was somehow meant to be.

That evening he took a green box from his pocket. 'These belonged to my mother,' he said. 'I'd like for you to have them.'

I fumbled with the clasp, and when I finally got it open I saw two rings sitting side by side.

I waited for Tim to say more.

'See if they fit.'

I hesitated over which finger. Was this a proposal? I didn't want to assume.

'Your left hand,' he said, but not romantically, just like I might not know the form.

They slid on easily.

'Keep that one,' Tim said, when I went to take them off.

Our fingers touched as I gave him back the wedding band.

'I'll write to the bishop,' Tim said, slipping the box into his pocket.

Back at the library the next week, I held my left hand out to Sarah. She admired the twinkle of the sapphire surrounded by all the little diamonds. 'Very pretty. You'll be the first woman to have not had sex with her bridegroom since Princess Diana.'

'Bit quick, isn't it?' Stephen said, when I called him to say we were getting married.

'Tim doesn't want to live in sin.'

'Does that mean you haven't had sex with him?'

'None of your business.'

'He doesn't think you're a virgin, does he?'

'Fuck off.'

'You'll have to mind your language once you're a vicar's wife. I can't believe you're marrying someone I haven't met. What's he like?'

'Believes in God. Doesn't drink, smoke, swear. Good at maths. He was an accountant before he became a vicar, but his heart wasn't in it.'

'Bet he earned more. Don't make much, vicars, do they?'

'Money isn't everything,' I said.

'Whatever,' Stephen said. 'What am I going to talk to him about? Does he like football? Cars?'

'Don't think so. You'll have to extend your conversational repertoire. Will you give me away? We're short on relatives generally. Tim's mother is dead and his father won't set foot in a church.'

'Bit extreme.'

'He thinks believing in God is evidence of an inferior intellect. He gave Tim his mother's rings for me, but that's as far as he'll go. All we've got between us is Mum and you.'

'I'll step up to the plate,' Stephen said. 'And I won't swear or tell any "as the actress said to the bishop" jokes. Can I pay for something? I just got a bonus and I'm flush.'

I was glad we were on the phone then, so he couldn't see my eyes fill up. That was how Dad would give us money. 'I'm flush,' he'd say, keen to share his good fortune.

'We're not having a fancy wedding,' I said, 'just a church service. I don't know what we'll do afterwards.'

'Let me host a meal, then. They call it a wedding breakfast, don't they? You tell me what time and how many guests, and I'll do everything else.'

There was a moment, at the church door, when I hesitated, but I thought it was more about missing Dad than not feeling sure. Stephen winked and gave me his arm, and we walked up the aisle together. I said my vows and meant every word, though it did strike me that 'until death us do part' might mean a very long time.

Stephen had booked an Italian restaurant. He was charming with all the church people and made a sweet and appropriately funny speech. Tim did a good job, too, though there was a hefty whiff of the pulpit and he gave star billing to God. I saw Stephen and Sarah exchange a look. Then I ate my tiramisu, chatting to Janet, who said she was a bit giggly as she'd allowed Stephen to tempt her into a second glass of Prosecco. It was then that she told me all I ever had to do as the wife of a vicar was be myself. I looked at her kind face, rosy-cheeked, and hoped all would be well.

'Do you feel like Madonna?' Stephen whispered as we said goodbye, and, when I didn't answer: 'Shiny and new? Touched for the very first time?' And I punched him on the arm, and he shoved me and we both laughed, and everyone said how nice it was that we got on so well. Then Tim and I left them all there in the restaurant and went off to the hotel.

I wasn't wearing a big white wedding dress but a cream silk shift. Tim lifted it over my head, folded it, and put it on the armchair next to the bed. Then he fumbled with my bra. 'I can't do this,' he said, crossly, which I chose to find endearing. He was still wearing his dog collar. I put my hand up to it, but he caught it in his. Then, somehow, we were undressing separately and scrambling into the bed. We lay there a bit, both on our backs. At least he hadn't turned the TV on. I wished I'd had more to drink. This would be the soberest I'd ever been for first-time sex. I considered telling that to Tim and then decided against it. He might not see the funny side.

Stephen phoned me the week after my wedding. 'Wotcha, Sis. I liked Sarah. Do you mind if I ask her out? Does it matter she's your colleague?'

'Not at all,' I said. 'She wants to leave anyway. She only really likes self-help books.'

'She knows about us, doesn't she?'

'What do you mean?'

'Dad. Us being mental.'

'I've told her a few things over the years.'

'Excellent. I should have thought of going out with your friends years ago. They're prepped.'

And that is how I got married, and my two favourite people fell in love with each other. Sarah is now Stephen's wife before she is my friend, though she is still that and I am grateful, because I have no others from my former life. They were all freaked out by Tim or didn't like the sober version of me. There is little point in being sad about it, so I try not to dwell on my friend Sally, who came for dinner but left early after Tim spent the evening lecturing her about the evils of her job in advertising. I walked her to the bus stop. 'He's a bit intense, but he really is concerned about people getting into debt buying stuff they don't need.'

'He's entitled to his opinion,' Sally said, 'and I don't much care about that. What I can't stand is the way he sits around as you serve him like some kind of hand-maiden. He's not even that nice to you.'

'He's a good person,' I said, 'he's just got his mind on higher things.'

'That stops him saying thank you for his lasagne, does it?'

'He says Grace.'

'He thanks God for his bounty but doesn't bother with you. That doesn't feel right to me.'

And she gave me a short fierce hug and never came around again.

Three

Do I have to tell it all? Track my disillusionment step by sorry step? I'm not sure I could. Sometimes I lie awake in the night listening to Tim snore, trying to figure out what went wrong. Where did he go, that kind man wearing the silly scarf? It's a mystery I can't fully solve.

Now I think it wasn't a first date, that day in the cafe, but a job interview. Tim wanted a junior disciple rather than a wife. He'd seen me looking cheerful among the needy at the homeless centre and thought I'd fit the bill. But we were at cross purposes from the start, because I'm not a particularly good person and not at all self-sacrificing. I just genuinely loved doing the book club and was always moved and humbled by the people who came to it. Tim thought this would apply to all church activity, that I would bring my shining eyes wherever people needed support, so was confused and disappoint-ed when I turned out to be a reluctant helpmate who would always rather read in the bath than tag along on his current mission of mercy. He wanted a selfless do-gooder and ended up with an eccentric bookworm. And I wanted to be loved for myself but got a man who gives most of his heart to God. There are three of us in this marriage, and I am definitely the least important.

I'd find it all easier with a bit of laughter and chat, but Tim is almost always in a bad mood. To be fair to him, it *is* hard being a vicar. There's a lot to do and not enough time to do it in. And it's not just about looking after souls. Vicars are also property managers, health and safety officers, and feel under pressure to do marketing, fundraising and social media, trying to grow the congregation while keeping the current lot happy. Tim wants to minister to those who are most in need, not stroke the egos of people who don't have enough real problems to worry about. He's grumpy about weddings. He bans photos during the vows and still says, 'We don't want to be distracted by clicks,' even though everyone uses a silent smartphone now. He used to prefer funerals and would come home full of pride that he'd delivered a meaningful send-off, but now he is more likely to be aggravated by the increased use of technology and the resulting glitches; slideshows that won't load, malfunctioning speakers, playlists that get interrupted by adverts. He doesn't have much of a sense of humour – his one joke is to say, 'Let's not throw the baby out with the baptism water.' He's not tactful and lacks the ability to smooth things over, so gets bogged down in all the squabbling among the volunteers. And there are always quarrels over the flower-arranging rota, or how often to allow visiting bell ringers, or whether the various suppers should be hot or cold, or who is making the sausage rolls for the endless fundraising teas.

My biggest mistake was to assume that someone doing so much for their fellow man must be full of love for humanity. But Tim isn't. He wants to save souls and improve lives, but he finds actual flesh-and-blood people a bit challenging. He only really loves God.

Assumption, as Stephen likes to say, is the mother of all fuck-ups. You might be wondering why I stayed. I do too. I don't especially believe in marriage, even. All through my childhood, my mother was threatening to leave my father – it got to the point where I wished she'd get on with it. My best friend, Kitty, also had parents who looked as if they would be better off apart. But there is a peculiar power to a marriage. In the early days, I felt like I'd gone all in, put all my money on the black of Tim's cassock. I didn't want to admit that I'd made a mistake, didn't want to cope with Stephen or Sarah being kind but smug. I could imagine Stephen saying he knew it was too soon, could hear Sarah quoting from some book about why women do foolish things in the name of love. And I dreaded being on the receiving end of my mother's opinions, which were already loud and clear in my ears: *Well, I knew it wouldn't last . . . You never stick at anything . . . You'll have to get a move on finding another man if you want to have a baby.*

I did want a baby. A family. And Tim meant well. Was it fair to him to chuck it in because he wasn't a laugh a minute? Perhaps it was my expectations that were too high. I still thought he would be a good father. I could imagine us with two little boys, walking down the street in our family unit of four. And I wanted that, those tiny hands in mine. So I decided it didn't matter very much that being with Tim didn't feel a lot like love. Maybe it would all work out. And I would have my boys. He would give me my boys.

I would love them equally, I knew that. I wouldn't be like my mother. It was never much of a secret, her preference for Stephen. Even my name felt like she couldn't be bothered to make much of an effort. Ann with no 'e', and no middle name. So sparse! I did once ask her why Stephen had a middle name and I didn't. She gave me a look and said, 'Least said, soonest mended,' which was one of her favourite expressions. 'That's not for little ears,' was another, and, 'What you don't know won't hurt you.'

Then we heard her admit it one day: to Mrs Kelly, another English woman who had married an Irishman and regretted it. 'Ann is difficult,' she said, 'always has been. Stephen, though. I love the bones of him.' And I felt Stephen clutch me, his breath against my cheek. My face was burning. By the time Mrs Kelly had gone, I had decided to pretend not to care. We ran into the garden and I tried not to catch Stephen's eye.

Later that night, he sneaked into my room after lights out. He often did this, as we liked to tell each other stories and we knew he'd get off more lightly than I would if Mum caught us out of bed.

'You're not difficult,' Stephen whispered through the darkness. 'I love you best. I love the bones of you.'

28

Stephen. My little brother. Eleven months younger than me. Irish twins. We looked after each other through the turbulent years of our parents' marriage, as our mother ricocheted between trying to change Dad and accepting him as he was. They were a mystery to us, our parents. How could they ever have liked each other? We knew the facts. A pub in Liverpool. Dad just paid off and with money in his pocket; Mum the day before she turned twenty. Their eyes met. She liked to tell the story to all these women who'd come around and sit in our kitchen. We'd crouch on the other side of the serving hatch, eavesdropping. 'Love at first sight, more fool me,' Mum would say. She'd wail, 'I was too young.' Or, 'He'd not kissed the Blarney Stone so much as eaten it.'

There was a photo from their wedding day on the mantelpiece in the sitting room. They looked happy enough. Mum was pregnant with me. 'If I'd not fallen,' we'd hear her say; or, 'If I'd not caught on.' Dad was off getting drunk when I was born. We heard that a lot. That she was ill, had needed a blood transfusion, and he was nowhere to be found. He turned up two days later, smelling of booze.

The Irish ladies were more likely to advocate tolerance: 'Sure, he's a good provider. And he loves the children.' The English ones would say his behaviour was unacceptable and that she shouldn't put up with it. Though if Dad came home while they were there, they'd perk right up and laugh at all his jokes while fiddling with their hair and looking at him from under their eyelashes. 'He could charm the birds from the trees,' they'd say to

Mum. She'd reply, 'If he was less charming, I wouldn't be in this mess.'

I didn't want to be like her. My marriage might not be perfect, but I was not going to complain to anyone who would listen. I would make the best of it.

But I knew nothing of the reality of having a child. Now, if I could travel through time, I would visit my younger self and say, 'Do not even think about having a baby with someone you don't fully love.'

We'd moved to Doncaster by the time I got pregnant, and I was surprised by how vulnerable I felt, how much my idea of myself as a modern woman, as a capable person, fell away. I had no friends outside the church. At first I enjoyed the borrowers in the library taking an interest in the pregnancy, but by the time I went on maternity leave I'd had enough of people touching my bump without asking, and opining on everything from epidurals to breastfeeding. As I got larger and more ponderous, all I really wanted to do was stay at home, but Tim was still keen for me to do errands with him and I usually agreed. If I'd been able to refuse, say that I just wanted to lie on the sofa and daydream, then what I came to think of as the car park incident would never have happened.

I was enormous by then, and it was a baking hot day. Tim parked right at the edge of the car park and strode off towards the supermarket. I was summoning up the energy to waddle after him when a man approached me. I could see straight away he was what Tim called 'disorganised' and what my mother would have described as 'a sandwich short of a picnic'. He held his hands out towards my bump: 'Baby.'

'That's right,' I said, in what I hoped was a calm tone. I could see Tim disappearing into the distance. Not in earshot, probably, unless I shouted.

'Baby.'

He was coming closer. He was grubby, with bloodshot eyes and a gap where his front teeth should have been. Some more robust, not-pregnant version of me would have been able to defuse the situation. I doubted he meant me any harm. But all I knew was that I didn't want him to touch me. I started to back away. I couldn't see Tim at all. I got behind a car. The man was making a horrible noise, a kind of throaty chuckle. 'I'll catch you,' he said, feigning a movement in one direction and laughing when I went the other way. 'You won't escape.'

Ten years later, I can still feel the fear in my body. My mouth was dry. All I could hear was the thud of my heart.

Then a large black car pulled into the space opposite.

A man got out and narrowed his eyes.

'Need some help?'

I nodded and it's all a blur, what happened next, but the man with no teeth didn't like being told to leave me alone. My rescuer opened his passenger door and helped me to sit down, then stood calmly in front of me as the man shouted at him. Tim heard the commotion and came back. He gave me a quick glance but seemed to be more concerned about the shouting man.

'He was about to attack this lady,' said the rescuer.

'That's my wife,' Tim said.

'You should take care of her, then.'

Tim tried to minister to the shouting man, who stopped shouting and ran away. The rescuer helped me stand.

'Thank you,' I said, 'I'm so grateful.'

'Good luck.' He let go of my hand. As he walked past Tim towards the supermarket, I heard him say, 'You should have a think about your priorities, my friend.'

I asked Tim to unlock our car. 'I need to sit down,' I said.

'What do you want to do?' Tim asked.

'What do you mean?'

'Shall we still go shopping?'

I shook my head.

'Shall I go?'

'I'd rather not be left alone here. Can you drive me back first?'

All the way home I cradled my bump, hoped the baby had not been distressed by my racing heart, and thought what a sad situation it was that I would rather be driving off with my rescuer than with my husband.

Stephen came to stay, bearing a bright-yellow travel system that was a pram, a pushchair and a car seat all in one. He assembled it and showed me how it worked.

'Everyone will see you coming. You won't get run over. Look, it's even got a holder for a cappuccino.' It stuck out among all my other things, which had been donated by church people and looked like I'd gone into a charity shop and swept everything from the baby shelf into a bin liner. Stephen didn't like that the cot was second-hand, questioned whether it was hygienic to have hand-me-down clothes, and tried to take me to Mothercare in the shopping centre for a last-minute spree.

'I'm fine,' I protested. 'I don't need more stuff. All babies really need is love.'

My mother offered to come for the birth, but I put her off. 'At least Tim won't be out getting drunk when you're in labour,' she said. 'Not like your father.' I held my phone away from my ear as she told me all about her suffering and Dad's failings, for what felt like the thousandth time.

Tim wasn't drunk, of course, but he was distracted. My contractions started on the same day that the fixed pews were due to be removed from the church, and it was all going wrong. This was Tim's big project. He'd thrown himself into the fundraising and the planning. The new seating would be more comfortable, flexible and democratic, Tim explained to the midwife, when he reappeared after taking yet another phone call. I tried to concentrate on my breathing as he said words like 'skip', 'council', 'permit', 'incompetence', 'unhelpful'. I felt like saying, *The miracle of childbirth that you so often preach about is happening right before your eyes. Would it not be an idea to pay attention to it?*

I loved Sam immediately. What a simple sentence that is: both all that needs to be said and nowhere near enough.

Our eyes met across a crowded maternity ward and that was it. I always felt like we were on the same side. His gaze was steady and I loved to watch him encountering the world. It felt private and sacred, the bond between us. Our organist and next-door neighbour Tess once said, 'He only has eyes for his mummy, doesn't he?' and I felt an urge to describe it, this rush of love and connection.

'I love him so much,' I said, 'I would die for him. Cheerfully. I'd be crucified for him.'

She laughed. Not unkindly, but I didn't like it. 'Enjoy it while it lasts. Soon he'll be a teenager and you'll never see him.' I tried to smile and she lowered her voice. 'Sometimes I wish I could be crucified for my children rather than have to put up with their boring father.' Then she guffawed as though she'd cracked an excellent joke, but her husband, Nigel – a golfer who had great tufts of hair growing out of his nose and ears – was deeply dull, and I found the whole exchange unsettling.

I felt under pressure, not only to go to church and be active in the community but to do it all perfectly. Tim and everyone else wanted Sam to be continually present but never needing attention or making any noise. 'What will you do if he starts crying?' I asked Tim, when there was an idea that Sam could represent Jesus in the nativity service. 'Jesus must have cried,' Tim said, but in the end they stuck with a doll wrapped up in a blue blanket, and I couldn't help thinking that Tim looked much more comfortable holding that fake baby than he did with Sam.

As soon as Sam was mobile, it was tricky to keep him still. He wanted to be on the go all the time, and I hated the way I had to try to tame him into 'appropriate' behaviour. And my efforts were never good enough. 'We thought we'd like having a young couple,' Nigel said to me, peevishly, one Sunday morning after church. I was pregnant again and feeling sick, and Sam and I both had rotten colds. Sam had been even more boisterous than usual, and I'd been even less capable of restraining him. I stared back at Nigel, at the nasal hair making a bid for freedom down his upper lip. He didn't complete his sentence but I saw it all in that moment: that they liked the idea of a vicar living out the Christian ideal of marriage, but they didn't want the reality.

More and more, I felt like an extra who had wandered onto the wrong set. When it was my turn to supervise the playgroup, I'd watch the way the children mixed up all the toys, so Noah would be at work in a plastic sweet-shop and a rather ancient Sindy doll would be sailing the ark. I used to look at that Sindy, with her scraggy hair and bright-blue eyes. I felt a bit like her, as though a giant toddler had picked me up and plonked me down in the model vicarage, and then not bothered with Tidy Up Time. I was stranded, a toy in the wrong box, but I didn't know what I could do about it, and now that I had Sam I didn't want to be put back in the right box unless he could come too.

I bore myself when I dwell on the various times I've felt let down by Tim or life. And perhaps I should have been more grateful for what I had, as my mother's favourite saying that things can always get worse was about to come true.

The last thing I remember is standing in the kitchen as Sam played with bricks on the floor. Then a bolt of pain. When I woke up, I was in hospital and Tim was sitting by my bed. I was fine, he told me, I would be fine.

I looked down at the drip in my arm.

'The baby?' I asked.

'There wasn't a baby,' he said.

He told me that my pregnancy had been ectopic, that instead of being in the womb, it was in my fallopian tube. This was common, he said, though less common for it to suddenly rupture with no warning. I'd needed surgery, he told me, and would have died without it.

'So there was a baby?'

'There was a pregnancy. It was non-viable. But they never are outside the womb.'

Viable, I thought. *My baby wasn't viable.*

Tim had come home to find me on the kitchen floor, he said. Blood everywhere and Sam crying. It was a good job that his meeting at the school had been cancelled, he said, and went on to explain why, as though I might need reassuring about the commitment levels of the members of the St Mary's Easter Pageant planning committee.

'Where is Sam?'

He was fine; everything was fine; he was with Tess. I should focus on getting better. I could probably come home tomorrow, they'd said.

Tim looked at his watch.

I want Sam, I thought, but I didn't say it. Sam had started to string words together. I could picture him reaching out his little arms and saying, 'Where Mummy? Go Mummy. Want Mummy.'

Tim stood up. 'I'd better get down to the community centre. The men's choir have got their dress rehearsal.' He put his hand on my head and shut his eyes. He didn't speak but I knew he was praying. Thanking God for sparing me. When he opened his eyes, he told me that the doctor had said there was no reason why I couldn't get pregnant again.

When I got home, I found Sam's clothes in the corner of the kitchen, next to the washing machine. I marvelled that neither Tim nor Tess had thought to put a wash on, had not considered how I would feel to see the little blue-and-white stripy dungarees streaked with blood, and be reminded that Sam was crying as I lay there bleeding and unable to care for him.

Sam had always been a good sleeper, but now he'd get upset when I tried to put him down, so I let him nod off on me. All I wanted to do was be still and quiet, and to be with Sam. Other people were a challenge. They kept telling me I was lucky. Lucky that I had recovered so quickly, lucky that I hadn't had a non-viable pregnancy that lasted longer and created more complications and distress. I think they thought it would cheer me up, to hear anecdotes of worse-off women who'd been more physically and emotionally damaged than I was in the quest for a child. 'If a baby isn't going to be healthy, then nature should do its work, and the sooner the better,' Tess said, when she brought round a chicken pie, and told me about her colleague's niece's baby who had been born with its organs on the outside of its body. 'There but for the grace of God,' she said. That afternoon, as Sam slept on me, I dozed too. I dreamt that my organs were no longer inside me, that my heart had been re-sited, torn from its relative security behind my ribcage and was now precariously stuck on the outside of my chest, showing its fragile workings to the world.

Not long afterwards, Tim gave away the yellow pram. He didn't ask me and didn't understand why I was upset about it.

'You said Sam didn't need it any more,' he said.

'It was a gift from Stephen.'

'But she needed a pram,' he said, and started telling me about the woman he'd given it to.

I didn't want to hear. I said, 'I hoped *we* might still need a pram.'

He looked impatient, like I was missing the point. 'If that happens,' he said, 'we can get another one.'

I never did get pregnant again. It could be that my surviving fallopian tube doesn't work properly. Though sometimes I think a bit of me did not want to have an-other child with a man who expressed so little grief for our lost baby and then gave away his pram.

The other day, I was down at the seafront and saw two little boys holding hands. The smaller one had orange trunks and a blue top with little white sharks. His older brother had the orange top and shark shorts. My hand went to my tummy. I had to sit down on a wall. I watched them toddle off towards the beach and felt lonely on Sam's behalf. I think his life would be better had he not been denied his little brother. And mine might be better if I had more than one hand to hold.

Four

I fetch the magnetic seagull notepad from the fridge. It was a housewarming gift from Sarah, who is now training to be a therapist. She said she thought the design would suit our coastal location. I didn't tell her we are surrounded by the real thing. One swooped down and pinched Sam's pasty not long after we arrived. They nest in our chimney and I wake up every day to their call.

I chew the end of my pen. The thing with lists, Sarah says, is not so much the reminder of what to do, but the sense of accomplishment in ticking things off. She's a bit worried about me, I think, keeps sending me links to articles about how unchecked maternal anxiety benefits neither mother nor child.

Make Chilli, I write at the top. *Clean Bathroom. Change Beds.* I turn on the front hob ring, take the mince out of the fridge, and squash it down into the pan with a wooden spoon. I get an onion from the larder. It's a struggle, the tough skin resisting the pressure of the blunt knife. I try a different knife. It's no sharper, but the serrated edge helps. Success! I peel off the outer skin and slice the white flesh. My eyes prickle. Oh, the bliss of an onion. So cheap and versatile, and such handy cover. Tim and Sam have no idea that so much of what they eat is marinated in sadness.

We moved to Cornwall because, somewhere along the way, I became a woman who can't disagree with her husband. We'd been in Newcastle for four years and I thought we were settled, but then Tim got into trouble when he said prayers with a newly married lesbian couple, and one of their friends posted a photo on Twitter. Vicar, happy couple, altar in the background. It did look like a wedding, and because gay marriage isn't allowed in church, lots of people were furious and said Tim should be sacked, and then lots of other people defended him. Tim wanted to explain so he used the church's Twitter account – he'd never done that before – to say that it wasn't a wedding, it was saying some prayers to meet a pastoral need. But that didn't make anyone less angry, and it annoyed lots of the supportive people. So then Tim tweeted that he would happily conduct gay marriages if it were up to him, but it wasn't, which led to lots of predictions that he would burn in hell, and one not very convincing death threat. Then the archdeacon rang up and told Tim to stop saying things on Twitter, and that he'd better pray the tabloids didn't pick it up. Sam thought it was funny. 'Dad's gone viral,' he said. But Tim felt very misunderstood.

He went on retreat for a week in the Brecon Beacons

and came back talking about Father Robert, who'd been in the next bedroom. He hadn't always been called Robert, Tim said. His name was Siegfried when he arrived in England in 1945 on a naval destroyer with his widowed German mother, who had just married a major in the British army. 'He is so full of God,' Tim said, then went on and on about Father Robert's parish, St Brida, a beautiful church right by the sea, at the edge of a town with the same name. A Celtic cross by the front door and a holy well that provided water for baptisms, though you had to be careful not to dip too enthusiastically and disturb the breeding newts. It had been a site of worship since the sixth century, when St Brida crossed the Irish Sea on a leaf. I couldn't see where all this talk was leading, but then he came to the point. On the last day, on their final walk, Father Robert had confided in Tim that although he didn't want to, he was going to have to retire. He suggested that Tim should come and serve God by the sea.

'He said he'd find it easier,' Tim explained, 'to leave St Brida in the hands of someone he trusted.' I saw his chest swell, and then he was off. The history, the almost tropical climate on the south coast of Cornwall. Palm trees in the graveyard. Dawn services at Gull Point.

'Will you have other churches?' I asked.

'It's a rural parish, so yes,' Tim said, shortly, as though I were asking an irrelevant question. *He's made up his mind*, I thought. We'd left Doncaster because Tim was fed up of looking after several small churches but I could see he didn't want me to point out the unpalatable truth that he would run himself ragged dashing from place to place, and all the communities would still feel neglected.

'What about Sam? He'd have to get used to a new school in his last year of primary.'

Nothing about Sam's education has been easy. So quick and clever, but he's always struggled to sit still, use cutlery, hold a pencil, and not spill everything. When he was six, his school said he was hypermobile and he'd grow out of it, but at ten he still can't write well and no one knows why. At least he can read now. After years of pain, he picked up *The Hobbit* the day after his ninth birthday and finished it. Though he isn't interested in trying anything else. He just reads *The Hobbit* again and again.

'He'll have to change schools soon anyway,' Tim said, 'for secondary. Maybe it's good timing.'

I wasn't convinced, but I could see that nothing was going to get in the way of Tim's desire to follow God's call. I didn't say that I'd rather not risk it, that I'd be back to square one again and so would Sam. It was hard arriving in new places and having to be careful not to say something that could be misconstrued. I could already see myself ending up in disgusted headlines on the front of the *St Brida Gazette*: *Vicar's wife fails to say thank you; Vicar's wife gets giggles in church; Vicar's wife refuses to bake scones for patronal festival*. So many ways to get it wrong.

But I kept my misgivings to myself. It would be a long process. Months. Tim could change his mind or take against someone on the interviewing panel. Or they might not like him and not give him the job. Maybe it wouldn't matter – in this instance at least – that I was unable to stand up for myself and my son.

Tim got the job. When I told Sam, I presented being by the seaside as a positive thing, but he said that global warming meant it was a bad idea to live by the coast. He was quite sanguine about it. 'Rising sea levels, Mum. We'd be trying to get to higher ground if we were sensible. Or selfish.'

We started packing up. Father Robert had moved to an almshouse up country, which sounded Dickensian to me, but he would apparently be happy there in the company of other retired vicars. Tim was stressed waiting for confirmation that the vicarage was ready for us, and then told me the delay was due to a backlog in the diocesan property department, and we should just move down anyway and not wait until the repairs were done. I was distracted because the book club was about to start – we'd chosen *Rebecca* by Daphne du Maurier in honour of the upcoming Cornish move – so I didn't question if this was wise. I looked around at the women I had got to know since we arrived four years before. Not kindred spirits exactly, but I had grown fond of them, and they of me and of Sam. We discussed the book and they all thought the heroine was a bit of a drip, and questioned how she did not see that she'd basically married a murderer. But they liked the descriptions of the flowers, and said maybe the garden at the new vicarage would be full of rhododendrons and hydrangeas and azaleas.

They said how envious they were at the prospect of our exciting new life, and I wondered if it could be true. Maybe it would be a good move for us, and we would all feel better breathing in salt-tanged air. I resolved to try to have a good attitude about it. Perhaps Tim would be happier, which would lead to Sam and me being happier. A fresh start by the sea.

Five

We arrived in St Brida to see the late-afternoon sun glinting off the stone of a magnificent mansion.

'Is that our house?' Sam said, as we drove up the hill.

'No,' said Tim. 'The Old Vicarage has been in private hands since the 1960s. We're in the New Vicarage.'

'So is our house even better, then?' Sam asked.

'There it is,' Tim said, as he pulled into a gravel car park. 'They built it when they sold the other one.'

'It's not as good, is it, Mum?' Sam said.

'Not as grand, certainly,' I said, taking in the pebble-dash and thinking that Tim had forgotten to mention we'd be living on the edge of a car park. 'But we don't need a huge house.'

'Who are those people?'

A bald man with a white beard stood next to two short women, one with a shock of dyed pink hair.

'Our welcoming committee,' Tim said and jumped out of the car, hand outstretched. He introduced us to Derek, the church warden, Barbara, and Doreen with the pink hair. We exchanged pleasantries about the journey as I noted the dingy net curtains in the windows.

When I moved towards the front door, Doreen put out her hand to stop me. 'We always go in through the kitchen.' I followed her around the side of the house, trying not to consider it a bad omen that the very first thing I attempted to do was wrong.

Walking into our new home was like stepping into a malodorous TARDIS. Everything was brown or orange, including the lino in the kitchen, which looked like it should be burnt or sent to a museum. I tried to maintain a neutral expression.

Then Sam said, 'What's that horrible smell?' at the same time as Barbara said she'd put a casserole in the oven, and in an effort to absolve the casserole I said, 'Damp, I think. And tobacco. Did Father Robert have a dog?'

'He had a springer spaniel called Lucky,' said Doreen. 'Well, she had the look of a spaniel. She was a stray. Turned up at the church porch one day shivering, and Father Robert took her in. She was very well behaved. Used to take herself down to the pier for a swim.'

'Has she gone to the almshouse?'

'She got run over,' Doreen said. 'By a tourist who didn't understand the one-way system. Father Robert was never the same again.'

'I wish we could get a dog,' Sam said. 'But do they all make houses smell like this?'

In the silence that followed, I failed to find a tactful way of saying that houses should never smell like this.

'Father Robert did like his pipe,' Barbara admitted. 'He set himself on fire once.'

'How?' Sam asked.

'Smoking in bed,' Barbara said, 'which you must not do, young man.'

'I'm only ten,' Sam said.

Tim said he couldn't smell anything, and Derek admitted there was a bit of an issue with damp and warned me not to hang anything in the built-in wardrobes upstairs, as it was worse up there because there were no radiators. He said we might be eligible for a grant towards the downstairs flooring – the common areas – but maybe to wait until after the damp had been looked at.

'What's common areas?' Sam asked.

Derek said, 'Places that visitors go.'

'So they'll pay for things to be nice for visitors but not for us?'

'He's a quick one, isn't he?' Derek said.

'So sharp he'll cut himself,' added Doreen.

Tim and Derek went off to the church together. Barbara said we'd find it chilly upstairs, but there were hot-water bottles under the sink. She gave me instructions about the casserole, and how to heat up the apple pie, and said she'd come around the next morning to see how we were getting on.

They left, and then Doreen poked her head back around the door to whisper that we'd probably need to add sugar to the pie, because Barbara never put enough in. 'Stingy,' she said with a snigger. 'Don't ever let her make you a tea. She makes one bag do three cups.'

'Let's explore,' I said to Sam.

We found great patches of mould in the larder and lots of boxes of service booklets and carrier bags of what looked like jumble stacked up against the wall of the dining room. The smell was at its most potent in the study. It didn't look like Father Robert had taken anything away. The bookcases were full of mainly religious books with one shelf of poetry, and there was paperwork all over the desk. Upstairs was freezing. We discovered peculiar brownish circles on the main bedroom ceiling, and a dried-out flannel on the edge of the bath.

'Why is it all so dirty?' Sam asked.

'Father Robert lived here on his own for forty years,' I said. 'It doesn't look like he was houseproud. Your bedroom isn't too bad. Let's start with that.'

I opened all the windows, put the yellowing net curtains in the washing machine, and filled the first of many buckets with hot water.

When I texted Tim to ask what time he'd be back, he said Derek had invited him to share his supper so they could continue talking. I thought how pompously churchy that phrasing was. Not, 'I'm going over to Derek's,' but 'Derek has invited me to share his supper.' I imagined Derek parcelling out one tin of economy sardines onto two bits of toast, and Tim saying a long grace that included plentiful references to new beginnings and the joy of fellowship. Then they'd tuck in, discussing the loaves and the fishes while glorying in the sacrifice of not having quite enough to eat.

*

'What's this giant flap?' Sam asked, as I dished up the casserole.

'It's a breakfast bar,' I said. 'I've not seen one for years. They're out of fashion now, but we had one when I was little.' I showed him how to fix it in place. 'Uncle Stephen and I used to sit on opposite sides and kick each other underneath.'

'Why?'

'Just messing about. If we made a noise, Granny would tell us off, so the trick was to stay under the radar.'

'Can we have our tea here?'

'As long as you don't kick me.'

'I'm really proud of us,' I said, as I tucked Sam in. 'We've worked so hard today.'

Sam looked happy and cosy in sheets that we'd warmed with a hot-water bottle. He held on to my hand as I read him a chapter from our book of Greek myths, about Achilles' mother dipping him in the River Styx.

I'd hoped he'd go straight off to sleep, but when I finished he sat up in bed. 'We're not supposed to believe in Achilles and his mum, are we?'

'No, it's a myth.'

'So why should we believe Bible stories?'

I hesitated. 'I don't think we're supposed to believe in the literal truth of the Bible. Not the Old Testament, anyway.'

'What's literal truth?'

50

'That it actually happened. That Eve ate the apple. That Noah had an ark. Those are stories, like Achilles. We're supposed to believe in the New Testament. Jesus.'

'That he was God's son and came to earth and was crucified to show God's love for his people?'

'Yes,' I said, though I could hear the lack of conviction in my voice. It did sound far-fetched, put like that.

'Would Dad let me be crucified so that all the homeless people know that God loves them?'

'Of course he wouldn't.'

'Would Dad let me be crucified to prove a point?'

'Dad wouldn't let you be crucified for any reason.'

'But Dad likes God, doesn't he? So he must think that was the right thing to do?'

I ruffled his hair. 'I don't think my theology is up to this, Sam. You could talk to Dad about it. Dad likes a bit of God chat.'

'He doesn't like God chat with me.'

I looked down at his little face. It didn't feel fair to disagree. Tim, so keen on debate with grown-ups in dog collars, never responded well to testing questions from Sam, and was annoyed when Sam asked if God cared that he ate with his fingers or decided that the Garden of Eden must have been a con trick, because who would say, 'Don't touch that,' and go away unless they wanted someone to go rogue?

I stood up. 'It's getting late. Prayers, please.'

'Do I have to say my prayers?'

'Dad likes you to. Just say a quick one.'

'Can I do it in my head?'

'Yes,' I said, though I suspected I was being duped. I kissed his forehead and left him to it.

I woke up the next morning to find that a bit of our bedroom ceiling had fallen in during the night.

'You look like a ghost,' I said to Tim, who had plaster dust in his hair. I examined the doorway of the spare room. 'Our bed will never get through there,' I said. 'We'll need to make do with those single beds until the ceiling can be fixed.'

I wondered if Tim might apologise or at least acknowledge the state of the house, but he was solely focused on the day ahead. Derek was picking him up early, he said, to take him to his other parishes. St Michael's first, then St Anta.

After Tim left, I washed up the breakfast dishes while Sam played in the garden. I watched through the window as he ran around in enormous circles. I decided that, although the decor was gruesome, I quite liked the shape of the kitchen. It was just as well, as I'd be spending a significant chunk of my life in there.

Barbara didn't wait for me to answer the door, just knocked and opened it, singing out, 'Only me.'

'I'm still in my nightie,' I said.

'Never mind,' she said, though I hadn't been apologising. 'I see you've taken down the nets at the front. Everyone using the car park will be able to see in.'

I nodded towards the machine. 'I'm giving them a wash.'

'Doreen should have done that,' she said. 'If it was necessary. It was my job to do the food and hers to do a clean.' She lowered her voice as though scared we might be overheard. 'The thing with Doreen is, she's not reliable. And since she had her cataracts done, she thinks she can see without her glasses but she can't. She's leaving smears all over the candlesticks, but won't be told.'

I tried not to comment as I gave her back her dishes and enthused about the casserole. I didn't mention the pie. Doreen had been right about the sugar, and Sam and I had struggled with the claggy pastry and overwhelming taste of cloves, though Tim had chomped through the lot when he'd finally come home.

I could see that Barbara was planning to hang around, so I explained about the ceiling malfunction and that I had to track down some single bed linen.

She waggled her finger at me. 'Just you wait a jiffy.' She went into the dining room and came back with a bag of sheets and some extremely unlovely purple floral eiderdowns.

'They belonged to my parents. I'm glad they won't go to general jumble. Give you a hand, shall I?' And before I could respond, she was charging up the stairs and we were making the beds together as I tried not to think about when the sheets had last had a wash.

'I must get dressed,' I said, hoping she'd take the hint, but when I came downstairs she was talking to Sam in the kitchen. She helped me peg the net curtains out on the washing line and still showed no sign of leaving, so I said Sam and I wanted to see the church, and she offered to walk us there.

As soon as we were out of the car park, it was beautiful, looking down over the church to the harbour and across the bay to a white lighthouse. We passed two large stone posts marking the entrance to a drive.

'That's Boscawen Hall,' Barbara explained. 'The family have lived there for generations. They're trying to run it as a going concern now, Billy Boscawen and his wife, Betsy. She's full of newfangled ideas. Yoga retreats and sea swimming breaks. Weddings, of course. Guests can walk straight up the drive after the service.'

'How lovely,' I said.

'Not always.' Barbara sniffed. 'They get drunk, then walk through the church on their way to their hotels. Doreen found something very nasty in the Angel Garden one Sunday morning, if you know what I mean.'

It took me a second, but the disgusted look on her face helped me along. At least the amorous guests weren't too drunk to take precautions, I thought, but I manufactured an expression of shock for Barbara's benefit.

'And people were sitting in the lychgate the other night. Fag ends everywhere. Derek had to sweep them all up, which isn't easy, what with his back.'

'What's the lychgate?' Sam asked.

'This,' Barbara said, as we reached the porch-like structure at the edge of the churchyard. 'There's been one here since medieval times. But this was built after the Great War as a memorial.'

'It's like a hobbit house,' Sam said. 'What's it for?'

'It marks the entrance to sacred ground. And coffins rest here before burial.'

'On this?' Sam said, putting his hand on the stone platform. 'Dead people lie on this?'

'For centuries. You'd think people would have more respect than to treat it like a bench.'

'It does look a bit like one,' Sam said.

'They should know better,' Barbara said. 'But you're a kind boy, giving them the benefit of the doubt. Be careful of that step. Lynn tripped over it last year on her way back from the harvest supper. She broke her sandal strap, and her ankle was completely black and blue.'

We walked into the churchyard, and Barbara showed us the oldest known grave. 'Doesn't look much, does it? The inscription has all worn off. But he was the vicar here and died about 1650.'

Then she stopped in front of a tall granite memorial engraved with lots of names. 'Another vicar. This is the one they built the Old Vicarage for. He had eight children when he arrived and then had two more.'

'So the Old Vicarage would have been the new vicarage when it was built?' Sam asked.

'Yes!' Barbara clapped her hands together and looked delighted. 'Yes, it was. It's a beautiful house. But his wife didn't get to enjoy it for long. She died giving birth to their tenth child.' She pointed to her name. 'She was called Jane. There's a monument to her inside the church.'

'So many children,' I said.

'I wish I had some brothers and sisters,' Sam said.

'Do you?' I tried to keep a neutral expression, aware of Barbara's eyes on me, scanning for information.

'Yes, but I'd rather have a kitten or a tortoise.'

I laughed, and as we walked down the path, Barbara invited Sam to visit her cat, who was getting on a bit but liked to be played with.

I sat on the bench next to the holy well, enjoying the inscription on the brass plaque: *Dear God, be good to me. The sea is so big and my boat is so small.*

Barbara and Sam looked for newts as she explained he shouldn't touch them and must never, despite the temptation, lick one. I couldn't see why anyone would be tempted to lick a newt, but Sam accepted it as sensible advice.

'Would I die?'

Barbara put her head on one side. 'Probably not,' she said. 'But don't take the risk.'

'If I did die, would I be buried with that other vicar's family?'

I shivered. 'Let's not worry about that.'

'But would I?'

I stood up. 'I really don't think we need to plan your funeral. But no. You wouldn't be put in with anyone else.' I held my arms out in case Sam needed a reassuring hug, but he darted up the path towards a huge tree with oddly spiked leaves.

'Do you know what that is?' Barbara called after him. Sam shook his head.

'It's a monkey puzzle tree. They say the devil sits at the top, and if you try to climb it, he'll get you.'

Sam turned and looked at us both. 'I don't believe in the devil,' he said, firmly. 'People just say stuff like that to make children behave.'

Barbara chuckled. 'You are an interesting boy. What do you want to be when you grow up?'

'Ordinary,' Sam said.

Just when I thought we'd be stuck with her all day, Barbara said she'd better get a move on. 'Ken can't be left alone for long,' she said. 'He'll be moping and wanting his dinner.' She was sorry she couldn't show us the church, but said I must look at Jane's monument, and Sam would like the old set of punishment stocks in the porch. 'Doreen says we should get them out again for vandals and litterers.'

'Barbara's nice,' Sam said, as she trotted off. 'Is Ken her cat?'

'I think he's probably her husband.'

As soon as we opened the church door, we saw the stocks leaning against the wall.

'Look, you can see the holes for their feet,' Sam said. 'Imagine being pelted with rotten fruit and old cabbages. They can't really start using them again, can they?'

I shook my head. 'Doreen will have been joking.'

Sam put a hand through the hole for the head. 'I wouldn't want to be put in the stocks, but I wouldn't like to do the throwing either, would you?'

'Definitely not.'

'Doreen might like it,' he said.

I bet she would, I thought.

We found Jane's memorial, a tablet in front of a statue of Mary holding Baby Jesus. I read a bit out to Sam, how she was a bright and admirable example of the virtues that befitted the wife of a minister. 'Gentle, meek, quiet, self-denying, humble.'

'Boring,' Sam said, and went off to examine some skulls adorning a plaque on the other wall as I skimmed through the rest. Clearly, Jane did all her good works so silently that it was only after her death that everyone realised quite how wonderful she was and got up a subscription to raise the monument. I read through it again, wondering how Jane managed to do so much good while having nine children to tend, and whether I would be happier if I were either more self-denying or less so.

As we walked back through the churchyard, I was drawn to a small granite headstone with only a name, dates, and the epitaph: *Brief is life but long is love.*

'Look, Sam. Rosina Lucy died almost exactly a hundred years ago.'

'Maybe she had Spanish flu.'

I wondered how many ten-year-olds would make that connection. I used to praise Sam for his knowledge but it made him self-conscious, and we work better if I treat him like a person whose company I enjoy rather than a child whose development I am tracking.

'What do you think of the epitaph?'

'Don't be soppy, Mum.'

When we reached the lychgate, Sam turned around and looked back down at the church, the sea, the lighthouse.

'It's like a postcard. The only rubbish thing here is our house. Why can't Dad smell how bad it is?'

I shrugged my shoulders. 'Perhaps his nose is blocked or his sense of smell doesn't work. Dad doesn't really care about his surroundings.'

'He probably thinks we're lucky to have any kind of house.'

'You're right,' I said. 'He probably does.'

It wouldn't matter how many children we had; Tim would never arrive in a new parish and ask for anything to benefit himself and his family. And standing with Sam looking up at the sky and down to the sea, catching glimpses of granite through the trees, I thought maybe he was right. Plenty of people in this unfair world would feel lucky to have shelter. If Dead Jane the perfect vicar's wife had landed here, she'd have meekly and efficiently got out her scrubbing brush. And if Mary had been given a room at the inn, she wouldn't have complained about the flooring or the net curtains, let alone the pong from the innkeeper's dog. Who was I to turn my nose up because of a bit of damp?

Six

Here I am a month later, knocking up a chilli and trying to count my blessings. There are some. Sam's class teacher is kind and patient, and he's settled into school. And the smell is largely gone, though it lingers in the study, where Tim doesn't want me to disturb anything.

We don't see Tim much, as he shuttles between his three parishes trying to get know everyone and sort out everything Father Robert let slide. And he has the problem of the wrong grave to deal with. The last thing Father Robert did was get muddled at a funeral and bury someone in the wrong place. It was the undertaker's mistake, Tim insists loyally, but even he admits that Father Robert should have noticed they'd opened up the wrong grave. Instead he went right ahead and buried this woman with a man she'd never met. The mistake was only discovered when the first occupant's daughter came to visit and found her father's grave disturbed. She was very upset to realise someone else was taking up the space reserved for her mother, who was in a care home and would probably be needing it herself before long. There needed to be an official exhumation, and Tim was very stressed about it. I tried to cheer him up by making a joke about post-mortem wife-swapping, but he did not find it funny – 'It's not a laughing matter' – nor did he appreciate Sam saying that 'The Wrong Grave' sounded like the title of a detective story.

The frying pan has seen better days. All the non-stick has worn off, and I have to keep stirring to make sure the mince doesn't catch on the bottom. As I'm folding in the onion, the phone rings.

'Vicar not in?' Doreen says. 'Never mind. You'll do. Could you pop down?'

'What's the problem?' I don't want to leave the chilli unfinished. I need the promised feeling of accomplishment that will come from ticking it off my list.

'I don't want to explain on the phone,' Doreen says.

I sigh and turn off the hob.

I let myself out of the door and feel the crunch of gravel under my feet as I cross the car park and look down at the sea. Our curate Bryony, who is running a mindfulness workshop next week, says it rests the eyes to look at the blues and greens of nature, to lose ourselves in the beauty of the natural world. God's world. That's what she said when she was encouraging the congregation to sign up for her day in the church hall – tea, coffee and light lunch supplied. Get away from your phone screens, she said, get off your emails, stop obsessing over the headlines, and feast your eyes on the colours of God's world. I saw Barbara and Doreen exchange a look. I don't think either of them has a smartphone. I imagined them meditating together, got the giggles, and had to sink to my knees and pretend I was indulging in a bit of extra prayer.

'It was loudest here,' says Doreen, standing by the vestry and raising her arms. Her burgundy jumper clashes with her pink hair. 'It's stopped now. I thought it might be beetles. Or woodworm.'

'And what did it sound like?'

'A sharp tapping. Could be a ghost.'

I laugh.

'I'm not joking,' says Doreen, sitting down on a pew. 'I'm susceptible. My granny was a spiritual healer.'

'Do you think it's someone trying to talk to you?'

'Could be,' she says. 'I used to have a little old lady sit at the end of my bed when I was a girl. It happens less now. Which might be for the best. It's a gift and a curse, if you know what I mean.'

I attempt a sympathetic nod and wonder how soon I can escape.

'You'll have heard about Lillian Holt?' Doreen asks.

'Yes, Tim's over at the hospital.'

Maybe Mrs Holt has shuffled off her mortal coil and immediately popped in to say hello. Though she didn't look that keen on Doreen in life, so I can't imagine she'd come to her first once free from earthly constraints.

'Cracked her head right open, I heard. Massive heart attack.' Doreen looks excited. 'You know she's had three husbands? And plenty more friends besides, if you get my meaning.' She drops her voice to a whisper. 'All fur coat and no knickers, that's what my mother would have said about her.'

'Gosh,' I say. I say 'gosh' a lot when I'm not sure how to respond, which is much of the time. I've tried saying nothing at all, but that's hard to pull off without appearing unfriendly or bored.

The big door creaks and we both turn around. I half expect a ghostly presence, but it's Barbara: 'I thought I saw you come in. Could I have a quick word?'

'I'll be out in a moment.'

Barbara ducks outside again and I turn back to Doreen, who is clearly annoyed at the interruption and doesn't want to lose her opportunity to tell me spiteful stories in the hope I will pass them on to Tim.

'I don't know what to suggest. It's a bit beyond my area of expertise, I'm afraid.'

'I'll just carry on,' says Doreen, waving her duster. 'I thought I should let you know about it. There are lots of dead people here, aren't there? In the graveyard. So not that surprising. You'll tell Father Tim for me?'

Tim tells people just to use his first name, but some of the older parishioners stick to what they are used to and I suspect he rather likes the title.

'Of course.'

'Better not mention it to Barbara. She might get unsettled. We don't want her on the whiskey for breakfast again, do we?'

She leers at me, and I have no idea if she is joking.

The sun has come out and is dazzling after the cool dark of the church. I blink and look around. Barbara is sitting on the bench down by the holy well.

'Beautiful day, isn't it?' I say, gesturing out at the view over the harbour.

'It won't last.' She's carrying a green hessian bag, and I see a little trowel and a pair of gardening gloves. 'I've been putting flowers on my parents' grave. A nice bunch of pinks. And weeding it. I pull up all the plantains but leave a bit of clover for luck.'

We sit in silence for a minute, and then she announces that she doesn't want to do the church laundry any more.

'It's getting a bit much for me. I'm not as young as I was.'

Ghosts and now laundry. I want to ask why she's telling me, but I know why. Because laundry is women's work. Because all the women of the parish ran around after the unmarried Father Robert who was famously incapable of looking after himself, but now expect me to assume all those caring duties. Which I am doing, so they are right.

'Do you have any thoughts about who might take over?' I ask, trying to dodge her attempt to pass the buck to me.

'Doreen is too busy, though I don't know what with. Lynn says her leg isn't up to it. I asked Lillian Holt – I thought she'd be glad to help – but she said it wasn't her sort of thing.'

'Gosh,' I say.

'I know. Damn ruddy cheek. As though we can all just pick and choose what we do. Anyway, she's in hospital now.'

Barbara sounds a bit pleased, as if ending up in hospital is a fitting consequence for the laundry refusal. 'Doreen rang to tell me to mention her in my prayers.'

From Barbara's shifty expression, I deduce there is scant chance of Lillian Holt getting any prayers out of her.

'I could keep asking, I suppose,' Barbara says.

I cave in and ask her to explain what's involved.

'It's not the job that it was, because Bryony looks after herself. The altar cloths need doing at least every three weeks and often two. It depends how much candle wax drips. And whether anyone spills the communion wine.'

'Oh dear,' I say, thinking of the blood of Christ getting splashed all over the show and causing problems for the laundress. That was probably not what Jesus died for.

'Father Tim has a steady hand,' says Barbara, 'but I watch Bryony waving her arms around and I shudder, knowing what I'll be dealing with later. It's a big job and it takes a lot of ironing, especially that embroidered panel at the front.'

'Well, don't worry,' I say, and wonder how often I say this when people are not worrying at all, just congratulating themselves on shifting their responsibilities to me.

A magpie flies down and perches on a gravestone nearby.

'I think that magpie is following me around,' I say.

'You don't want that,' says Barbara. 'One for sorrow.'

65

'I keep asking him where his friend is, but he won't tell me.'

'Robins, now,' Barbara goes on, 'they're a hopeful bird. Soul carriers, you know. When you see a robin, it's a lost loved one popping down to say hello.'

'What a consoling thought.'

'It's true,' Barbara huffs. 'It's the actual truth.'

According to who? I think, but move quickly to smooth over my offence. 'I didn't mean it wasn't,' I say, 'I just meant it's comforting to think about.'

'The day after my father died, God rest his soul, my mother saw a robin on the kitchen windowsill. It sat there all morning.'

'Beautiful.' I compose my features into my vicar's wife mask – benign, slightly soppy, not too clever – and we sit together in silence, until I judge I've given enough time to paying tribute to Barbara's father's birdlike apparition and say I must get home and finish making our tea before picking Sam up.

'He's a smashing little fellow,' Barbara says. 'Enjoy it while it lasts. Boys grow up self-centred. He'll be off on one of those, what are they called? Mind-the-gap years. He'll go to Argentina and you won't hear a word for six months. You won't know if he's even alive.'

I flinch before I can stop myself, then say goodbye and walk up through the gravestones. As I pass Rosina Lucy, I cheer myself up by talking to her in my head. *What do you think? Was anything Doreen said true or just attention seeking? And what do you make of Barbara stuffing me with the laundry while frightening me about Sam?*

I can't envisage even an older, more organised version of Sam getting himself to South America. At least Barbara is thinking he'll survive long enough to do it, and not come a cropper due to snogging a newt. And all that nonsense about the robin being a soul carrier. I suppose it's comforting for Barbara to believe her dead father visited her mother. I can't imagine my dad inhabiting a bird's body to hang out with Mum the day after he died. Or that she'd have welcomed him if he had.

Tim doesn't make it back for tea. Sam says the chilli is 'not bad', and I fill him in on Mrs Holt's accident.

'What's happened to her tortoise?'

'Tortoise?'

'He's called Frisky because he likes running away.'

Like Mrs Holt herself, if Doreen is to be believed.

'Probably her daughter is looking after him.'

'I hope he isn't too lonely.'

Sam is in bed by the time Tim gets home. I heat up chilli as Tim sits at the breakfast bar and complains extensively about the roadworks on the bypass and the inefficient traffic light system.

'There you go,' I say, putting the plate in front of him. I almost add, *you'll feel better with some food in your tummy*, but I remember just in time that he is not my child.

He bows his head and says a few words of grace.

'How is Mrs Holt?'

'Still alive. Worried about her granddaughter.'

'Why?'

'Wants to leave her husband. Mrs Holt says Beth has made her bed and now she'll have to lie in it.'

'How old-fashioned,' I say in surprise. I like the look of Mrs Holt, who has the air of having seen things. 'Doreen told me she's had lots of husbands.'

Tim looks pained. 'Should you be gossiping with Doreen?'

'I wouldn't call it gossiping. She was talking at me. What's wrong with Beth's husband, anyway?'

'Does there have to be something wrong with him?'

'There usually is. When someone wants to leave someone. Why does Beth want to leave him?'

'Because she has no moral fibre, according to Mrs Holt. She doesn't want to do her duty and just wants to have a good time.'

I can't tell from Tim's tone whether he agrees with Mrs Holt, who has a lot to say for someone who is nearly dead.

'There's nothing exactly wrong with wanting to have a good time, is there?'

'I don't suppose there is,' says Tim.

The kitchen fills with a silence broken only by the noise of his chewing.

'Mrs Holt says she can't say goodbye while her mind is troubled.'

Mrs Holt, I think, is having a fine time having everyone at her beck and call.

'She wants me to talk to them. Beth and her husband, Justin. I'm seeing them on Saturday morning. So I'll have to get my piece for the parish magazine done tomorrow.'

That's Tim's day off up the spout, then. We're supposed to do something together but it hardly ever happens. We did go to St Ives last week, though even that was part of Tim's religious tourism. He wanted to see the place where St Brida landed on her leaf, as he has plans to lead a pilgrimage in her footsteps. It rained nonstop, and the church that has a stained-glass window with her in it was locked. We ate our packed lunch in the car, looking out to Godrevy Lighthouse. I told him a bit about Virginia Woolf but he looked bored, so I tried to make a joke that St Brida herself must have dealt with tribulations greater than a bit of rain and a locked door, but he did not find it funny. I could have that on my gravestone: 'Her husband did not find her funny.'

'Sam was in good spirits, after school,' I say. 'We played Pontoon and his number work is good. He's quicker than I am at working out his possible routes to twenty-one, at knowing when to stick and when to twist.'

'Pontoon?' Tim stands up. 'Isn't that a gambling game?'

'You can gamble at it.' I stack the dishes in the sink. 'Like most card games. We didn't, obviously.'

Tim goes into his study and I do the washing-up. Am I unreasonable to be upset at his lack of appreciation? It is dispiriting to toil away only to have my efforts with Doreen rebranded as gossiping, and for Tim's only comment about our child to be the suggestion that I am getting him into gambling.

My father was a big card player. 'Don't get married to your hand,' he'd say, when he was teaching Stephen and me how to play poker. He meant that you had to know when to fold, that you shouldn't be so bedazzled by your pocket pair of aces that you end up over-committed. *I don't get married to my hand, Dad*, I think. *But it might be a problem that I'm married to my marriage.*

As I scrub a bit of burnt chilli off the bottom of the pan, I realise I have forgotten to tell Tim about Doreen and the ghostly noise, and about Barbara and the laundry. I catch sight of the seagull notepad on the fridge. There is only one tick. I did not get around to cleaning the bathroom or changing the beds. I am too tired now. Those pleasures will have to be deferred until tomorrow. I think of Mrs Holt and Beth and that curious expression. She's made her bed and now she has to lie in it. Does she? Does everyone? Do I?

Seven

On Friday morning, after dropping Sam at school, I walk back the long way, via the seafront. As I approach the cafe next to the beach, my feet slow and I find myself climbing the steps, asking for a table outside, and ordering a coffee from the waiter, who has a snake tattooed all down one arm.

I look out at the sea. There are a few people swimming or on paddleboards. I am not yet used to living in a holiday destination while not being on holiday, though I can now spot tourists. They are always photographing the sea rather than looking at it, and they have louder voices. The woman at the next table is one, tucking into smoked salmon and scrambled eggs, and trying to persuade the man opposite her that they should relocate. 'We don't even like London any more,' she says between mouthfuls. He doesn't look convinced. The conversation continues. She urges the move, pointing out how much more they'd get for their money. They could buy somewhere with a large garden and build an office in it and both work from home. They'd be much healthier with all the fresh air and access to nature. She knows a woman who no longer needs to take allergy tablets, and someone else whose asthma has improved. 'It's the salt in the air,' she says, 'and getting away from all the pollution.' The man nods along, but there is something stubborn in the set of his mouth.

'You could take up surfing,' says the woman. 'We could get a van. Swim all year round. You need to start in the summer and just not stop. That's how to acclimatise.' Then, finally, desperately, as though she is playing her trump card: 'And it would be great for if we have kids.'

It backfires. The man's expression doesn't change, but he picks up his phone. The woman's eyes fill with tears and she rummages in her bag. I think she is looking for a tissue, but she too pulls her phone out and applies herself to it. She should leave him. He has no intention of giving her anything that she wants. And she thinks she wants to move house, but what she really wants is a baby. That man won't want to do either of those things with her. But the woman is now laughing. 'Look!' She holds out her phone to show him something on her screen.

'Ridiculous,' he says. 'Who does she think she is?'

'And this!' the woman cries. 'This is even worse!' And they re-bond by mocking the Instagram posts of someone called Poppy who has badly behaved but aesthetically pleasing children or possibly dogs called Otis and Juno, and I can tell that the woman will stick around for as long as the man will let her, even though surely only heartbreak lies ahead. And I wonder why I can so clearly see what other people should do with their lives but haven't got much of a clue about my own.

The tide is out so I walk the next bit over the rocks rather than on the road, picking my way carefully over the seaweed-covered stones. A woman with curly grey hair is holding hands with a little boy in blue wellies who reminds me of Sam at that age.

'Look,' he says to her, holding out a pebble. 'Love heart.'

'Put it in your pocket,' she says, 'and you can give it to Mummy later.'

The little boy looks so pleased and proud. I smile at the woman and turn my head away.

When I am nearly home, I see a tall man with unruly hair wearing a T-shirt that says: 'Jesus Loves You' in big letters. It's only when I get closer that I see the smaller letters beneath it: 'But I don't, so fuck off.'

On Saturday morning, I iron Tim's surplice while half watching Sam out of the kitchen window. He is playing in the big camellia bush at the bottom of the garden. It is two or three metres high, and every so often he falls out. Perhaps I should stop him. but he looks like he's enjoying himself.

Tim is cheerful when he comes back from seeing Beth and Justin.

'So have you convinced them to stay together?'

'I rather think I have.'

'What was the problem?'

'Beth felt unappreciated.'

'Well, that will do it,' I say, as I fill the kettle.

'Justin is stressed about work. He moved to a different building site but the job isn't as promised. And they are trying to buy a house, but prices are going up faster than they can save. Beth didn't know how much it was bothering him. She likes to have her nails done and he thinks it a waste of money. But they've agreed she could go easy on treats until they've bought a house.'

'So you've saved the day.'

'I think so, yes.'

'My hero,' I say, as I throw the tea bag into the bin.

'He's a bit of a rough diamond,' says Tim. 'Swears a lot. Fs and Cs. He said to her, "I'm sorry when I don't treat you right, but I'm never a C-word on purpose."'

'Did he say "C-word"?'

'No, the real word.'

'What did she say to that?'

'Hugged him. Said the nails are because she likes to be pretty for him. He said, "You don't need to do anything to be pretty. You *are* pretty."'

'How wonderful. What a slice of life to see on an ordinary Saturday morning. The ballad of Justin and Beth. I love it.'

And I do. My heart lifts at the thought of this young couple appreciating each other again, and that Tim has had a role in making it happen.

'Should Sam be doing that?'

I join Tim at the window. Sam is wobbling around at the top of the camellia.

'I know it looks a bit dangerous. But he's having fun.'

'It's not doing the bush any good.'

So what? I want to say but don't. *Don't ruin it,* I want to say. *I quite like you at this moment. Don't mess it all up by being mean to our son, by caring more about the bush than about him.*

'He needs to let off some steam,' I say.

Tim turns away from the window. 'They're coming to church tomorrow. Beth and Justin.'

'Wow. Church Growth. That will swell the congregation. Young people, too.'

Maybe Beth will enjoy it so much that she'll volunteer to help with the laundry.

Tim is tired after his afternoon wedding. The bride's side of the family were already drunk, and the much older groom told her off about it as they were signing the register. He was particularly annoyed that her guests had smirked and fidgeted through the Lord's Prayer being read in Cornish by his niece, who is doing her A levels and doesn't need to have her confidence eroded. 'I don't know what you thought would happen,' the bride snapped back. 'You can't expect everyone to enjoy something they don't understand.'

The reception is at Boscawen Hall, but they didn't ask Tim up for a drink. Tim doesn't enjoy wedding receptions but takes not being invited as an indication that the couple are disrespecting God. It is obvious to me that

God is irrelevant to most people getting married. They only want the setting; the church is merely a backdrop and the vicar is an extra. I have tried to suggest that it is pointless to care, but although Tim likes to air his grievances, he doesn't want advice, so I am stuck having to commiserate with him about things I think he should learn to ignore.

We are supposed to do something as a family on Saturday nights. Sam and I like playing games and cards, but Tim suggests we watch a film. Sam wants *The Hobbit*, but Tim says he's not interested in goblins. 'There aren't many goblins in it, Dad,' Sam explains, but we end up with Tim's choice, a DVD Doreen has given us. It starts off OK; it's about a little boy doing a kindness project at school. I feel almost happy sitting on the sofa next to Sam, thinking about the importance of optimism and planning a kindness project of my own to cheer myself up. We pause the film so I can get us each a bowl of ice cream, which I jazz up by sharing out a tube of Smarties over the top. I remember what Sarah has told me about trying to find the joy in small things, and I'm pleased with how pretty and colourful it all looks. But then the film takes a dark turn into domestic violence and bullying. Sam keeps fidgeting and pretending he needs to go to the toilet. 'Just eat your ice cream,' Tim says, and I can feel his aggravation, and the ice cream burns in my throat and I don't know how to say, *We should stop watching this*, and, *What was Doreen thinking, recommending this to us?*

And we do all finish our ice cream and crunch through our Smarties, but the film gets worse and worse, and the little boy ends up being stabbed by the bullies, and then Sam runs out of the room crying and hides under the dining table, and Tim is shouting at him not to be silly, and finally I manage to say, 'We should have pulled the plug on that earlier. It was too much for him,' and then Tim shuts himself into the study. I wish I could either run away or stomp off, but instead I coax Sam out from under the table, calm him down, and do what I always do in response to Tim's outbursts, say that Dad is a bit tired.

Later that night, I step into the garden and hear a woman's voice slicing through the night air: 'Everyone focuses on the birth. Does it hurt? But that's nothing. You stop drinking and take folic acid and do what you're told and cross your fingers. And then you've got this baby and you've got to keep it alive.'

Wedding guests on their way home from the hall. She sounds a bit squiffy, unaware of how loud she is. I wonder if they are sitting in the lychgate and smoking, leaving piles of cigarette ends for Barbara and Derek to complain about tomorrow.

'And you keep thinking it will get easier and it never does. It just gets different. Night feeds, then leaving them at the school gate, then watching them get their heart broken. I mean, I'd die for my kids, wouldn't you?'

'I'd rather kill for them.'

It's a man's voice. Up until then I'd assumed she was talking to a girlfriend.

Her voice softens. 'What do you think life would be like if we'd had children together?'

'We'd have driven each other mad.'

She laughs. I can hear the invitation in it.

'We were never cut out for the domestic, were we?'

They must be old flames reunited at the wedding. Friends of the older groom, probably, rather than the younger bride. I wonder where their current partners are.

'We were too high-octane,' he says.

'It was good, wasn't it? When it was good?'

'The best. We burnt brightly. I still think of you. Much more than I should.'

I peel myself away. I can hear the way this is going. I hope they don't regret it in the morning. Or leave anything behind in the Angel Garden.

Sunday is our wedding anniversary, but Tim has forgotten. I'm not trying to catch him out. I would have said 'Happy Anniversary' when I woke up, but he was already in the study with the door shut. I make bacon and eggs for breakfast as a treat, but before I can mention it, Tim orders Sam to stop wriggling on his chair, tells him off for picking up a mushroom with his fingers, and then loses it when Sam knocks over his orange juice.

'Come on,' I say to Sam, as the study door slams. 'Let's get some fresh air before church.'

We walk down into town. The shops are still closed and we are the only people in the usually bustling high street. We stroll along, looking at the crockery in the window of the charity shop and the display of blue glass bottles in the antiques emporium. I stop in front of the bookshop. 'We could come back when it's open,' I say. 'See if you want to choose something new. Branch out from *The Hobbit*.'

'I like reading *The Hobbit*, Mum,' Sam says, kindly but firmly, and we turn and retrace our steps.

'Why is Dad always in a bad mood on Sundays?'

I look down at Sam. I can't deny that it's true. Tim *is* always in a bad mood on Sundays. 'I think he feels under pressure.'

'But why? He likes church, doesn't he? That's why it's his job.'

We turn onto the pier, and I feel the breeze against my cheeks.

'People do get stressed about work. Even when they enjoy it.'

'Did you go to church before you met Dad?'

'No.'

'Did he make you?'

'He suggested it.'

'Do you like it?'

My desire to be loyal to Tim battles with my need to be honest with Sam. 'Not always, no. But can you be discreet about it?'

'What's discreet?'

'Not telling people.'

'Like lying?'

'More like being tactful. I want to tell you the truth, but it would be awkward for Dad if you ran around shouting, "Mum hates church!" from the rooftops.'

'I wouldn't shout anything from the rooftops.'

'It's just a saying that means telling a lot of people.'

'So you don't like church, and you don't want anyone to know, but it isn't lying.'

'Pretty much.'

We've reached the end of the pier. I look out at the boats bobbing about on the water, point out to Sam that we are seeing the lighthouse from a different angle. 'Barbara used to come here with her granny, you know, but there was a turnstile then and you had to pay tuppence to get through.'

Sam doesn't want to be deflected. 'Religion is the cause of loads of wars, Mum.'

'I know, sweetheart.'

'What's the difference between Catholics and Protestants?'

'Catholics have mass, and confession. No women priests. More about Mary.'

'But what do they believe? What's different about that?'

'I think it's to do with communion,' I say. 'Catholics believe that God is present in the wine and bread. Protestants think it's symbolic.'

'That's it? Doesn't feel like a big enough reason to torture and murder loads of people.'

'No,' I agree.

'And do we have to go to church, you and me?'

'Yes,' I say.

'Why?' Sam asks.

I look out at the lighthouse. Why do we? I can't think.

'Is it because Dad would kick off if we didn't?'

'He likes to have us there,' I say, in what I hope is a diplomatic modification of Sam's truth. 'We go to support him.'

I look at Sam's face, the way his forehead wrinkles as he tries to figure out this strange world.

And because I have reached the edge of my ability to respond truthfully to Sam without criticising or contradicting his father, I ask if it is too early for ice cream. Sam thinks it is never too early for ice cream.

You can tell a christening party from the regular churchgoers because they are more dressed up. Some of the younger women are wearing short skirts and low-cut tops. Doreen stares at them with disapproval. I can almost hear her saying, 'What do they think this is? A nightclub?'

In his sermon, Tim asks if people have noticed the green of his stole and explains the different colours of the liturgical year. They'll see him in purple at Advent, and in white at Christmas. He is wearing green today because we are in Ordinary Time, that bit of the church calendar after Pentecost and before Advent. He has been pondering this notion of Ordinary Time, he says, and how it is easier in many ways to lead a spiritual life during the big festivals but that how we conduct ourselves in Ordinary Time is just as important. I know what's coming next, because he wrote about it in his introduction to the parish magazine and kept reading his drafts to me. *Is any time ordinary? Surely all time is valuable because we can use it to grow closer to God. Every moment is precious because it is a gift.* Tim places his hand on his stole. Green is the colour of life, he says, and growing new life, and the new life can grow into God's love.

'Which brings us to today's baptism,' he says, and talks about the importance of prayer as the first step into a relationship with God. My mind drifts. I'm off the case with praying. It feels like attention seeking, like I am tugging at God's apron strings. 'How many ears does God have?' Sam said when he was younger. 'And doesn't he get bored of everyone complaining all the time?'

Now Tim is talking about how Jesus showed his scars to Thomas to prove his identity. This is one of his favourite subjects. Tim can bring anything round to poor old Doubting Thomas. And he loves talking about the scars of the world. He is full of compassion when trying to heal other people, but lacking in it when it comes to his own son. He's never intentionally cruel, and I'm not sure he knows how unloving he sounds. I bet he'd be shocked if I told him that the only words he has uttered to Sam today are variations on 'Sit still,' 'Use your fork,' and – shouting – 'Why do you have to be so clumsy?' And there I go again on the mad merry-go-round of my own thoughts. He's not bad enough to leave, is he? Or is he?

Once, in Newcastle, one of the book-club mums complained about her husband being sharp with the children, and I tried to say something about understanding how she felt. We were in the kitchen at the vicarage making trays of sandwiches for the school leavers' party and she stopped slicing her cucumber, looked at me strangely, and then said, 'The most important thing we can do for our children is love their fathers.' And I felt reproved and applied myself to grating my enormous block of cheap cheddar.

Tim leads baby Hector and the rest of the christening party towards the font at the back of the church. The rest of us turn in our seats, and I see an unfamiliar young couple a few rows away from me who must be Beth and Justin. She is holding the order of service and those expensive nails are indeed spectacular; gold and turquoise and studded with little jewels.

The godmother's peacock fascinator is wobbling and she is bursting out of her dress. Hector's father keeps having a quick squint down her cleavage. I hope Hector's mother doesn't notice.

'As Mary knew the joy and pain of childbirth,' Tim says. *Oh yes,* I think, *that about sums it up.*

Finally, it is over. I let Sam run off outside and go to help Barbara with the urn. When Tim joins us at the back of the church, he accepts a cup of tea from Barbara and a custard cream from a plate offered by Doreen.

'It's amazing,' Beth tells him. 'Granny's better. The nurse says they've never seen anything like it, and that if she carries on like this, she'll be able to come home in a couple of days.'

'Thank the Lord,' says Tim.

'Thank you, Vicar,' says Beth, pointing one of her remarkable talons in his direction. 'Granny says it's all your doing. A miracle.'

As we walk back up through the lychgate, I apologise for forgetting to tell Tim about Doreen's ghost and Barbara's resignation from the laundry and say that yes, I can see it was not ideal for him to find out over coffee and I understand it is not good for us to look so divided and disorganised.

We crunch over the gravel of the car park in an unhappy silence. How has this happened? Tim has just been congratulated for performing an actual miracle. Shouldn't there be a bit more joy sloshing around?

'Amazing about Mrs Holt,' I try, as we get home. Tim doesn't respond. He retreats to his study and closes the door.

Later that afternoon, I am ironing in the kitchen when Stephen phones me from his car. He is driving up to Manchester for an early meeting the next day with one of his biggest customers. The last couple of times we've chatted he's been exhausted, so I'm relieved to hear him sounding buoyant. 'You're on good form.'

'Painted the front door today. Took it off its hinges. Heat-gunned it. Very satisfying. And don't tell anyone, but I'm chuffed to be on the road and giving bathtime the swerve. I love my family, but I do like a night in a hotel on my own. Bottle of wine, my choice of telly. There might even be a bathrobe.'

'Living the dream,' I say, wedging the phone between my head and shoulder so I can carry on with the sleeve of Tim's shirt.

'Happy anniversary.'

'You are clever to remember.'

'It's the day I met Sarah, isn't it? We always know. Doing anything special?'

'We had a lovely day.' I don't like lying to Stephen but nor do I want to expose Tim to him. They have nothing in common, my husband and my brother. Tim disapproves of Stephen's consumerist lifestyle, and Stephen can't fathom why anyone would work such long hours for almost no money. They can't see each other's good points, and over the years I've got into the habit of not sharing anything that would reinforce what they already think of each other.

'How's the new gaff?'

'Amazing views,' I say, feeling pleased that I've ducked out of telling another lie. 'Like something out of a fairy tale or a romantic comedy.'

Stephen shouts, 'Twat,' and then apologies. 'Just some dude in a Mercedes behaving like a bellend.' Then he says they are thinking of coming to Cornwall for a week in the summer. 'Bella really wants to see Sam and Alice has been learning about climate change at school. She keeps making all this alarming artwork and is refusing to fly anywhere.'

'That's brilliant, isn't it? Don't we all have to stop getting on planes?'

'Theoretically, yes.'

'But actually. I mean, she's right, isn't she?'

'But I want to go on holiday. I want to go somewhere I know it won't rain for two weeks, and I can sit by a pool and have someone bring me colourful drinks with umbrellas in while someone else is entertaining my children in a safe and nourishing way. I want to read a thriller – nothing too modern; maybe Nazis or horse racing – and then go water-skiing in the afternoons. I want to be surrounded by beautiful people, and in the evening I want to eat garlicky seafood and have a silly pudding with a sparkler in, and more drinks and maybe a brandy or two, and then I want to go to bed and sleep well because I know there is no work so I don't have to go into the office and deal with cunts.'

I start on another shirt. 'Well, you can't always get what you want.'

'If it was up to me we'd force Alice to come on expensive foreign holidays, but Sarah thinks we should be supportive. So, Cornwall it is. Sarah has found us a place with views and hot tub. It had better not rain.'

'You might want to manage your expectations about the rain. But as the locals say, if you don't like the weather you just need to wait five minutes and it will be different.'

'Fair enough. Should I ask Mum?'

'Please, no.' I shudder.

'We could pick her up on the way down.'

'It's not the logistics I'm worried about. Did I tell you about her housewarming present? She sent me this sign that says, *Every family has a story. Welcome to ours.*'

'Jesus.'

'I know. She made it at a crafting class. I've hidden it

in the cupboard under the stairs. I can't cope with her, sorry. I'll have a rubbish time if she comes.'

'She gets on with Tim, doesn't she?'

'She butters him up and asks him to explain bits of the Bible to her. And she loves Sam. It's only me she can't stand.'

I finish the shirt. I usually give in to Stephen — and everyone else — but I am determined to hold my ground over this. I look at the ironing basket. Still almost full. It's so relentless, laundry, washing and drying and ironing bits of material, just for them to be worn and dirtied again.

Stephen sighs. 'OK, then.' I can hear him thinking, *I tried my best.* 'Can't imagine her in a kayak, anyway. Did I tell you I'm going wakeboarding?'

'What's that?'

'Like water-skiing, without the skis,' he says. 'You get towed behind a boat. And do tricks in the air.'

'Be careful.'

'Who are you, my mother?'

'Shut up.'

That night, I read for a while before closing my book and putting it on the table. I glance over at Tim. He is stuck into one of Father Robert's books about Julian of Norwich. She was visited by Christ on her deathbed, and then didn't die but lived in a cell built into the church wall, sharing her visions of divine love. That would suit Tim, probably: not to have to worry about earthly love and the boring business of remembering wedding anniversaries or being patient with your offspring.

I slide down under the purple eiderdown, feeling the warmth of the hot-water bottle against my feet and trying not to think of Barbara's dead parents. Time to count my blessings again. I am not cold or hungry. I live with a man who tries to be a good person, who doesn't hit me or chase other women or disappear off on benders like my dad used to do. Often they work, these pep talks, but tonight it doesn't feel like enough. I'm so bored. Is it wrong to want something to happen? Pointless, probably. And tempting fate, maybe. Things can always get worse, as my mother likes to say. I give my head a little shake to try to dislodge her. Perhaps I am getting my period. I think back to Sam asking me about a tampon he'd found in my bag.

'I have these things called periods.'

'Do all grown-ups have them?'

'Only women.'

'Does it hurt?'

'Sometimes.'

'Will you die?'

'No.'

'Will you get better?'

'They'll stop when I get older.'

'I bet you're looking forward to that,' he said, and I laughed, though I knew he was being serious.

I hear Tim reach out for his lamp, and then the light goes off. His voice breaks into the darkness.

'Do you want me to come into your bed for a bit?'

I lie still, considering the question. Not 'Can I?' but 'Do you want me to?' I open my mouth. Words don't come. I could be asleep. I was almost asleep. Might he be able to believe that I am asleep? I continue to lie still. At some point, much later, I do sleep.

Eight

I'm sitting on the bench in the churchyard, watching the comings and goings on the harbour. I'm avoiding Tim because he's smarting over last night's PCC meeting and his failure to organise a strategy day to respond to the bishop's vision for the future. I can't bear to hear it all again; how Bryony suggested they get away from the parish for some blue-sky thinking, perhaps to the M&S cafe on the bypass, but Barbara said it was too far. So Derek said he would drive Barbara there and back but wanted to know whether the costs of coffee and sandwiches – they couldn't just sit there all day not consuming anything – would be covered. Then they disagreed over how to conduct the survey that needs to be done so they can discuss it at the strategy day. It must be online, Bryony said, for environmental reasons. But Barbara pointed out that some of the older parishioners would only fill it in if it was printed out. Derek offered to help her do it on the computer and she responded defensively, saying she wasn't worried about herself, but that Doreen would never be able to manage and nor would Lynn or Lillian Holt. Tim said that Lillian could use a computer because she'd sent him a very nice email when she came home from hospital. Barbara then went off topic and started lobbying for Pet Church, a monthly service for animals. Her cat would benefit from the company. Derek had reservations about how sanitary it would all be, and then Barbara said she had to go home because Ken was still in pain after his run-in with the Korean barbecue hot plate at the Tranquillity noodle bar, and she might have to change his dressing.

'I thought Ken hardly left the house,' I said. 'Barbara told me he is a martyr to his sciatica.'

'Well, he must have done,' Tim snapped, as though I was focusing on the wrong thing, and bemoaned again the fact that the meeting had closed without anyone making a decision about anything.

'You need a strategy day about how to set up a strategy day,' I said, trying to lighten the mood.

'How can Barbara think a full day is too much? What else does she have to do, exactly?'

'Sounds like she's got a lot on, looking after Ken and entertaining her depressed cat,' I said, but Tim paid no attention to me and carried on complaining about how hard it is that there isn't anyone under seventy on the PCC, and that Derek is being difficult about going on the safeguarding course that the diocese say is necessary if he wants to continue being a worship leader. I asked him if he'd mentioned that I could set up a book club, and he said he did but they'd tried it a few years ago.

Nobody but Barbara bothered to read the books, and Doreen could only manage large print editions. 'That might have changed now she's had her cataracts done,' I said, but I could see Tim wasn't interested in the one contribution I might enjoy making to church life, so I resolved not to mention it again.

Now, sitting on the bench, I watch the shadows on the path from the monkey puzzle tree. I could be mindful. I know how to do that now. I only went to Bryony's meditation class because not many people signed up, but I quite enjoyed it. We did it in the church hall, and started by concentrating on eating a Malteser and then learnt that we are not our emotions.

'Thoughts are like clouds in the sky,' Bryony said, arms outstretched. 'Sometimes they are dark and stormy. Other times they may be soft and wispy. They can fill the whole sky, or they may dissolve, leaving us empty.' She taught us to ground ourselves by directing our breath through our feet. After lunch – tuna sandwiches, apples and gingernuts – we moved on to loving kindness meditation, which involved wishing well for ourselves and other people.

'Isn't that the same as prayer?' Barbara asked.

'It's not a million miles away,' Bryony said, 'but a different approach. Start by thinking of someone you love in an uncomplicated way. Maybe a child.'

'What if you haven't got anyone like that?' Doreen asked.

'You can think of a pet.'

'I haven't got a pet.'

'You can think of a warm light or a favourite tree,' Bryony said, with a hint of impatience. 'A spiritual leader. God, if you like. Anything that will help you feel loving.'

'Can it be a dead person?'

'I don't see why not.'

'I wouldn't choose a dead person,' Barbara said.

'It's all right for you,' Doreen shot back. 'You've got that cat.'

'Think about your son,' Barbara suggested.

'He wants to split up with his wife,' Doreen said. 'I'm not sending him any loving kindness.'

Bryony intervened. 'We're straying from the point. All we're trying to do is start with the simplest, purest love we feel. Because love is a muscle. Love is a tool.'

I made a note to remember that bit to tell Stephen later.

'Once we are all up in the energy of love, we'll be extending our compassion to people with whom we have a more difficult relationship.'

Barbara elbowed Doreen in the ribs. 'You'll be fine when we get to that bit. You'll be spoilt for choice.'

Once everyone had shut up, I did get into it, and enjoyed wishing good things on Sam and Stephen and Sarah and Alice and Bella, and on Tim and even on Barbara and Doreen. Afterwards I walked home through the churchyard, sat on this bench, and felt almost calm. And it was a great success in general, so Bryony is going to do regular 'Mindful Monday' evenings in the church hall, with Barbara bringing an apple pie for afterwards.

I can't recapture it today, though. Should I try a prayer? *Lord, if this is supposed to be my life, please help me to endure it.*

Then my phone rings. I fish it out of my pocket and look at the screen. Stephen.

I answer it. Silence.

'Are you there?' I ask. 'Hello?'

'Sorry,' he says. I can hear the pain in his voice. 'Sorry to do this. But I need to press the panic button.'

London, July 2019

Nine

On my way down to the train station, I see Doreen's pink head bobbing along the bottom edge of the churchyard. She's carrying a litter picker and a half-full bin liner. I try to speed up but the noisy wheels of my suitcase betray me, and her face lights up with greedy curiosity as she hurries across. 'Barbara said you're going up to London.'

I don't want her to think I'm gallivanting, so I tell her my brother isn't very well.

'What's wrong with him?'

I hesitate. I am all for lowering the stigma and shame around mental health but really don't want to talk to her about it. I compromise.

'Overwork, I think. Stress.'

'Stress!' Doreen snorts. 'That didn't exist when I was young. All these new diseases. Disorders and whatnot. They sound made up to me.'

I assume my vicar's wife mask while wondering what would happen if I obeyed my instincts and told her to fuck off.

'My daughter-in-law hardly eats anything. She's got gluten, which means no bread, and now she's off dairy too. That doesn't leave a lot to go on. My son is a bit browned off. He used to look forward to Fridays because it was takeaway night. It's no reason to leave your marriage, I said, her not wanting to eat pizza any more.'

I enjoy the novelty of being in genuine agreement with Doreen.

'I'll support him in prayer, your brother,' she goes on. 'What's his name?'

'Stephen.'

Doreen nods. 'Stephen. Yes, rest assured. He'll be in my prayers.'

I smile, but perhaps I don't look sufficiently grateful as Doreen rushes to convince me of her powers. 'Barbara said it did her the world of good when I prayed on her hip.'

'I'm sure it did.'

'And Lynn's ankle. And that time she was attacked by a hydrangea and her elbow went septic. And I prayed hard for Lillian Holt, though she gives your husband the credit for getting her out of hospital.'

'I bet it all helped.'

'I do properly hold people in prayer,' she insists, thrusting her head towards me. 'I don't just say I will and then not do it.'

'I wouldn't dream of mistrusting you.'

It is only when I collect my tickets from the machine at Truro station that I realise Stephen has bought me First

Class. I cross over the footbridge and walk down to the far end of the platform. I sneak a look at my fellow passengers. A man in a suit with a briefcase. Two women a bit older than me, chatting happily. An elderly couple in tweeds. Both my case and rucksack are charity shop bargains that have seen better days, and I feel a bit scruffy for Stephen's treat. Nervous, too. The tweed-wearers look like churchgoers. I would not like to be spotted indulging in luxury travel, even though it is a gift.

Once on board, I do enjoy sinking into the comfy seat. The tweedy couple tell the guard they are on their way to their grandson's wedding in Edinburgh, and will be getting a taxi from Paddington to King's Cross to catch their connection. He reassures them. They'll have plenty of time. The chatty women sit at opposite sides of a table with their laptops. 'No talking until Newton Abbot?' says one. 'Agreed,' says the other, and they tap away at their keyboards.

I get my book out but can't settle to it so look out of the window instead. The sky is full of fluffy white clouds. As we chug up through Cornwall, I look out at the sheep and cows, at the boat yards and sea views. There is a partially submerged wreck and even a herd of deer. It is almost like meditation, this staring out of the window, though I can't say I have stilled my thoughts. As I watch crows picking over a freshly ploughed field, as I admire a row of neatly thatched cottages and look at the distant people on beaches and boats, my mind is flicking between Sam and Stephen. My allegiance feels stretched.

When I told Sam I loved him this morning, he said that love was a scam, designed to get people to do stuff.

'But I love you so much,' I protested.

'I'm your child. You are programmed to look after me.'

'It feels like love to me.'

He shrugged, and then Tim said I'd be late if I didn't get a move on. Sam let me embrace him but kept his arms by his sides rather than hugging me back.

'You will look after each other, won't you?' I asked.

'We'll be fine,' Tim said, but without any warmth or reassurance in his tone.

I sigh so loudly that one of the women looks up from her laptop screen. She gives me a little smile and I return it.

If I am going to do this, I might as well feel good about it. There is no point in fretting about Sam. Often he and Tim do get on when I'm not there. Better, I sometimes think, than when I am in the way. It's not an especially cheering thought, that my family functions best when we are not together. I sigh again, rest my face against the window. As the journey rolls on, my preoccupations shift with the geography. Sam and Cornwall fade, and Stephen and London get brighter.

'Wobbly' was the word Stephen used when he told me about it over the phone, all those years ago. 'I'm a bit wobbly,' he said. He was on business in New York, before he worked for himself. In his last call he'd talked of signing big deals, drinking vodka martinis, and eating pastrami on rye. I was expecting more highlights but he said, 'I don't think I can get home on my own. I don't think I can get on the plane.'

'What do you mean?'

'Can't explain. Will you come?'

He booked me onto a flight the next day. In a taxi from JFK, I looked out of the window at the skyline, thinking of all the New York novels I had read. I would never have expected that I would first see the city in real life because Stephen – strong, resilient Stephen – needed rescuing.

He was waiting for me in the hotel lobby. His face was pale with a greenish tint. He needed to pace, he said; it helped if he kept moving. It wasn't the first time, he admitted, as we walked the streets near his hotel. Over the noise of the traffic and the honking of all those yellow cabs, he told me he'd been to hospital twice in the last six months, convinced he was about to die.

'That's how I feel now. Like my heart is about to pop. But there's nothing wrong with me, they said. It's panic. I think I'm having a heart attack but what I'm actually having is a panic attack.' He shook his head. 'What a twat.'

'Why didn't you tell me?'

He shrugged and looked away. 'Embarrassed,' he mumbled.

'But you've picked me up off the floor a few times. You've never judged.'

'It usually makes sense, your stuff.'

'And yours doesn't?'

He sighed. 'You tell me.'

There were things he had to do five times, he said. He needed to check locks and flick light switches, and make sure he left his toothbrush and his shower gel in the exact same position.

The night was drawing in. I looked across at his tormented face through the dusk. 'What happens if you don't?'

'The plane will crash. I won't make the sale. I'll get fired. I'll die.'

'Like, really?'

'Probably not. But I think I will. I know it's nuts. Or part of me knows. But another part thinks I've got to do it all, or else.' There was a tremor in his voice. 'It's exhausting.'

I linked arms with him as we walked on.

'I don't really understand,' I said.

'You won't be able to,' Stephen said. 'It's mental. I do know that. But if I could logic myself out of it, I'd have done it.'

'Have you seen anyone?'

'The doctor at A and E said I should tell my GP.'

'You need a bit of therapy, don't you?'

'Fuck knows. All I care about right now is getting home. Thanks for coming. I really don't think I'd be able to get on the plane without you.'

The next day, Stephen drank three Manhattans in the hotel bar before we left for the airport, explaining he'd worked out the optimal amount of alcohol to take the edge off his fear without making it more likely he'd do a runner. He was jittery in the cab but friendly as we went through check-in and security. When I commented that he seemed himself, he did a strange mirthless laugh. 'I am capable of seeming myself,' he said. 'I've chaired huge meetings thinking I'm about to peg it, and no one ever knows.'

He clutched my hand for the entire duration of the flight. He was clammy, with a sheen of sweat on his face. 'Just talk to me,' he said. 'But not about anything horrible or depressing.' So I embarked on a stream of non-challenging conversation. The time I painted his face with nail varnish not knowing that it wouldn't just rub off; when we fell off the rope swing over the pond and got covered in mud. But relaying our child-hood was full of trip hazards. I didn't want to mention Dad so I switched to the library, the funny things our borrowers asked and how they would get book titles slightly wrong. *Captain Corelli's Mandarin. We Need to Talk About Brian*. I told him about my colleagues. Fran-cis, who always wore a three-piece suit and had a gold pocket watch. Belinda, who ignored people when they said thank you but would hiss, 'You're welcome,' if they didn't. And Sarah, who was so tiny she couldn't reach the top shelf even when she stood on a kick stool. I told him about Gavin, who played his guitar enthusiastically at Rhyme Time and might be secretly in love with Archive Andy. I described the ladies who came on Wednesday nights for Knit and Natter, and how Sarah, who liked to eavesdrop on them, said they should rebrand themselves as Stitch and Bitch.

'What do they talk about?' Stephen asked.

'Husbands and hysterectomies,' I said, 'and how painful and inconvenient they both are.'

'Don't stop,' he said. I was out of material so started retelling the Narnia books, but not as though I was reading, more like I was describing stuff that had happened to a friend of mine called Lucy when she went to live in a large country house. 'And then, she came out of the back of the wardrobe and there was all this snow.'

I got him home and went with him to the doctor's, as he admitted he might bolt if he had to go alone. He was prescribed a course of Cognitive Behavioural Therapy and that helped a bit. 'I understand more, anyway,' he said. 'I get flooded with adrenaline. My body goes into fight or flight. Triggered by stress, apparently.'

'Could you do a less demanding job?'

'Where would the fun be in that? I don't want to be skint as well as mad. No, I need to manage myself. Exercise is good. Helps burn it all off. They're called rituals. The things I do. Obsessive because I can't stop thinking about them, and compulsive because I can't stop doing them.'

'And can't you stop?'

'No. But it could be worse. If there's a continuum, I'm between a footballer who believes in his lucky pants and someone who can't leave home because they get too scared they've left the gas on.'

'You can leave the house.'

'Yes. Locking up can be tricky but I don't have any problems with appliances, touch wood. Thanks for coming to save me.'

'I will cross any ocean,' I said. 'You have a lifetime guarantee. It's like in Narnia, that horn they blow to summon help.'

'Fuck Narnia,' he said. 'I'm going to think of you as my own personal panic button. I'll try not to be trigger happy.'

He's had good times and bad times. Periods of stability punctuated by more wobbles. At one point he thought he'd have to stop flying, but he went on a course guaranteed to cure flight phobia and it worked well enough that he's only as anxious on a plane as he is everywhere else.

He doesn't always need me, and less since he met Sarah, but I drop everything when he does. His anxiety hasn't got in the way of his productivity and he has all the external markers of success. To outsiders he appears robust, thick-skinned even, like he has everything. Only Sarah and I know how much his internal world is vulnerable to fire and flame.

Tim is not particularly sympathetic. Given his preference for lame ducks, I thought he might like Stephen more when he knew what lay hidden just beneath the surface of all that bonhomie and confidence. But it doesn't work like that. When I went to Tim's study yesterday to say that Stephen needed me, I stood in front of his desk, wishing I felt less like a schoolgirl in the headmaster's office. Tim looked up, but I could see he wanted me to go away so he could get on with his sermon. When I explained, he said, 'How long will you be gone? What about Sam? I've got two weddings on Saturday and the opening of the Men's Shed next week.' I told him I'd only be away for three days, would come home on the Monday night sleeper train, and suggested we ask Barbara to help. I didn't say what I wanted to, which was that I wasn't going to ignore my own brother's mental illness so that Tim could be free to give all his focus and attention to the problems of strangers.

At Newton Abbot, the two women congratulate each other on having done loads of work and discuss the romantic problems of a mutual friend called Rachel who has embarked on an unwisely enthusiastic relationship with a man she met at her gym.

'She knew he was boring about his allotment but she ignored it because he was encouraging about her leg presses. But now she's trying to reverse out and he's trying to ramp up.'

'Their treadmills are not in sync.'

'She said she's losing her sense of self, that she always does it with men. Goes full steam ahead and then realises she's forgotten who she is.'

'I like the courgettes, though, don't you? That's a plus.'

'A supply of courgettes for family and friends is not a good enough reason to put up with a bore.'

'What is?'

'Nothing.'

'Unless you have kids.'

'Oh, yes. If you have kids, you'll put up with almost anything.'

'You need to go to the loo,' shouts the tweedy man at his wife.

He probably doesn't know how loud his voice is.

'Go on,' he urges, when she doesn't immediately jump to it. 'We don't have much time at Paddington. We don't want what happened to you in Penzance to happen again.'

The old lady blushes.

Perhaps this is where all romance leads. Bladder problems and recriminations.

Ten

At Paddington, I am assailed by the noise and smells of London. I cross the concourse through the press of people and go down into the Underground. There are huge billboards everywhere selling perfume, make-up, handbags, a revolutionary anti-pollution moisturiser.

On the Tube I sit opposite a poster with a happy, jolly baby advertising fertility treatment. This baby will not cry or sulk, wants only to stare lovingly and gratefully into its mother's eyes.

My mind goes to my little lost baby. *I've got Sam*, I tell myself, and imagine for a moment being a different woman, one who longs for a baby but can't have one. I feel my face crumple with the pain of it. The man opposite glances at me. I compose my features and wonder what life I lead in that other universe where neither Tim nor Sam exists.

When I change trains at Earl's Court, the same man is opposite me again. About my age. Sturdy. Solid. Dark hair and blue eyes with a scar across his cheekbone. There is an alertness about him. He looks poised for action. The other passengers are all buried in their phones. I look at the man and am tempted to catch his eye and smile. *It is only you and I*, I think, *who are paying attention to this current moment*. But I'm not in church now, I remind myself. I'm not in the place where I am supposed to befriend strangers, and it might not be welcome here.

A couple get on, speaking a language I don't know. They are holding hands. Or rather, she is holding his hand in both of hers. She has beautifully manicured nails with square-cut tops. Their fingers interlace. *That is what love looks like*, I think. That absorption. I can study them as much as I want because all their attention is on each other.

The possibility of holding hands with Tim is so remote. There must have been a time when I loved him but I can't access it. I try to remember being in that cafe with him after church. When did our eyes first meet? I liked the way he wore that scarf, not caring that it was garish and wonky. He was wise when we talked about my dad. He was good, I was sure of it. I sneak another look at the man opposite. He looks purposeful, useful, efficient and decisive. He wouldn't be pushed around by Barbara and Doreen and the PCC. If he told Derek to go on a safeguarding course, Derek would go.

The hand holders get off at Turnham Green, and just as we are gathering speed again, the train judders and then screeches to halt. All the passengers look up from their phones.

'A jumper, I bet,' says the woman next to me.

'Sorry?'

'A jumper,' the woman says again, 'That's what it felt like to me. Someone jumped in front of the train. It's happened to me before. Just before Chiswick Park, that was. We'll be stuck here for ages. They send people to clean it all up.'

I feel sick. What can I do? I try to remember what I learnt from Bryony. Feet. I need to feel my feet on the ground, imagine my breath coming up from the centre of the earth. I look down at the floor. How can I ground myself when it is only the train carriage beneath my feet? And then air.

The man opposite stands up and looks out of the window on both sides. He sits down again.

The tannoy crackles: 'Ladies and gentlemen, due to passenger action we will be here until further notice. We'll get you on the move as fast as we can, but there will be a delay.'

'Passenger action,' says the woman. 'That's what they're calling it these days.'

Another woman snorts, as though the worst thing about this situation is the language used to describe it.

'What a terrible death,' says a man wearing bright-orange trainers.

'The coward's way out,' says a pair of brogues.

'Instantaneous,' says the flip-flops. 'Even if you do end up cut to pieces.'

Several grumble that it shouldn't be allowed, that precautions should be taken. One man claims to have a friend who works for Transport for London, that they are working through the hotspots one by one, increasing the security. A woman tells a horrible story about the fate of her neighbour's cousin's son after taking medication that was meant to treat his acne. 'He was only seventeen,' she says. 'He went doolally.'

It echoes around my head. What an awful word. And the way she said it with relish, drawing it out.

A woman says that at least we are not actually underground, that it would be more depressing if it was dark, that we'd feel more trapped, and a man says that most passenger action happens at the outer stations. The woman asks why and I hope for a moment that maybe people want a last look at the sky, but the man with the friend in the know says that the stations that are not underground have fewer precautions. He starts to tell us about suicide pits, but I feel sick again and hunch my shoulders to my ears to try to block him out.

Then, as though there has been an invisible signal that this is enough talking to strangers, the passengers all re-apply themselves to their phones, messaging and calling and expressing irritation at the interruption to the day. My hands are trembling. I manage to text Sarah. She sends a row of heart emojis. If I let her know when I'm moving again, Stephen will walk down to meet me.

Through the window of the train, I see a cluster of men in high-vis clothing walking down the track. I take another deep breath. I'm not sure it is helping. Maybe I should try to pray for the person's soul. *Lord, in your mercy, hear my prayer.* I might be sick. Or faint. The man opposite me looks calm. Good in a crisis, I bet. If I get to a point where I might pass out, I will ask for his help. I close my eyes and recite the Hail Mary in French. *Je vous salue,*

Marie, pleine de grace. It calms me, but then I start thinking of French exchange trips, and remembering how we couldn't keep our side of the bargain. Stephen had been to Honfleur to stay with Eduard, who chain-smoked and let him ride his scooter. But then everything changed. Stephen said to me, 'I suppose Eduard won't be able to come here now.' I asked Mum. She snapped at me that the French exchange was the least of our problems, which did turn out to be true as, not long after Dad's funeral, we found out we had no money and had to go and live with Mum's parents. I say the Hail Mary again. And again. I count to fifty in French slowly. Then the Hail Mary again, and I do that until the driver thanks us for our patience and the train moves.

There's another flurry of activity as all the passengers send updates to the outside world. I text Sarah again.

'Could have been worse,' says the woman next to me. 'I was hours outside Chiswick Park. They must have found it all.'

As I get off the Tube, I see two men in high-vis vests at the end of the platform. One of them is holding what looks like an industrial-sized roll of dustbin liners. I think of Doreen and her litter picking around the graves and then I look at the size of the roll, clock what they must be for, am struck again with the horror of it. My legs might collapse from under me. I manage to get to a bench on the platform and sit down. I could melt into a puddle on the floor. I close my eyes.

'Excuse me.'

It is the man from the train.

'Are you OK?'

'Not really,' I say.

'You're very pale. You could do with some water. Do you have any with you?'

I nod, only now realising how dry my mouth is. My arms feel oddly numb. I look towards my little rucksack. My water bottle is there, tucked in the side pocket.

'Shall I?'

I nod again.

He gets the bottle, unscrews the cap, sits next to me and holds it up to my mouth.

I drink. I feel a dribble go down my chin and wipe it with the back of my hand. My arm feels like it is moving in slow motion.

'That will do you good.' His voice is steady and confident. 'You're experiencing shock. Adrenaline is having its way with you. You'll feel better soon.'

We sit for a while. I don't know how long. Eventually I swallow a few times and get ready to speak.

'Thank you,' I say. 'You're very kind.'

'Not at all.'

'You must think I'm mad.' My voice sounds odd, like it doesn't belong to me.

'Not at all,' he says again.

'My father—' I begin. But I can't carry on.

'That's OK,' he says. 'I could tell. I was keeping an eye on you in case you hit the deck.'

'Years ago.'

'That's the thing with trauma,' he says. 'Time doesn't behave in an ordinary way.'

'Doesn't it?'

'Our brains go a bit haywire. And memory can be all over the place. Things gets stuck.'

I shut my eyes and I am there, walking towards the front door, seeing black through the dappled glass, opening it to find the policeman. Mum's white face. In the big black car with Stephen. At the church looking at the shiny handles on the coffin. I can picture Dad's friends at the wake, can hear Tommy Mac's lowered voice. I'm with Stephen outside the pub as the sound of singing floats out through the back door.

'Breathe,' the man says. 'Breathe in slowly. Aim for your belly. Good. And out. That's it.'

We sit a bit longer. The numbness is gone, though my hands are a bit tingly. I finish my water.

'Thank you,' I say. It doesn't feel adequate. 'I mustn't keep you any longer.'

'Your colour is much better. Do you have far to go? Shall I call someone for you?'

'My brother is meeting me,' I say. 'He only lives around the corner.'

'Can I do anything else for you?'

'No, thank you. I'm grateful for your help. I'll sit here a few more minutes and then make a move.'

He stands up. 'Make sure you take it easy. Don't go climbing any mountains.'

I watch him walk away. By the exit he looks back, as though checking I'm still OK. He nods, then heads up the stairs.

I've lost all sense of time. I feel a bit floaty and not fully real, like I might be having a dream and will shortly wake up and puzzle over what it meant. I become aware of my surroundings: the grey of the platform, the metal seat underneath me.

My phone beeps. I manage to get it from my bag. My hands are still shaky.

It's Stephen: *Where are you?*

On way, I text back, my fingers clumsy, and then I carefully stand up.

When I come out of the station, Stephen is talking to someone. As I get closer, I see it is the man from the Tube.

'And here she is,' says Stephen. 'My sister, Ann.'

The man holds out his hand.

'Jamie,' he says.

His handshake is firm and warm. I almost thank him again, say something flippant like, 'My knight in shining armour,' but somehow I don't. I meet his eyes, understand that he is leaving it up to me if I want to tell Stephen what happened.

'I must deliver my sister to Sarah,' says Stephen, 'but we'll see you tomorrow night.'

'Will you?'

'You're coming to ours for dinner, aren't you? With Suzannah.'

He frowns. 'I said I'd talk to a friend of hers who is writing a book. That's not you, is it?'

115

Stephen laughs. 'No way. Liam is the writer. He's coming too.'

Jamie nods. 'Until tomorrow then,' he says, and his eyes flicker towards me as he smiles again.

'Look how lean he is,' Stephen says, as we watch him walk down the street. 'I'd kill for his BMI. He's super fit. Was in the Marines. He's a security consultant now. Advises high-net-worths.'

'What makes someone a high-net-worth?'

'How much money? I don't know; it's all relative, isn't it?'

'Would you like that much money?'

'I'd like to know I was capable of earning it. I'm not sure how much fun it would be if you had to worry about the kids being snatched.'

Jamie is almost out of sight. I turn and look at Stephen. I know from his face he is struggling. His skin has that greenish tint and there is a tightness around his eyes. 'And what's happening tomorrow night?'

'Dinner party at ours. Not that he seemed to know anything about it.'

'Do you really feel like throwing a party?'

'I don't feel like doing anything.' He looks at me. 'Are you all right? You're a bit pale.'

'Someone jumped in front of our train.'

'Sarah said.'

'It never gets easier, does it?'

'No, it never does.'

Our eyes meet, and for a moment the street recedes. London has vanished, the concrete replaced by water, and I feel like we are in a boat together, being tossed on a sea of pain. Then Stephen reaches out for my suitcase. 'Jesus, what an ugly object.'

'I can wheel it if it cramps your style.'

'I'll survive.'

As we walk towards Magnolia Road, Stephen tells me that he's been in this state of what he calls heart-attack city for nearly two weeks now. 'I'm all over the shop. Feel like shit. Can't sleep. Can't concentrate.'

'Did anything trigger it?'

'Getting injured didn't help. Stupid wakeboarding. I took up a posh-twat sport and then got injured like a posh twat. Tore my medial collateral ligament. I won't be able to train for months.'

'That's upsetting.'

'It is. All that fitness down the drain. No more marathons for a while. And my cuntiest customer is being even more cuntlike than usual. He's American so he's litigious. A cocktail of shit. But nothing that should—'

'I didn't mean to suggest there must be a logical reason,' I say. 'Sorry. Just trying to get a handle on it.'

'Don't apologise. Jesus. Forty-three and I still need my big sister to come and bail me out.'

I put my hand through his arm. 'What do you need from me? What can I do?'

'Keep me company. I feel less like my heart is about to explode out of my body when you're around. Sarah wants me to cut down on work, but that won't solve anything. We're thinking of leaving, you know. I don't like the way things are going in the States. I want a Plan B in case America ceases to be a functioning democracy. New Zealand, maybe.'

I'm trying to take all this in when a van parks up ahead of us and the driver takes out a large oblong package.

'Look at that.' Stephen points. 'An ultra-wide monitor. I want one of those.'

'Haven't you already got one?'

'I've only got thirty-four inches. That one is forty-nine. The extra real estate would be handy for meetings. Agenda on one side, minutes on the other, video in the middle.'

'Wow,' I say. I'm not trying to be sarcastic, but Stephen looks at me like he thinks I am.

'It's not technology one-upmanship,' he says, defensively. 'Or trying to spend my way out of the existential void, which is what Sarah says I do. It would be genuinely useful.'

'I'm sure.' I think how strange it is that Stephen wants to emigrate with his whole family to avoid global meltdown but can also be cheered up by the prospect of a new monitor.

We walk across the footbridge over the railway at the bottom of Magnolia Road. Stephen stops in the middle and looks down at the track.

I stand next to him but face the other direction, looking towards the street at all the pretty terraced houses painted in different pastel shades. I hear a lot about what happens here from Sarah, who runs the book club and is on the street party committee. It often sounds like a more enjoyable and upmarket version of church life, where fun is allowed and no one has to worry about God.

Stephen kicks his foot against the wire netting of the bridge. 'There's something I want to tell you.'

'Go on.'

'I'll have to work up to it.'

He looks dreadful, with a sweaty sheen on his forehead.

'You've got until Monday night. But wouldn't it be better to get it off your chest now?'

He grimaces. 'Can't.'

'In your own time, then.'

We stand for a while, and I wonder what it could be. We had an odd conversation just before he married Sarah where I asked if he'd been upfront with her about all the wobbles. He was outraged that I would feel the need to check. 'Of course I have,' he said. 'And whose side are you on, anyway?' We were both a bit drunk. It was before I was pregnant with Sam. He'd come to visit us in the new parish and kept making jokes about Doncaster being the casual-sex capital of the UK. Tim went to bed early and we stayed up drinking the whiskey Stephen had brought as a housewarming gift. My memory is hazy, but I think the evening ended with me promising that I would always support him, even if he behaved badly. I would always put him first.

I can see he isn't going to tell me whatever it is now. I look towards the street again and see a man waving at us from the attic of the second house along.

I nudge Stephen, who raises his arm in reply. 'That's Liam. Looking out of the window instead of getting on with his book. You'll meet him and Juliet tomorrow night.'

'You are lucky to live here,' I say, as we walk down the steps.

'I'd like more space. But Sarah doesn't want to move. She loves our friends. I said, we'll make new friends, but she thinks we shouldn't take it for granted, the set-up we have here.'

'She's right.'

'You're always moving. You settle in easily to new places.'

'No, I don't. I just put a brave face on it.'

'Really?'

'Yes. I'd love to have interesting neighbours to invite for meals. I don't think moving would solve any of your problems, anyway. You're just trying to distract yourself.'

We've reached his house. He opens the white wooden gate. 'Am I? Maybe it's like that thing people say about going on holiday. You get to the other side of the world only to realise you've brought yourself with you.'

'There's no escape from the self.'

'Fuck,' says Stephen, as he puts the key in the lock of the very purple front door. 'Then what hope is there for me?'

Eleven

We walk into a beautiful smell of chocolate and flowers and Sarah throws herself into my arms. When I haven't seen her for a while, I'm always surprised by how tiny and pretty she is. She's wearing yoga pants and a pale-pink top, and looks like the domestic goddess she is. As we hug, Stephen tells her about bumping into Jamie and him not knowing about the dinner. 'He thought he was just talking to Liam.'

'Oh dear,' she says. 'I think Suzannah is trying to trick him into a couples' activity.'

'All above my pay grade, thank God.' Stephen adds that he has a couple more hours of work to do. He'll take my case up; I'm in the attic bedroom next to his office.

Sarah gives him an exasperated look as he climbs the stairs.

'I wish he'd just stop,' she says, when he is out of earshot.

She takes a chunk of her smooth blonde hair into her hand, mimes pulling it out, then ushers me into the kitchen.

'See how frustrated I am? He exhausts himself earning money, then comes up with crazy ideas to spend it. He's still going on about underground extensions. I keep saying, over my dead body. He'll literally have to kill me and cover me in concrete before I let him inconvenience all our friends by digging up half the street.'

I laugh and then apologise.

'I suppose it is a bit funny,' she groans. 'Sorry to bang on before you've even sat down. Settle in and I'll make some coffee.'

She busies herself with the machine as I soak up the atmosphere. Everything is so clean and tidy and bright; an open-plan space with a kitchen and a dining table, and then a cosier area down by the French windows that lead out into the garden. Rainbow the cat is asleep on the blue sofa.

Here and there, a sign of my nieces. A whiteboard that says *We love you, Mummy* in neat cursive handwriting. Pretty pink glittery things. A miniature handbag, purple headphones, a tiny toy lipstick. Even the Lego bricks are in pastel shades.

I peep through the archway beside the fridge into the utility corner. Washing machine, tumble drier, a mop and bucket, supplies of toilet roll, kitchen roll, and capsules for the washing machine and dishwasher, which have been decanted from their ugly packaging into jars with black labels written in chalk pen. Medicines are on a higher shelf in boxes, each with their own label. *Are you hot?* says one. *Are you itchy? Are you bleeding? Are you a cat?*

'You're so organised,' I say. 'It's very calming. If I ever have a full-scale nervous breakdown, can I recuperate in your utility cupboard?'

'You'd be welcome.' Sarah gestures me towards a small blue mug on the enormous kitchen island. 'Though why do you need to wait for a crisis to offer yourself rest and comfort?'

I laugh. 'That's such a therapist question.'

Sarah wrinkles her nose. 'Is that bad?'

'Not at all. I love that you care about me. Most of the people in my life are into self sacrifice and see God as the only answer to a problem. It's good to be reminded there is another perspective.'

'I wish Stephen felt the same,' she says. 'He's supportive of my training but snippy if I try to share what I've learnt. He doesn't want to be improved, he says, just wants a beer and a moan.'

'I'm always up for being improved,' I offer, 'so don't hold back on the insights. But Stephen has never been keen on what he calls navel gazing.'

'Perhaps that's what all my training is about. Maybe I wouldn't want to be a therapist if my own fucking husband would sort his shit out.'

I look at her – my friend, my sister-in-law, who hardly swears. 'Come here,' I say. We embrace again. 'You'll be a great therapist, and all your clients will be lucky to have you.'

When I ask what I can do, Sarah says I'm already helping because Stephen calmed down from the moment he rang me, which meant she could relax a bit too. What she'd love is her own version of a beer and a moan. Her friend Juliet is collecting the girls from school and giving them tea, and she wants to spend that precious slice of time unburdening herself while doing her food prep.

She gets out a chopping board and a roasting tray, explaining that she lives on vegetables, pretty much, cooking huge batches which she eats for all her solo meals including breakfast with yoghurt and a spoonful of sauerkraut. I make a face.

'It's good for the gut,' Sarah assures me, as she dons a blue-and-white striped apron. 'And you get used to the taste.'

She lines up courgettes, red peppers, onions, an aubergine and a bulb of garlic, and puts an empty Tupperware box by her side. She takes the bulb of garlic, slices across the bottom, then presses each individual clove with the flat of a large knife to release it. She throws the garlic into the roasting tray and the discarded skin and ends into the Tupperware.

Then she sighs and says that Stephen has been a non-stop nightmare since his wakeboarding injury, when, because he couldn't move much for a few days, he just lay on the sofa flicking between news channels in between work calls and winding himself up about the state of the world. 'He wants me to research visas to New Zealand. Should I take him seriously?' She attacks a courgette. 'I mean, he could be right about imminent global meltdown, but it could be coming from the same bit of him that believes he's got to touch his toothbrush five times to make sure the girls don't get kidnapped.'

She moves on to a plump red pepper. 'He can't run because of his injury, and I don't know how he'll regulate himself without exercise. He's doing lots of counting and checking. He doesn't want anyone to know, which I understand, but I don't want to be dishonest with the girls. Alice asked me why Daddy kept turning the lights on and off, and I didn't know what to say.'

Her voice breaks. 'I don't want to start making up justifying reasons. I can't tell her that he's checking they're properly off, can I? That's what I say when he goes back to rattle the front door, that he's making sure he's locked it properly. But they're not stupid. Soon one of them will say, but he's already checked it five times. What do I do then? I don't want to try to convince them it's normal behaviour, do I?'

'It's hard.' I think of all the compromises I make when I try to interpret Tim to Sam and can see how tricky it is for Sarah to respect Stephen's desire for privacy while not being dishonest with her daughters.

'And it's not just the girls. All my friends think I have a perfect life. Which I do, in lots of ways. I'm not complaining, but it would be so much easier if I could just admit I'm knackered because he's up all night thinking he's having a heart attack. If he had asthma, or arthritis, or angina, I could say, couldn't I?'

'You mean it would be easier to explain?'

'More that he wouldn't be ashamed about it. That's the problem. I'm not ashamed of the wobbles. He is. But I'm getting increasingly hacked off that he won't get help. Will you talk to him about it? There's more chance he'll listen to you. Will you try?'

'Of course.' I doubt it will work, but it feels kinder not to tell Sarah that right now. She could do with a bit of hope even if nothing comes of it.

'There.' She casts the chunks of aubergine into the tray. 'All done. There's something therapeutic about making food, don't you think?'

'Not for me,' I say. 'I'd happily never cook again.'

'You don't like it at all?'

'Can't bear it.' I feel a thrill at the disclosure. I could never admit this in the vicarage kitchen. 'I liked watching you, though. You're so neat. When I do peppers, I end up with seeds all over the place.'

Sarah throws the contents of the Tupperware into the kitchen bin. 'We should compost really, but Stephen says he doesn't want to be surrounded by rot.'

I say she's probably got enough on without feeling guilty about her failure to compost, and she cheers up when I share how Bryony's initiative of communal composting came to a halt when Doreen opened the lid of the big green bin to see a fat rat sitting on top of the eggshells, potato peelings and old flower arrangements.

Sarah makes us both another coffee – decaf this time – and we sit on either end of the blue sofa. Rainbow is a bit disgruntled to be disturbed but then curls up on my lap and I enjoy the warmth of her as I look out of the French windows at the garden with its two sheds and a pretty red rose climbing up a trellis against the fence.

'And you'll help us get through this dinner party to-morrow night?' Sarah says, crossing her legs under her as though she is about to start doing yoga. 'Not cooking, obviously, just moral support. Keep Stephen on an even keel.'

'Can't you cancel it?'

'Stephen hates cancelling things. Makes him feel weak. So we all have to keep calm and carry on. I know exactly how it will pan out. He'll be stressed out before-hand, then the life and soul during, and he'll collapse afterwards. But he'll be better because you're here.'

'Who's coming?'

'Juliet and Liam, who live down the road, and Suzan-nah – a mum from school – with her boyfriend Jamie. Well, I say boyfriend. He's elusive, apparently. Goes abroad for work at a moment's notice, hasn't invited her to his flat, no social media presence. That's a red flag, apparently. Bigamists aren't on the socials.'

I consider telling Sarah about what happened on the Tube, but I don't want to explain or take the focus away from Stephen. I remind her I met Jamie earlier, with Stephen.

She nods. 'Handsome, isn't he? It's that James Bond vibe. Women go giggly around him, and men stand up straighter and suck in their tummies. You watch. And he didn't know about dinner?'

I shake my head.

'I think Suzannah is trying to pin him down. We were having coffee one morning after drop-off, and when Liam said he wanted to talk to military people for his new novel, she offered Jamie. Somehow I ended up hosting this dinner. Juliet says it won't work, Liam would be better off taking Jamie to the pub.' Sarah sighs and looks out of the window. 'It's all a bit silly and teen-age, really.'

I tickle Rainbow under the chin, thinking that it is a bit. But I'm pleased I'll see Jamie again. 'And none of these friends know about Stephen's wobbles?'

'No, it's only you and me that have any idea. He doesn't want any bleed into his working life; thinks it would be bad news, professionally. Liam had some type of breakdown a few years ago when he was stuck with the book he was writing. That's not a secret. But Stephen says it's one thing for Liam, as a writer, to talk about going mental, but that no one would want to buy networks from a nut job.' Sarah's eyes moisten. 'His words not mine, obviously. I did tell Juliet once that we're not as perfect as she thinks we are.'

I reach out and give her hand a little squeeze. Her skin is soft. 'You do look perfect, that's the thing.'

She sighs and then laughs, 'Liam thinks so too. He's always threatening to put us in a novel but says he'd have to give us a dark secret. He's obsessed with our dishwasher because it projects the finishing time on the floor in blue light. Like Gatsby's dock, or something. I don't understand him half the time. He's always quoting from literature, expecting everyone to get the references.' She stands up and stretches her arms to the ceiling., 'And as you used to say in the library days, I like the idea of reading more than I can face the actual slog of it. I'm on one novel a month these days, for our club, and that's plenty.'

As Sarah gathers our coffee cups and takes them over to the sink, I stroke Rainbow and think that if I lived here I'd spend every single spare second lying on this sofa reading a book.

Twelve

'Now you can open your eyes,' Alice says.

I'm standing with my nieces in front of the mirror in my room. They've been making me what they call 'red-carpet ready'. I've been manicured, pedicured, dressed in Sarah's clothes, and given 'a statement lip'.

'You look so pretty,' says Bella.

The dress is fine – they finally found one that isn't indecently short on me – and I'll wait until the girls are in bed before I tone down my cheeks, and rub off the gold eyeshadow and most of the lipstick.

'You can wear this if you like,' says Bella, pulling off her diamanté headband with built-in cat ears and holding it out.

'That is so kind, but I don't want to stretch it.'

'We need to do perfume,' Alice says, brandishing a bottle. 'I got this from Mummy. What you do is spray into the air and walk into it. Did you know that?'

'No. I just put a bit on my wrists.'

'We saw it on YouTube,' Bella says. 'Can I walk too?'

'We can all do it together.'

The girls discuss the logistics, and after a brief tussle over who is doing the actual squirting – Alice wins because it was her idea and she has longer arms – we hold hands and step forward into the scent of roses.

Sarah has transformed the dining table into a thing of sparkling beauty, all crystal and silver. I touch one of the thick, white napkins, enjoying the feel of the material against my fingers. I have nothing like this in my house. The feeding of humans is a functional business. Apart from holy communion, of course. When Tim is doling out the body and blood of Christ, he uses a silver cup and a linen cloth.

Stephen is lying on the sofa, Rainbow asleep on his legs. He's still wearing his dressing gown and has spent most of the day either working in his office or playing a computer game that involves shooting terrorists. I suggested a walk, but he said he needed to chill out. Since I arrived, I've learnt a lot about recent innovations in telecoms, how to train for a marathon, what to consider when buying a trail bike, and how to use the telescope he keeps in his office. He's yet to get anywhere near telling me his secret.

'Why do you look like a chorus girl?'

'Alice and Bella have been styling me.' I show him my manicure. My nails are silver on one hand and pink on the other.

'Quite a neat job,' Stephen says.

'I'm unrecognisable. Mum would say, *What are you doing dressed up like a dog's dinner?*'

'*It's not a fashion parade,*' Stephen trills, in a frighteningly good imitation.

'*It's like Blackpool Illuminations in here,*' I return.

'*It's not a hotel. You can't come and go at all hours.*'

I laugh. '*I wish to God I'd never met your father and let him ruin my life by knocking me up with you.*'

Stephen looks pained.

'Bit much?' I ask.

'Bit much,' he says.

Sarah comes in still wearing her apron, but she's red-carpet ready underneath. She leans down to kiss Stephen's forehead. 'Come on. Shower.'

'Rainbow doesn't want to be disturbed.'

'Our guests will be here in an hour,' Sarah says firmly, 'and you look like Stig of the Dump. I've done dinner and Ann has amused your children all day. You just need to clean yourself up and make a jug of Pimm's. Can you do that?'

'Yes, ma'am.'

I phone home and Sam answers. He's in good spirits. Barbara taught him to play a Cornish card game called euchre, but then had to go home because Ken is tied to the house until his fungal infection clears up and he can put his shoes on again. Dad had two weddings today, both with late brides and annoying photographers. They had a pizza for tea but Dad had to go out again because Derek's mother has had a funny turn. Sam is watching *The Hobbit* and will put himself to bed if Dad isn't home in time. I say goodnight and think how grown-up he sounds, my little boy with his middle-aged churchgoer line of chat.

Stephen decides Pimm's is boring and he'll make negronis instead. He throws me an orange from the fruit bowl, and I slice it as he sloshes gin and red vermouth into a jug.

'You're going for it,' Sarah says.

He adds liberal amounts of Campari. 'The chances of me getting through this evening without vast amounts of alcohol are zero. Who are you sitting me next to?'

'Juliet and Suzannah.'

He makes a face. 'Suzannah does my head in.'

'Why?' I am curious about her, this woman Jamie must like, though not enough to consent to being pinned down.

'Hard work.' He gets three tumblers, fills them with ice cubes, and pours the red liquid over the top. 'I love that sound, don't you? The crack as ice meets strong liquor. Orange, please.'

I add a slice to each glass.

Sarah picks hers up. 'What shall we drink to?'

'Survival,' Stephen says, and takes a huge gulp.

Sarah goes to put the girls to bed and I chat to Stephen, sipping away at the delicious, bitter liquid, thinking it's a good job Barbara and Doreen can't see how luxurious it is for me to come to my brother's aid. Stephen tells me Suzannah is high maintenance. Juliet works in PR and can be funny about her nightmare clients. Liam is a good laugh, though not when he bangs on about writer's block. 'And don't encourage him to talk about that prison he visits. So depressing.'

'It's probably depressing to be imprisoned there.'

'Don't you start. I don't have room for it, that's all. I give plenty of money to charity, but I can't bear the details of how they've all been failed by society multiple times. I don't want to listen to it again and again.'

The doorbell rings.

'Here we go,' Stephen says.

'You sound more like you're going into battle than throwing a party.'

He knocks back the rest of his negroni. 'Hell is other people. But Sarah loves this kind of shit.'

We hear her coming down the stairs.

'She'll get the door.' Stephen positions himself behind the island, almost like he is barricading himself in.

Juliet, Liam and Suzannah all arrive together. Juliet has auburn hair piled up on her head, and Liam looks like an ageing but still cool pop star. With his northern accent, he could be a third Gallagher brother. Suzannah is blonde and beautiful, which should not surprise me, I think. Of course Jamie would have an attractive girlfriend.

'Jamie not with you?' Stephen asks her, as he gives them all a drink.

'He's making his own way here.'

There is a sour note to her voice, and I can tell this was not the plan. She wanted to arrive with him, like a couple. She raises her eyebrows slightly when we are introduced, and I realise I've yet to tone down my make-over. I explain, and Sarah says the girls have requested a final goodnight from me.

I am almost at the foot of the stairs when the bell rings. I feel a flutter of anticipation as I go to the door.

Jamie is even better looking than I remember, and because there is a step down from the front door, we are at the same eye level. I thought he had blue eyes before, but they look grey now.

'I hoped I'd be seeing you again.' His voice is warm. 'You've been OK?'

'No further problems.' I step back to let him into the hall. 'Thanks again for looking after me. You were ever so kind.'

'It was a pleasure. You've certainly got some colour back in your cheeks now.'

I laugh. 'My nieces have been playing with me like I'm a giant doll.'

'I thought that must be the case. Unless I'd read you very wrong.'

'You didn't have me pegged as a fan of gold eyeshadow?'

He shakes his head slowly, and I like the idea that this man has an opinion about me and who I am. I wish we could just stay here in the hallway and I didn't have to share him with the rest of the party. Or his girlfriend.

I point Jamie towards the kitchen, then head upstairs. I kiss Alice and Bella goodnight and sing them a lullaby each, which is lovely; Sam still likes a story and a tuck-in but no longer wants a song. I go up to my room and take off most of the make-up. I still look different. Maybe it is the effect of the negroni. Or the mascara is making my eyes look sparkly. I picture Jamie standing there in the doorway. What was it he said? *I hoped I'd be seeing you again.*

Downstairs, I pause as I open the kitchen door. They are all standing in a group by the island, and I feel like I've wandered into a TV programme about sophisticated London life. I hope it is a comedy and not the sort of drama where the pleasant neighbour turns out to be a serial killer. Stephen looks like he's having a whale of a time, attentive to all his guests, topping up glasses. Sarah has lost her worried expression. If I didn't know what was happening beneath the surface, I'd be too intimidated to join in and would want to scuttle straight back to the land of custard creams and hot-water bottles. Then Stephen looks across at me. I see a flash of relief cross his face and remember that the real him wants me here.

He beckons me into the space between him and Juliet.

'Another negroni? Or a glass of champagne?'

'I'm not sure I should. I hardly drink these days.'

'You only live once,' he says, handing me a flute. He puts his arm around me. 'Now, Liam was just telling us about the Young Offender Institution he goes to every Friday.' He gives me a squeeze. 'They've all been failed by society again and again.'

Liam says, 'Yesterday I met a lad called Jason. I told him I had a character in my novel called Jason. He asked what he was like. I said he was half Irish. Jason said,

I'm half Irish. I said, he likes dogs. Jason said, I like dogs. And then he said, I bet your Jason hasn't stabbed anyone though, has he?'

There's a ripple of laughter, and Liam talks about how funny and bright so many of the lads are, but often hardly able to read and write. Education has not worked for them, he says, has done them more harm than good, and I think of my Sam and his strange scribble.

Sarah and Juliet look interested but I can see Suzannah is a bit bored and as soon as Liam pauses she jumps in and asks about his new novel.

Liam looks awkward and inches closer to Juliet as though seeking reassurance, 'It's early days, but I want to create an homage to *Anna Karenina.*'

'Doesn't she throw herself under a train?' asks Suzannah.

I glance at Jamie and our eyes meet. His mouth turns up ever so slightly. Not quite a smile, but something steadying. I look at his hand holding his glass and think back to the way he offered me my water bottle on the platform.

'That's the thing,' says Liam. 'In nineteenth-century fiction, adulterous women do end up dead by their own hand. I want to write an old-fashioned story of sin and betrayal but explore what happens now. If we break society's rules, do we have to be punished for our transgressions?'

'And do we?' Sarah asks.

'I don't know yet. I haven't decided what will happen to my Anna.'

'Nothing bad has to happen to her,' Suzannah says. 'Everyone has affairs now. They either get over it or the marriage breaks up. No one kills themselves over love any more.'

'Men have died and worms have eaten them,' Liam says, rather grandly, like he's quoting something. 'But not for love.'

'Exactly,' Suzannah says. 'And can't you even get remarried in church now?'

They all look towards me. *They must know,* I think. Of course they do. Stephen and Sarah will have told them about me. 'You can,' I say. 'But people don't take marriage vows lightly. My husband had a situation recently where the groom's parents didn't want the bride's sister to be matron of honour because she was divorced.'

'What happened?' Juliet asks.

'Tim encouraged tolerance and got the parents to relent. But they still believed she was wrong, even though they agreed to be forgiving. And when one of our parishioners thought she was dying, she asked Tim to talk to her granddaughter and persuade her not to leave her husband.'

'And did he?' Liam asks.

'He helped them clear up some misunderstandings. The young man apologised to his wife.' I am emboldened by the drink. 'He said, "I know I'm difficult. But I'm never a cunt on purpose."'

'That's rather sweet,' Juliet says.

'I'll make a note,' Liam says. 'And try it out the next time I annoy you.'

She leans towards him and chinks her glass against his. I feel a flicker of envy.

Liam turns back to me. 'More tales of vicarage life, please.'

'Tell them about the communal composting,' Sarah says. They all laugh when Doreen lifts the lid to see the rat, so I carry on about Doreen's ghost and how she later told me she thought it might have been a seagull banging its beak against the vestry window. I detail the recent hullabaloo over the brass cleaning, how Doreen was furious when the other ladies suggested her poor eyesight was leading to smudges on the candlesticks. I say that Lynn is still using this funny green foam called Oasis in her flower displays even though Bryony has banned it because it is bad for the environment.

'Contraband Oasis,' Liam says. 'Brilliant. Do you have a graveyard? I love reading all the names and epitaphs. So many stories. And all those beloved husbands and mothers. You'd think no one bad ever died.'

I tell him about Perfect Jane and her memorial. I describe the war graves area; white stones with red roses planted among them, how so many of the young men died at sea and on the same day. 'It's very beautiful. We've got a huge monkey puzzle tree and lots of hydrangeas and rhododendrons. Several benches looking out over the harbour towards the lighthouse.'

Liam sounds excited. 'A lighthouse?'

'Where is this?' Jamie asks.

'In Cornwall. On the south coast.'

'St Brida?'

'Yes.'

'I thought it sounded familiar. That's where I'm from.'

I stare at him. 'You grew up there?'

'Just around the corner from the church. My father is buried in your graveyard. Not far from the monkey puzzle tree.'

I have a sudden terrible thought. 'I do hope your mother isn't one of our brass cleaners.'

Jamie laughs. 'She moved up country to live with my sister after Dad died.'

'Do you go ever back?'

'I've no relatives there any more, but you must know Billy and Betsy?'

'We live at the bottom of their driveway.'

'Billy and I served together. I'm sort of an uncle to their boys. And now they're all grown up, Betsy is always trying to drag me into helping with the sheep.'

'What a coincidence,' Sarah says.

I feel oddly flustered and like I am too much the centre of attention. I glance at Suzannah. She is not pleased by this development, does not want Jamie to have a connection to anyone but her.

'You don't have a Cornish accent, do you?' Sarah asks Jamie.

'It comes out if I'm knocking around down there, talking to the lads at the boatyard.'

'Do a bit for us,' Liam says.

'He's not a performing seal, Liam,' says Suzannah, an edge of ownership in her voice.

There's a silence. Then Jamie grins. 'Thass all right, my handsome,' he says, and claps Liam on the shoulder.

Sarah picks up her oven gloves. 'Let's eat.'

Stephen and Sarah take either end of the dining table. I'm next to Sarah with Liam on my other side. Jamie is opposite me with Suzannah next to him. My eyes are drawn to him, to them. They look more like strangers meeting for the first time than a couple. There is none of the familiarity and ease between them that I see in the others. But there would be none of that between Tim and me either, if he were here. I wonder what I'd make of my own marriage if I was watching it across a table. I'm glad Tim's not here. I couldn't relax if he was, I'd be too worried he was about to launch into a lecture or start talking about God. I look down at my napkin, fiddle with the embroidered edge. It's a big thing, to realise I don't enjoy being with my husband. Maybe I'm drunk.

Juliet is telling everyone about how Liam is so obsessed with lighthouses that their romantic child-free mini-break was scuppered when he made friends with a retired keeper in the pub, and they then spent the whole weekend out on his boat. I laugh along, thinking that some of her frustration might be real, but it's so obvious that she loves him and would rather be on a boat with him than doing something more appealing with someone else.

Sarah serves salmon with lemon caper butter and garlic-crushed potatoes to a chorus of appreciation and compliments. As she passes around a tomato and watercress salad, she admits to never having read *Anna Karenina*. 'Should we do it for book club, Liam? Or will it encourage us into having affairs?'

'It's not an advertisement for adultery,' says Liam, 'more a cautionary tale: Women, if you go off with handsome soldiers, you'll end up disgraced and suicidal.'

'He's the bad guy, is he?' asks Jamie. 'The soldier?'

'You could read it, Jamie,' says Sarah, 'then come discuss it with us.'

Suzannah looks nervously at Jamie to see whether he will accept this further entrenchment into her life.

'I've never been much of a reader,' he says.

'What is it with straight men and book clubs?' Sarah asks. 'We don't have any. Except Liam, when he talked to us about his own book.'

'I'll come if you do *Anna Karenina*,' says Liam. 'Good research.'

'Count me out,' Stephen says. 'My contribution to book club is to make sure there is plenty of wine in the fridge and then clear off for the evening.'

'Philistine,' Sarah says.

'And how do you want Jamie to help you, Liam?' Suzannah asks, with that same proprietorial tone. Jamie doesn't quite flinch, but I can see he is not the sort of man who wants to be spoken for.

'I'm trying to get my head around what a modern version of Anna's lover might look like,' says Liam. 'Count Vronsky. He's respected by his regiment and expected to have a mistress, but he resigns his commission once he sets up home with her.' Liam looks at Jamie. 'How does that map against things now? Is there a higher moral standard in the military than in civilian life? What happens if people have affairs?'

'Depends quite a lot on who's involved,' Jamie says. 'Bad form to have one with the partner of someone in your command.'

'What happens? Would you get chucked out?'

'You might. Or get posted. Sent somewhere else at short notice. And then, if you had a wife, you'd have the job of explaining why.'

'You've never been married?' Juliet asks.

'No,' Jamie says.

There's a silence, as though we are all waiting for him to explain. When he doesn't, Sarah says she wouldn't want a military husband. 'I couldn't stand not knowing he was safe.'

'It puts a lot of pressure on relationships,' Jamie concedes. 'It's hard for people to be apart. Leads to lots of divorces.'

'You're not in the forces any more, though,' Juliet says.

Again, this sense that we are waiting for him to justify himself.

'I'm not much more reliable,' Jamie says. 'I get a phone call and might be gone for a couple of days or a month. Women don't like that. I've never had a pet, let alone a wife.'

'He's always on call,' Suzannah says. 'Has a special phone and everything. Can't go out of signal.'

It's still subtle, but Jamie's discomfort is more obvious this time – to me at least.

'Are you on call now?' Sarah asks.

Jamie smiles at Sarah. 'Hopefully my phone won't ring before I've finished this delicious salmon.'

Stephen says, 'You probably can't tell us who you work for.'

'You wouldn't recognise the names if I did. Lots of ultras are under the radar.'

'Ultras?' Stephen asks.

'Ultra-net-worths. They tend not to want attention.'

'The super-rich,' Stephen says. 'What are they like?'

'Not that different from other people. Less happy, usually.'

'Why?'

'They don't trust anyone. Always think they're being ripped off. And nothing is ever good enough. They have to up the ante all the time. It's a miserable life in many ways.'

'Not as miserable as being unable to feed your kids or pay your bills,' Juliet says.

Jamie nods.

'He knows that,' Suzannah says. 'That's not what he's saying.'

'We all know it, don't we?' Sarah gets up and starts clearing the table. 'There's no shortage of evidence that the rich and famous are screwed up. And yet we still envy them.'

'Maybe we think we'd do a better job of it,' says Liam, 'if it was handed to us. Money and fame. That we wouldn't be overdosing and needing to go to rehab. We would be purely and simply happy.'

As we eat our sticky toffee pudding, Liam asks Jamie more questions about soldiering; how he got into it, highlights of his career, best and worst bits. Jamie is polite but not particularly forthcoming. I can see Liam is hoping he'll stumble on the right question to make him open up but I don't think he's going to find it. Liam's not being disrespectful, exactly, but he clearly can't see why anyone would join the army in the first place and I'm not surprised Jamie doesn't feel obliged to put on a show for him. He does tell us about watching the sun rise over the desert from the back of a Chinook but says that military life is much less dramatic than everyone thinks, more about endurance and the ability to stay focused while hanging around.

'And how did you get that scar?' Liam is sounding desperate now. If I were him, I'd pull the plug and change the subject.

'Iraq.'

'What happened?'

Jamie puts down his spoon. 'An IED exploded. I caught a bit of shrapnel.'

Suzannah touches Jamie's arm, whispers something to him. He doesn't shrug her off exactly, but nor does he respond.

Juliet takes a sip of her wine. 'Of course, what we all really want to know is if you've killed anyone.'

There's a collective gasp. Stephen meets my eye and makes a 'What the fuck?' face.

'Steady on, Juliet,' he says.

She's defiant. 'Well, we do, don't we? I bet that's what we're all thinking.'

We look at each other and back at Jamie.

'Not me,' asserts Stephen. 'I was enjoying my pudding and minding my own business.'

I see a flicker of amusement across Jamie's face.

'I wasn't either,' Sarah says. 'I was thinking about PTSD, wondering how many soldiers need therapy, and if they get it.'

Suzannah looks a bit cross. I bet she thinks it's a good answer and that Jamie will like it. She won't say anything herself, I realise, because she wants the rest of us to think she already knows.

'I was,' Liam admits. 'And wondering what it feels like, both at the time and afterwards. If you get used to it.'

Jamie nods, and then his eyes rest on me. He doesn't say anything but there's an invitation in his gaze. I do feel an urge to tell him the truth. If none of the others were here, I might even do it. Some of it, anyway. I could tell him I wanted Liam to leave him alone and stop treating him like a curiosity. I wouldn't confess that I didn't understand why he was with Suzannah, or that a bit of me wished all the others would disappear so I could just talk to him.

The silence is stretching. We're still looking at each other and I'm not going to look away first. I feel caught in his beam, but don't want to escape. Then Sarah kicks me under the table, and I pull myself together.

'I reckon,' I say, lightly, 'that you must be good at interrogating people, because I could easily tell you all my secrets.'

Everyone laughs. I bet they're thinking, *What secrets could she have, this mousy woman?* But I don't much care. Sarah nudges me with her foot again and I cast around for something sensible to contribute, 'I wasn't speculating about whether you'd killed anyone but I was trying to get my head around how you live with the threat of death.'

His mouth turns up slightly. He knows I just made that up.

'That you might die, or your friends might die,' I add, and I can hear the sincerity in my voice. I might not have been thinking this, but it is real. 'I can't imagine it.'

'You shouldn't have to,' Jamie says. 'That's what the forces exist for. To protect civilians. To bear those burdens, including to take life, if we have to, and then work out how to live with what we've done.'

'At some cost to yourself, though,' Sarah says.

Jamie picks up his glass and raises it to us all. 'That's the deal.'

Juliet tings her glass with a fork. 'I don't want to skimp on my apology. I'm sorry, Jamie. It was a clumsy question. I see now that I shouldn't have asked.'

'It's natural to be curious,' Jamie says. 'But it isn't something that should be discussed lightly or without context. Out of respect for the enemy, as well as everything else.'

147

'It's not dinner party fodder,' Juliet agrees.

Jamie smiles. 'That's a good way of putting it.'

Sarah stands up. 'Perhaps we should all talk about something else over the cheese. Liam, you'll never believe this. Ann hasn't got a dishwasher.'

'What a fucking awful evening,' Stephen says, the minute they are all out the door. 'I bet Jamie was bored off his head. Liam came across like a nosy twat. Juliet behaved like she was his mum helping him get his homework done. Suzannah had a face like a smacked arse all night.'

'If she was hoping to pin Jamie down,' Sarah says, 'it had the opposite effect. I've never seen a man less in love. That thing about never even having a pet. Oof.'

Stephen pours himself a large glass of brandy. 'Doesn't want to be domesticated, does he? Can't say I blame him.'

'Hey,' says Sarah.

'It's different for me. I've got you. Any man would be honoured to be caged up with you. But why would Jamie want to sign up for book clubs and mini-breaks with Suzannah when he could be off doing lucrative shit for some billionaire?'

Sarah looks hurt. 'Caged up? Is that what it feels like? Do you mean marriage?'

'I don't mean being with you.' Stephen stretches out his arms, taking in all the debris of the dinner party; the dirty plates and glasses, the empty bottles standing on the side, the candles burning themselves down. 'Work, kids, home. Life. Not so much a rat race as a hamster cage. I'm just running around on my wheel.' He raises his glass to her. 'It's a nice wheel, I know that. In a nice cage. And I like the other hamsters I live with.'

Sarah narrows her eyes. 'You're drunk.'

'You could be right.' Stephen drains his glass. 'Whoops. All gone. I'll tell you a secret, shall I? I would like to get even drunker.'

'Don't look at me,' I say. 'I need sleep.'

'So do I.' Sarah takes the bottle of brandy and puts it back on the sideboard. 'We all do. I'm going to clear up, and you can help me or go to bed.'

Her voice is firm, like it was earlier when she told him to get off the sofa. And he obeys her again, taking the glass of water she gives him and shambling towards the stairs.

'Not our finest hour,' Sarah says, as I help her clear the table. 'But did you enjoy yourself?'

'Very much. They're all so different from the people I encounter at home. I liked Liam. It was just a bad idea for him to try to do his novel research with an audience.'

'And you liked Jamie,' she states.

I lift a pile of plates over to the island. 'He was very gracious over the killing thing, wasn't he? Impressive how he held his ground without making anyone feel bad. I wish I could do that.'

'And you liked him.'

I blow out the candles, gather up the napkins. 'I see what you mean about his effect on women, yes. Though I hope I didn't go giggly.'

'He was looking at you all night.'

'Was he?' I try to sound casual. 'My eyebrows are still a bit gold. Maybe he was looking at them.'

Sarah makes a little snorting sound and starts stacking the dishwasher. 'Poor Suzannah. Still, she might as well find out now. She doesn't want to be with someone capable of falling for someone else in an evening.'

I ignore most of what she says and respond to the bit about Suzannah. 'She was oddly possessive of him. I don't blame him for not enjoying it.'

'I bet he turns up. In Cornwall. To see those friends with the sheep. I bet you look up one day from polishing the candlesticks and he'll be there.'

'Don't be daft.' I'm about to add that she used to make up this sort of nonsense about Tim being keen on me, when I remember she was right about that to the extent I ended up marrying him.

'He likes you,' says Sarah, 'I can tell.'

'I think you're the one who's drunk.'

Upstairs, in the loft bedroom, I draw back the curtain and look out. By the light of the moon I can just make out the patchwork of gardens, with their sheds and trampolines and climbing roses. *Do all the people asleep in these houses feel like they are on the hamster wheel of life?* Perhaps that is what God is for, at the end of the day: to offer a promise of something more. Not that Stephen would find that consoling.

I think about what Sarah said about Jamie. He was looking at me, and I liked it. He made me feel like a person in my own right. Not a wife, or mother, or sister. For the first time in years, I felt like myself. *I hoped I'd be seeing you again.*

I shake my head. I'm not used to drinking; that's why I feel restless and strange. And I'm too far away from Sam. Only two days left now. Then I will go home, and my ordinary life will resume. I close my eyes and imagine Sam tucked up in bed at the vicarage, and me tiptoeing into his room, lightly kissing his cheek, and wishing him sweet dreams and an untroubled future.

Thirteen

The restaurant is plush and manly, and fitted out in dark wood with red-velvet furnishings and white table linen. The air hums with conversation and the chink of heavy silver cutlery on china plates. In the corner: a huge tank full of lobsters with elastic bands over their claws. I nudge Stephen.

'Poor fuckers,' he says, and averts his eyes.

This is Stephen's last chance to confide in me. From here he is taking me to Paddington, and I am catching the sleeper train home. I am ready to go, everything packed into a new suitcase, as Stephen has replaced 'that monstrosity' with a nifty red case he bought for himself before realising the boxy shape made it unsuitable for flights. Sarah insisted on giving me the dress and perfume I wore on Saturday night, saying they suited me more than her. I did manage to say no to a jar of sauerkraut.

When Stephen told me he'd booked us into his favourite steakhouse for a last dinner, I tried to refuse, saying

I'd had enough treats to last me for months. We went back and forth and then he said wearily, 'Do stop arguing. I can't talk to you anywhere near Sarah or the kids, can I? We need to get out of the house.' So I caved in and here I am, drinking a martini before I go home to resume my diet of mince and things on toast. Not that my mind is on food and drink. Even if Stephen can't bring himself to choke out his secret, I've got to fulfil my promise to Sarah and talk to him about getting some help.

The waiter brings over a chalkboard showing all the different cuts and weights of meat. After much deliberation and consultation, Stephen plumps for an enormous Nebraskan T-bone and I settle on a more modestly sized rib-eye. I must have it medium-rare, he says, because the fat needs to render. Triple-cooked chips, pommes dauphinoise, onion rings.

'Some salad?' I suggest. 'Something green?'

'If we must.'

The waiter leaves with our order.

'What a lot there is to it.'

'Serious business,' says Stephen, 'choosing a steak.'

The wine arrives, and Stephen sniffs it and then nods.

'How did you learn all this?' I gesture to the room, the flurry of waiters, men shaking out their thick napkins.

'I got that job in the restaurant, didn't I? I was fifteen when I started washing up there. And scrubbing mussels. Was waiting tables at sixteen. I learnt about food and wine, but I also got to observe wealth. No one is special, no matter how fancy their clothes. Everyone farts and shits.'

The steaks arrive on silver dishes. Do we want mustard? English, French, Dijon, wholegrain? We wield enormous knives as Stephen gets me to taste his steak so I can compare it with my own. We don't talk much as we eat. Stephen looks nervous. I'm feeling tense about how to broach the subject of therapy.

'At least now you know the difference between British and American beef,' he says, shovelling in the last of the chips. He leans back in his chair and lets out a long sigh.

'Contented?' I ask.

'Did I sound like it?'

'Not really.' I decide to go for it. 'Look, I know you don't like the idea—'

He interrupts, 'Don't tell me to have therapy.'

I look down at the table. I have spattered a bit of juice – blood – onto the white tablecloth.

'OK, but—'

'I can't do it because they will want to talk about Dad. And I can't. I literally can't. I just can't look back.'

His face is full of pain. All the confidence has vanished and he looks young, uncertain. Like he did on the day the policeman came. My stomach lurches, and I feel it: that sinking, tumbling sensation of being in freefall, of the end of innocence, like nothing would ever be the same again.

I reach out and touch Stephen's hand. It is as if we are frozen in this moment. We are here in the restaurant and we are also in our kitchen, wondering why the policeman has taken Mum into the front room and closed the door. And then Mum cries out and we look at each other, and we can't imagine what has happened but we know it must be bad. And I think we might never be able to get free. We could be trapped here for eternity.

But the waiter arrives. 'Can I tempt you with the dessert menu?'

Stephen grins at me ruefully as he takes it. 'The consolation of pudding.'

He orders a chocolate torte for himself, a lemon posset for me, and allows himself to be persuaded into a glass of sauternes.

When it comes, he swirls it around, sniffs, and offers it to me.

I take a tiny sip. It tastes expensive.

'Do you think I'm like Dad?'

I know it has cost him a lot to ask this question. The only time our mother ever listened to me was when I told her that, if she really cared about Stephen, she'd stop going on about how much like Dad he was. I hand him back the wine. 'You are kind and funny and good to be with. Dad was all those things.'

'I suppose he was.'

'You're not like him in loads of ways. You don't gamble. You always turn up if you say you will. You probably drink too much, but you don't get drunk like he did. You can stop, can't you? You stopped on Saturday night when Sarah said. Dad would never have let himself be sent to bed.'

Stephen laughs, but it is more like a bark. 'Do you remember what he used to say? When Mum tried to get him to slow down?'

I can see Dad then, standing at the bar at the Irish club, ordering another round. Mum wanting him to take us all home. I feel a tear run down my cheek. 'He used to say, *we'll be a long time dead*.'

By the time I come back from my little cry in the bathroom, Stephen has ordered two enormous glasses of cognac, and says he'll finish mine if I don't want it all.

'Is this what you've been worrying about, then? Is this why you pressed the panic button?' None of this is exactly new. I was expecting him to tell me something I didn't know.

He shakes his head.

The waiter is delivering a bottle of champagne to the next table. Four men in suits. I wonder what they are celebrating.

'Do you know how old I am?' Stephen asks.

'Of course I do. You're forty-three.'

He looks at me as though he's willing me to understand. 'And do you know how old Dad was when he died?'

'He was forty-three.'

Stephen swirls the cognac and looks down at it. 'I don't think I'm going to outlive him. I think I'm going to die before I get to forty-four.'

The men at the next table give a little cheer as the champagne cork pops, and for a moment I think I must have misheard. I ask Stephen to say it again and he does, still not looking up.

'Why do you think that?'

'Because I'm mental, probably.' He takes a sip of his drink. 'I haven't told Sarah, which, depending on how mental I'm feeling, is either cruel because we need to start planning for how she carries on without me, or good because it will worry her that I'm so mental I think I'm going to die at the same age as my dead father.'

I'm still grappling with his meaning. 'I don't understand. Have you had some terrible diagnosis?'

'Nothing as sane as that. I just think I'll die before my next birthday.' He sounds very matter-of-fact about it.

'So do you really think you are going to die, or do you *think* that you think you are going to die but know that you won't?'

He looks at me for the first time since his revelation. 'Bit of both.'

'So when you suddenly want to emigrate to New Zealand, or build an underground extension, or get a swanky new monitor . . . ?'

'It feels worth making other plans. But it isn't as cut and dried as that. It's more like all the possibilities are on the table. The cards are dealt but I haven't played the hand yet. I could still win big. But it's more likely I'll go down in flames.'

'And you don't want to— You're not going to do anything to make it happen?'

He shakes his head vehemently. 'I'd never do that to Sarah and the girls. I wouldn't be so scared, would I, of dying, if I was willing to do it to myself?'

'I suppose not,' I say, though none of it really makes sense.

'Don't make me tell Sarah. Or go to therapy.'

'Shouldn't you tell Sarah?'

'I can't. A lot of the time I manage to ignore it. That's my coping strategy. Work so hard I don't have time to think. But I won't be able to if Sarah knows. I won't be able to get it back in the box.'

I'm not sure of the logic of this, either, but can't see that arguing with him will help.

'What can I do, then?'

'I just wanted to tell you. And I wanted you to be prepared. You'd help Sarah and the girls, wouldn't you? They'll have plenty of money. I've got all the right insurance.'

'Of course I would. But it won't come to that. Does it help if I tell you it's not real?'

Stephen shrugs. 'Makes no difference. I can't reason myself out of it. Distraction is good. Take the piss if you like. I do feel better if I manage to get a laugh out of something. It won't do any harm anyway.'

'Got it.' I finish my brandy and Stephen asks for the bill.

'You know, another way you're not like Dad is that you've got more resources,' I say. 'We've got each other. Sarah is there to tell us both helpful things. I bet Dad didn't even know the words "coping strategy".'

'Poor fucker. There was no one to talk him out of it.'

'Maybe he didn't mean to do it,' I say. 'That is possible.'

'Come on.' Stephen looks at me as if I'm deluded. 'Even drunk people don't go and play on the railway line for no reason.'

I look down at the blood-stained tablecloth. 'Mum thought it was an accident.'

'She was just trying to protect us.'

'I'm not sure she cared about that.'

'Of course she did. It's a horrible thing to tell a child. You don't want them to know anyone would do that, let alone their own father. I'm never telling the girls.'

'But you don't want to lie to them, do you?'

Stephen doesn't respond. I hear Mum's voice in my head: *What you don't know won't hurt you. That's not for little ears.*

'I try to tell the truth to Sam,' I say. 'I understand why people want to protect their children. But we can't save them from the pain of life.'

'Can't we?' Stephen asks. 'I think I might try to for a little bit longer.'

In the taxi, I look out of the window at the lights as Stephen and the driver talk about football. Stephen's voice has changed again. He laughs a lot and keeps calling the taxi driver 'mate' as he commiserates with him on the performance of his team. I try to get my head around what he has told me. I am both upset by it, and not. Upset because I can see it is a horrible thing for him, but not, because it isn't real. I wish he'd tell Sarah. And I'll have to let her know I tried and failed with the therapy. There's not much more I can do without going behind his back, which feels impossible. As the taxi pulls into Paddington, I realise this is simply a longer version of that plane ride home from New York. He just needs me to keep him company until he's back on the tarmac.

'Look at you being all manly with the cabbie,' I say, once we are on the pavement.

'I do know how to speak man. Dad was good at that, wasn't he? It's a useful skill. I know men who are scared of their plumbers.'

As we reach the platform, Stephen asks if we could have a regular call. It will help him to contain it, he thinks. We agree to speak every Sunday night.

'Now, you don't need to wait with me. Go home and see your lovely wife. Reassure her you won't make her move to New Zealand.'

Stephen takes my hand. 'My big sister. My saviour. You do always make everything a little less shit.'

I look up at him, and it is as though the years collapse in on themselves and I see him at every stage of our lives. 'I love the bones of you,' I say.

We embrace. I smell his aftershave, feel a wisp of stubble against my forehead. My little brother. And then, from nowhere, I have the urge to offer a prayer. *Please God. Keep my little brother safe.*

Cornwall, August 2019

Fourteen

I pretend to be disappointed that my husband will be away for the entirety of Stephen and Sarah's holiday, but really I offer up a prayer of thanks when Tim says he is needed back in our old parish to lead the pilgrimage to Durham Cathedral.

We're having tea in the kitchen. Pizza and ice cream to celebrate Sam's last day of term. I pour out some lemonade and suggest we toast Sam's achievement at settling into a new school. 'Yes, very good,' Tim says, then explains how the curate who is supposed to be in charge has a stubborn fungal infection and doesn't think it's wise to subject his feet to the demands of a long walk.

'Ken has got one of those,' Sam says. 'Barbara thinks it's because he can't bend down to dry between his toes.'

I can see that Tim is mentally on the road to Durham in God's service and doesn't want to be distracted by Ken or foot ailments more generally. It will be a long drive, he says, but he can stop off to visit Father Robert in his almshouse. It is a big commitment of time, but it's important to honour the commitment of the twelve people who have signed up. He talks about his willingness to make a personal sacrifice and relates it to Jesus sending the disciples out with only one pair of sandals.

'What will you do on the pilgrimage exactly?' Sam asks, when he can get a word in.

'I will be open to what God asks of me.'

'And do you have to walk all the way back too?'

'No,' Tim says. 'We get the train.'

'Could Jesus get the train?'

'They hadn't been invented then.'

As I dish out the ice cream, I think how I'm not even surprised Tim isn't asking my opinion or acknowledging he'll be away from Sam for a chunk of the holidays. I sprinkle some hundreds and thousands, and stifle a laugh when Sam asks Tim what Jesus would have done if he'd got a fungal infection.

As Sam and I settle into life on our own, I can't deny that everything is easier without Tim around, needing to be fed and pointing out Sam's faults. We have an easy relaxed day waiting for Stephen and his family to arrive. I watch one of Sam's hobbit films with him. We agree we'd definitely say yes if Gandalf asked us to go on an adventure, and Sam perfects his impression of Gollum, doing an excellent job on the raspy voice. Then Sarah phones to say that Bella has been sick in the car, so they'll press on to the holiday cottage. Stephen will call around to see us later.

*

'Nice lino.' Stephen steps into the kitchen and looks around. 'It's like a seventies theme park.'

As Sam demonstrates the breakfast bar, Stephen tells him how hard I used to kick him when we were his age. 'And she once threw a saucepan at me.'

I protest, 'That was an accident. It slipped out of my hand.'

They are both laughing, but I can see that Stephen is taken aback by the state of the vicarage, and I can't face him coming further in right now so suggest a tour of the church.

'This is more like it,' Stephen says, when we get to the path. 'What a view.'

I hang back slightly so I can enjoy watching them, Stephen with his arm around Sam's shoulders as he chatters away. I love the ease of their relationship and how quickly they drop back into it, even when they haven't seen each other for a while. When Sam explains the lychgate I can see Stephen isn't keen on dwelling on all the dead bodies that have lain here over the centuries, so I interrupt with tales of eavesdropping on the drunk wedding guests.

'I didn't know that, Mum,' Sam says.

'You're always asleep.'

'What do they talk about?'

I remember the rekindling of old flames but can't recast it into anything appropriate for Sam. 'Love and clothes. Whether the bridesmaids suited their style of dress. If the groom looked silly in his top hat. Often it's old friends who haven't seen each other for a while. So they reminisce.'

'What's reminince?'

'Reminisce. Trade memories. Do you remember the time we did this or that or the other.'

'You and Uncle Stephen do that a lot.'

'It's one of the best things about knowing someone for a long time,' Stephen says, 'that you share memories together.'

'Why don't you do it with Dad?'

I hesitate. Sam is right, but it's never occurred to me before that we don't. It's probably too human for Tim when he could be thinking about God. 'I'm not sure. We could do it, though. You and I.'

Sam grins. 'Maybe, in the future, we'll say, do you remember that time we took Uncle Stephen to the church?'

Sam shows Stephen the stocks, pointing out the holes. 'Then people threw rotten food at you. Doreen says I'll end up here if I'm naughty. She gives me marks out of ten for behaving in church. I never get more than a six. She says if I go under five, she'll put me in the stocks.'

Stephen raises his eyebrows at me.

'I didn't know she said that to you, Sam,' I say. 'You know I'd never let her. Nor would Dad.'

'You wouldn't, but Dad might.'

Sam says it like it is no big deal, but my stomach flips. I avoid Stephen's gaze. I don't want to see either pity or censure in his eyes. 'He wouldn't, sweetheart. I promise you he wouldn't.'

'It doesn't matter anyway,' Sam says. 'I'm too fast for her. I could run away.'

We laugh and walk further in.

'That's cheery.' Stephen points up at the skulls that adorn a monument.

'The Victorians liked to remind themselves of death. That it is inevitable.'

Stephen grimaces.

I pat his shoulder. 'Not necessarily imminent, though. Come and look at Jane.'

Stephen reads the memorial tablet. 'She doesn't sound like a barrel of laughs. Too good to be true?'

'I've often wondered. Maybe she put on a brave face but boiled inside.'

'Is that what you do, Mum?'

I look down at Sam. 'A little bit, yes.'

'What makes you boil?' Stephen asks.

I tell them about the bellringing competition. I knew nothing about it and came home after being caught in the rain to find the dining room full of strangers. 'The main judge asked me to do them a round of teas, and when I went upstairs to change out of my wet clothes, he was coming out of our upstairs bathroom. It's that sort of thing that winds me up. People not respecting our privacy.'

'If you died, Mum, do you think Derek and Barbara and that lot would organise a tribute for you?'

'Doubt it.'

'That's not fair,' says Sam. 'You look after me and help at the food bank, and go to church even when you don't want to.'

'A few flowers, maybe. Bought from parish funds.'

'I think you'd deserve a statue.'

I put my arm around him. 'That means a lot to me, Sam. Anyway, I'm not likely to die any time soon.'

Stephen picks up one of the service booklets and points to the cover. 'Why does it say Ordinary Time?'

'That's the bit of the church calendar we're in. Because there are no big feasts. It lasts until Advent.'

'Jesus,' Stephen says, and then: 'Sorry. It's just, Ordinary Time. It doesn't feel like we're living through ordinary times, does it?'

'Why not?' Sam asks.

Stephen sighs. 'Naughty politicians doing silly things.'

Sam nods gravely. 'And the climate. Humans have destroyed the world.'

'Well, I don't know about that.' Stephen puts down the booklet. 'I'll tell you a secret, Sam. I can't think about climate change. It's too big.'

'But what if everyone decides not to think about it because it's too big?'

'I know. That's why it's a secret. I don't want other people thinking I'm a—'

He glances at me and back at Sam.

'Bad person. I don't want people thinking I'm a bad person. So it's a secret. For your ears only.'

'Like confession,' I say. 'That's what happens in Catholic churches. People confess their sins and get forgiven.'

'Who forgives them?' Sam asks.

'The priest.'

'Can Dad do it? If Dad was here, could he forgive Uncle Stephen?'

Stephen and I exchange a smile.

168

'Not quite,' I say. 'Maybe we could try. You and me.'

Sam reaches out and pats Stephen on the arm. 'We forgive you.' Then he shrugs. 'It's probably too late anyway.'

Stephen pulls Sam in for a hug. 'That's one way to look at it.'

That night I wake with a start. I was in the churchyard with Jamie. We were looking for his father's grave but couldn't find it. Then Stephen was saying, *I don't want to die*, and Sam was crying, *Please don't put me in the stocks*. I get up and check on Sam. He's fast asleep. He looks peaceful, as though it is only in my dreams that he is in any danger or distress. I stand and listen to the rhythm of his breath, drop a kiss on his forehead.

Back in my bedroom, I look out of my window. The church is beautiful in the moonlight. I've dreamt of Jamie a few times now. Not much happens. We walk and talk. Once we were on a boat. And in real life, I have looked for his father's grave. I don't have much to go on, but I've found two possible men who are the right kind of age with no named children. It's silly. I don't even know why I'm interested. Except I do. I like the idea of having some kind of connection to him, to that feeling he gave me of being a person in my own right.

We spend most of the next day at the beach in grand style as Stephen has all the kit down to a special mallet to knock in the red and yellow windbreaker. When Sam kicks off his trainers I see one of them has a hole. He does look like a poor relation in his slightly too small trunks, but the girls very sweetly share their body boards with him and they all splash around happily. Stephen does a continual inventory of everyone else's equipment – hardly anyone has just a towel and a book – and tries to persuade Sarah they need to get an inflatable sofa and a chiller cabinet.

I ask how their friends are. I am hoping for a snippet of Jamie, but instead I get a lot about Liam, whose children's book about time travel is going to be published, and Sandeep, whose son Sukraj keeps forgetting his EpiPen.

Sarah is trying to read *Anna Karenina* but can't get past the first few pages and her copy spends most of the day face down in the sand. She says she'd never have picked it for book club if she'd known how long it was. 'My name will be mud.'

'You must have shelved it at the library,' I say.

'I don't notice things about books the way you do. I can't believe you haven't read it. You've read everything.'

I don't say that I've never wanted to experience being in the head of a character who jumps under a train. It doesn't feel the right kind of chat for the beach.

Later we have a picnic in the vicarage garden.

'I wish we could have tea like this more often,' Sam says.

'What do you like best?' Sarah asks him.

'The prawns,' he says, 'and olives.'

'I like avocado best,' says Bella.

Back in the kitchen, Sarah wraps the leftovers in tin-foil and watches the children out of the window. They are taking it in turns to fall out of the camellia.

'Amazing, isn't it,' says Stephen, 'what the kids eat. We didn't get a sniff of an avocado growing up, did we? Mum thought spaghetti was exotic. What was that thing she used to make with mince and sweetcorn?'

'Spaghetti Verona. But mainly it was cottage pie, chops, a roast dinner on Sundays.'

'Angel Delight,' says Stephen. 'And fruit cocktail. Only ever one cherry we used to fight over.'

'Those pink wafers that stick to the mouth. Wagon Wheels, if we were lucky.'

Stephen opens the cupboards under the sink. 'I still can't believe you haven't got a dishwasher.'

'I'm very happy without,' I say. 'Don't go buying me one.'

'You wash, I'll dry, then. Like when we were kids.'

I wink at Sarah. 'He got bubbles everywhere if he was in charge of the washing-up liquid.'

'Tell me more,' she says. 'Was he very aggravating?'

'Actually, no.' I flick a bit of foam at his face. 'I can't pretend that he was. We always got on.'

Stephen swipes at me with the tea towel. 'Where does this dish go?'

I point towards the larder.

Stephen disappears through the door. 'Jesus,' he says. 'Sorry, but there's a fair bit of damp in here.'

'Cornwall is damp. We're on a list. But there's a back-log. A lot of church buildings need attention.'

Stephen's face shows his disgust. 'This can't be good for you. What does Tim think?'

'He cares more about our souls than our bodies. If asked, he'd probably say we were better off than a lot of people. Which is true.'

He shakes his head. 'It's like something out of a film. Living in squalor. I don't know why you put up with it.'

I don't know why I put up with it either, but Stephen's reaction makes me a bit defensive. 'Lots of people have to live in circumstances that are less than ideal.'

I can see that Stephen doesn't understand what other people have got to do with it. He changes tack. 'Why aren't you working? I thought you liked work.'

'I will do, in the future.' I put the last plate on the draining board and pull the plug. 'It's just been tricky settling in. Tim's got a lot on as it is without me going out to work and not being here.'

'And he'd rather be skint than have to do the dishes occasionally?'

I look at the grey water circling down the drain. 'Yes, actually, he would. And they all expect me to help. The parishioners. The last vicar didn't have a wife. They all said it would be nice to have a woman about the place.'

'Oh, for fuck's sake,' says Stephen, 'can you even hear yourself? I thought you were supposed to be a feminist?'

I watch the exasperation on Stephen's face. This was how we used to speak to each other when we were teen-agers. I want to fight back. I want to say, *Don't lecture me. I'm not the one who's made up a story that I'm going to magically expire before my next birthday.* But I can't say that in front of Sarah. And I feel too old and tired, worn out by all the compromises of my life. I can't stand to see it through his eyes. Any success I've had in looking on the bright side about my situation is fragmenting under his gaze. I sit down at the breakfast bar and rest my head in my hands.

'I don't know what happened to you,' Stephen says. 'You used to be so sparky. I always thought you could do anything.'

'When?' I say, staring down at the surface of the breakfast bar. 'When was I ever like that?'

'When we were kids. What happened?'

I look at him. 'What do you think happened? I lost the only parent who liked me. I had to look after you. Everything changed.'

It is impossible to stay upright. I lie down on the floor.

Sam comes in. 'What's going on? Mum?'

I should get up, I think. I need to reassure him. But I can't. I put my hand over my face.

I feel Stephen lie down next to me. 'We're playing this game we used to play as kids, Sam. It's called Floor.'

'What do you do?' Sam asks.

'You just lie down,' Stephen says. 'It's not hard. But you're not allowed to get up.'

'What's the point of it?'

'Well, a purist could say there isn't much point. But it's quite relaxing.'

'Let's get ice lollies, Sam, and go out into the garden,' Sarah says.

I close my eyes. I feel like a dam is about to burst. I hear the rustling around in the freezer, then footsteps, and the back door closes. At last. Sam has gone. It is just Stephen and me lying on the floor. I can let go.

Dad used to tell us a story about this time when he and his mate, Jimmy, had been digging a hole on a night shift and had stopped for a sleep. One of the bosses found them and shook Dad awake.

'Leave me alone,' Dad said.

'Do you know who I am?' the man shouted, furious.

Dad nudged Jimmy awake. 'Hey, Jimmy. There's a bloke here who don't know who he is.'

At this point, Dad would roar with laughter. Stephen and I liked to act it out. We'd get the dog to be Jimmy. We'd take it in turns to be Dad or the boss. I always wanted to be Dad. My favourite bit was the end. I knew it was wrong, the way Dad said it. I knew it should be 'doesn't' instead of 'don't'. But I liked Dad's way and I loved saying it. 'Hey, Jimmy. There's a bloke here who don't know who he is.'

It is difficult to remember the life before. I have flashes only, like I'm flicking through a photograph album belonging to someone I used to know. Dad asleep in the armchair. Dad cracking open a can of beer and saying, 'I deserve this,' before taking a hefty swig and ending up with foam on his upper lip. Dad with his arm around Stephen. The Irish club. The working men's club. Sometimes Mum and Dad would dance and we'd watch them, sitting with our bottles of pop and bags of crisps. When

Mum wanted him to stop, to slow down, to have less fun, Dad would say, *A man can drink and not be drunk*, or, *We'll be a long time dead*.

What I do remember is that I was obsessed with going to St Hilda's school to do my A levels. Kitty Graham was going, and I wanted to go too. It cost thousands of pounds, but I was about to take the entrance exams in the hope of a scholarship. I wanted to go even if I didn't get one, and Dad had promised I could. He believed in education, that was the thing. He was proud that my teachers would say I was exceptionally bright, an Oxbridge prospect. He liked to say that the world could be my oyster, and he loved the idea of me mixing with what he called 'quality people'. I was reading *Brideshead Revisited* and I wanted to meet my Sebastian, the friend who would make me feel like real life was beginning. I wanted to wear a gown – I wasn't sure exactly what one was – and ride a bicycle and be punted around by a young man wearing a boater. And read. And write essays. In my fantasies, my handwriting had always become more beautiful.

When Kitty and I went on the open day, a girl came out of the toilets with her skirt tucked up in her knickers. She walked the length of the corridor before the sniggers of the surrounding boys tipped her off. 'She'll never be able to come here now,' whispered Kitty. I thought Kitty was a bit unkind in her obvious satisfaction, but I accepted the truth. Yes, it would be impossible to ever get over the humiliation, and I was grateful that it wasn't me.

Later – after Dad's funeral – I kept thinking about that girl and wondering where she was. I thought that maybe if it had been me, I wouldn't have had to suffer what came later. That I had brought it on myself. I could have responded differently and I might then have averted everything that happened later. All of which could be laid at the foot of my pride. I had been punished to show that there are many worse things than showing your knickers to a gaggle of posh boys.

It was more difficult to stay in touch in those days before email. I wrote to Kitty Graham once or twice but she never answered, and as I got on the bus to the sixth-form college near my grandparents' house, I would imagine her living my lost life. Rowing, maybe. Playing lacrosse. Debating society. And I did not fulfil the promise of my potential. I was no longer a prospect for anything. The world was not my oyster. The girl I was had disappeared.

Eventually I stop crying.

'What's wrong,' Stephen asks.

'I don't know who I am.'

'Don't you?'

'No.'

'I know who you are.'

I reach for his hand and hold it.

'I don't remember much of life before,' I say. 'Do you?'

'Bacon and cabbage at the Irish club. Playing poker with Dad. You're right about everything changing. It was the end of fun, wasn't it?'

'It was.'

Stephen squeezes my hand. 'Thanks for looking after me.'

'I don't know why I said that. I didn't really look after you. People just kept telling me I had to.'

'You did look after me.'

'Dad kept saying it to me, before.'

'When?'

'For a while. If he was drunk, mainly. He'd say how he wished he'd had a sister, that life would have been different. He'd say it was good you'd always have me. Should I have known?'

'You were fifteen. How could you have known?'

'And I was nagging him about that stupid school.'

'What school?'

'I wanted to go to that private school for sixth form. Dad had been keen on it. But then he asked me if I really wanted to go, and would they not all be a bit stuck up. I said I did.'

'You don't think it was your fault, do you? Even I know it wasn't our fault. It was nothing to do with us, except we had to suffer the consequences.'

'Mum said it was.'

'What?'

'She said it. I heard her. In the kitchen, a few days after the funeral. She said, he was worried about that bloody school. She said I'd always been able to twist him around my little finger and he couldn't bear letting me down.'

'That's nonsense. She was upset.' Stephen squeezes my hand again. 'She didn't mean it. And Dad was right about one thing. It is good for me that I've got you. I don't know what I'd do without you. Though next time you go tonto, can you do it somewhere with a nice bit of carpet?'

By the time Sarah comes back in, we have finished the dishes and are sitting at the breakfast bar drinking tea.

'This is an amazing place,' she says. 'The views, and the garden. Think what people would give to be so close to the sea.'

She raises her eyebrows at Stephen.

'OK,' he says, 'I'll agree the location is good. And the rest of it is none of my business, I suppose.'

We plan out the rest of the week. I think Sam and I should go to church to support Bryony, but Sam argues that it is enough that he has to support Dad, so I agree he can go to the donkey sanctuary with his cousins instead. Sarah asks if I fancy a spa session with her at one of the hotels later in the week. Stephen will take the kids to the beach.

'You won't feel left out?' I ask Stephen.

'You'll be doing me a favour. I hate the spa.'

'He doesn't like being separated from his phone for that long,' says Sarah, with a wink.

At church, I quickly realise I much prefer the Bryony who runs Mindful Mondays to the Bryony who talks about God. She offers the opportunity for personal witness, inviting us to come forward and share how we have been experiencing God in our lives. Nobody moves. But then a woman I don't recognise shuffles to the front and talks about how depressed and miserable she has been lately, and how she doubted everything, but then God came back to her when she saw a blue tit on her bird feeder and knew it was a message for her, and that there are no coincidences, only God incidences.

Then Bryony tells a tedious story about thinking her parcel was lost in the post but it wasn't, and asks us to talk to the people near us and share a time when we too lost our faith and found it again. I feel put on the spot by this. And I haven't quite followed her reasoning. What if the delivery had ended up at the wrong address? Does contacting customer services show a lack of faith? Sometimes parcels do just go astray.

It gets worse when Bryony asks people to share back. Barbara says she lost faith that her tomato plants would flower, but they did.

'How wonderful!' Bryony exclaims.

Mrs Holt says that she thought she was going to die on a trolley but God spared her, and Bryony says, 'How wonderful,' again but doesn't sound quite as excited as she did about the tomatoes.

Bryony talks about prayer and gratitude. You can pray while peeling the potatoes for Sunday lunch if you do it joyfully and with gratitude. Where do we like to pray? Barbara says she prays just before bed. Derek likes to pop into the church every day when he opens up. Blue-tit woman likes to get into nature. And then Doreen says the only way she can get everything done in her life is to multi-task, so she prays on the toilet.

Bryony asks everyone to pray for all the people in the world who suffer most from the selfishness of the West – there is a long list – and for God's planet. She asks for help for all the political leaders of the world; that they will be supported in their burdensome duties and guided to make the right choices.

'Let us lift them up,' she exclaims. 'Let us raise them in prayer.'

We sing 'Shine Jesus Shine', and Bryony waves her arms in the air and encourages the congregation to follow suit. Barbara is really going for it, and even Doreen has one arm up. I feel under pressure but keep my arms by my sides. Mrs Holt is not moving, either.

My only sincere prayer is the thanks I offer when it is all over.

I walk out with Mrs Holt.

'I'm not doing all that arm waving,' she says to Bryony.

'You do whatever you like, Mrs Holt,' says Bryony. 'I'm just happy to see you here every week.'

'I'm a miracle, you know,' says Mrs Holt. 'That's what the doctor says.'

'I know,' says Bryony. 'God's work is great indeed.'

Mrs Holt doesn't look convinced by that. Maybe she doesn't want to share the credit for her sustained life with anyone, even God.

Sam arrives home full of stories about the donkeys. He looks different and I think it must be happiness and then notice he's wearing new clothes and trainers.

'We popped into Truro afterwards,' Stephen says. 'Did a bit of birthday shopping.'

The children go outside to play.

'I wanted to take him for a haircut, but Sarah said I had to check with you first.'

'I always cut his hair.'

'I know you do. It's completely fucking obvious. He's too old to have shit hair.'

'Is it that bad?'

'Don't you remember the weird kids at school? What did they all have in common? Older parents, sometimes religious; homemade haircuts; hand-me-down clothes. Are you trying to make Sam a pariah?'

I know Tim would disapprove if he were here. But he's not.

'OK, then. If he wants to, it's fine by me.'

Tim calls just after I've tucked Sam in. The pilgrimage is going well, but there is a domineering worship leader he finds annoying and one woman who keeps complaining that her feet hurt. He tells me all about his trip to the almshouse on the way up. Father Robert is poorly. He's short of breath and has grown a beard, as he kept cutting himself when shaving. He's had some tests – they put a huge needle into his hip – but says that whatever happens he doesn't want any treatment. 'He's not in a hurry for heaven but is content to leave his life in God's hands,' Tim says, admiringly, and then asks me, 'Was Sam well behaved in church today?'

I almost lie. Would he ever find out? But the abrupt change of subject has wrong-footed me, and I hesitate too long.

'Sam didn't go to church. He went to the donkey sanctuary with the girls.'

There is a silence.

'There were a lot of donkeys there,' I say, in the chirpy voice I use when I am trying to pretend all is well, 'but not much else. Some people complain that there is nothing to do except look at donkeys. But the kids all enjoyed it. They're going to the seal sanctuary on Thursday. I don't know if there's anything else to do there. Or just seals. I'm not going because there's no room in the car.'

As I hang up, I wonder if I'm frightened of Tim. Not that he'll hit me, or swear at me, but that he will disapprove. I must be, or else why don't I tell him I'm going to the spa with Sarah? Or that Sam is getting a proper haircut? Why can't I say that I don't want to go to church to listen to Doreen talk about praying on the toilet? How would I even form the sentence? *I don't want to go to church this morning. I don't feel like church this morning.* What is Stephen's expression when he doesn't want to do something? 'Just give it the swerve.' Sam gave church the swerve this morning. Maybe one day I will too. But I can't imagine it.

At the spa, Sarah and I coincide with a hen party taking photos of each other drinking Prosecco in the hot tub.

'Do you think they have any idea what marriage is like?' Sarah asks me, as we observe them from the safety of the herbal sauna.

'How could they?' I ask. 'You don't understand Planet Marriage until you've been there.'

'And then you find out it's not at all like the guidebook promised.' She sounds unusually bleak. 'Look, I had an ulterior motive for wanting to get you alone. Can I ask you something?'

I am about to respond when the sauna door opens and three young men come in and discuss the pros and cons of high-powered blenders. They're good for making ginger shots, one says, but his friend tells him blenders destroy the cell structure of plants and turn them into sugar. You should eat things in their natural state, he says, and you need thirty types of fruit and veg a week for your microbiome to thrive. It's hard going, though you can count all the different varieties of salad in a bag and all the different types of seeds. He's got a mix that has pumpkin, sunflower and caraway. 'I'm eating so many seeds,' he says, 'I feel like a bird.'

Sarah says she's too hot, and we decamp into the gardens and find a couple of loungers on a gravelled area near the plunge pool.

We both lie down. 'Go for it.'

'I'm not sure I should.'

'Ask me anything you like.'

She sits up, swings her legs over the side of the lounger. 'Is Stephen having an affair?'

I laugh. 'Sorry, but it seems so unlikely.'

'He isn't, then?'

'Not that I know of. I'm sure he isn't. What makes you think it?'

'He's odd, hyped up all the time. I'm used to the anxiety, but the secrecy is new. He goes out into the garden to make calls. Says he's phoning you, but why wouldn't he want me to hear?' Her voice is plaintive. 'I thought you might know about it.'

'Sweetheart.' I look down over the gardens towards the sea and wonder what I can say without breaking Stephen's confidence. 'There's nothing like that. He adores you. He is feeling troubled. I've tried to get him to talk to you or agree to therapy, and he says he can't. But it's not a lack of love, I promise.'

'That's a relief, I suppose.' She leans down, picks up a handful of granite chips, lets them slip through her fingers. 'I've only got to deal with a miserable husband, not a miserable husband who might want to leave me. Shall we try the plunge pool?'

Afterwards, as I wait for Sarah in the lounge, I text Stephen to say that if he won't tell Sarah, he needs to reassure her. He replies with a thumbs-up emoji. Across the room, the hen party are gathering. They have matching pink gift bags that say 'Bride Squad' in gold letters. 'I've got a lipstick and a hangover kit,' says a woman with black-framed glasses. They compare the contents of the bags and discuss the upcoming pitch-and-putt session. Not everyone is keen. The bride must still be in the changing rooms as there are a couple of borderline bitchy comments about how not everyone has her energy levels or competitive streak. 'She's only letting me be a bridesmaid if I wear contact lenses for the big day,' says the woman who got the lipstick, as she tests it out on the back of her hand. 'She says she doesn't want my glasses ruining her wedding photos.'

On Thursday, I wave them all off to the seal sanctuary. Sam's haircut is fantastic. He looks older and more robust as he trots off happily with his cousins, sliding into the gap between their massive car seats.

I peg out the washing, then go into the dining room and stare at the mountain of carrier bags. I don't even know who I would talk to about relocating it. *Vicar's wife is above storing jumble. Vicar's wife is selfish princess. Vicar's wife does not care about other people.* It's too tiring. Maybe I'll read a book instead. Something escapist. Give myself a few hours off from my own life.

There's a knock at the front door. Obviously the God I am never sure that I believe in does not want me to have time to myself. It won't be Barbara or Derek or any of the usual suspects, as they charge straight on in through the kitchen. I compose my features so I don't look bored or aggravated when whoever it is tells me that their car won't start, or asks for directions, or complains that there are empty lager cans in the Angel Garden.

I open the door.

'Oh,' I say, and can hear the pleasure in my voice. 'It's you.'

Fifteen

Jamie stands there in jeans and a blue sweater. He's vibrant against the gravelly background of the car park, and looks like he's stepped out of a photoshoot for an advert selling casual clothes to middle-aged men who aspire to health and fitness. I cast around for a normal way to greet him. 'This is the second time I've opened the door to you.'

Too portentous, I think, as soon as the words are out of my mouth, but he's smiling and I look into his eyes – blue again today – and feel a rush of whatever it is I experienced on the train platform and across the dinner table.

'That first time,' he says, 'you were expecting it to be me.'

'And today you are a surprise.'

'A good one?'

I nod. I don't trust myself to speak. I feel like I've lost control of my body. My mouth is smiling itself.

'I'm going to visit my dad's grave. Would you like to come with me?'

He is staying with Billy and Betsy, he tells me, as we walk down towards the church. It's a flying visit. Tomorrow he's seeing a client whose yacht has docked in St Brida and then he's heading back to London. I explain about Tim's pilgrimage, that Stephen and Sarah are here. I tell him how Stephen read out all the reviews of the donkey sanctuary that complained there was not enough to do apart from the donkeys, and how we all loved the response saying, *We are a donkey sanctuary, not a fairground. Don't come here unless you are interested in donkeys.* Jamie laughs. *A man who sees the funny side,* I think, *what a beautiful thing.*

'They've taken Sam to the seal sanctuary today. There's not enough room in the car for me.'

'So you've got a day to yourself,' he says. 'Any plans?'

'Not really. I was about to choose a book to read.'

We approach Rosina Lucy. 'This is my favourite grave.'

He stops. 'What is it you like?'

'The absence of clutter. Not "daughter of" or "wife of" or "mother of". Just her name and dates. But the epitaph has so much warmth in it.'

'Brief is life but long is love,' he reads.

I do like his voice. I look at him, standing there in the sunshine, and can't quite believe this is happening. I have an urge to confide in him. 'Rosina is the nearest I've got to a friend down here. I have little chats with her.' I look up at him. 'Do you think that's mad?'

'Whatever gets you through.' He winks at me. 'It's better than hard drugs or punching people.'

187

As we walk around the church, Jamie says he re-members being a Wise Man in the nativity here. He had a crown made from cardboard and sprayed with gold paint. He touches the back of his head. 'I can still feel the staple digging into my skull.'

'I bet you were a cute little boy.'

'My mum thought I was. She was cross I wasn't Joseph. And that I didn't have any lines.'

'When I was Mary, my mum said, "Don't they usually choose a pretty girl to be Mary?"'

Jamie looks down at me. 'That's horrible.'

I nod. 'Yes, it was. We don't get on.'

'Never?'

'I heard her tell one of her friends once that I came out of her with my nose in the air. That's depressing, isn't it? On my wedding day, she said, "I never thought you'd get married. I suppose you'll have a child now, and then you'll know how hard it is."'

'She sounds like a grade-A bitch,' Jamie says.

'Thank you,' I say. 'That's such a refreshing change from being told that she probably loves me deep down.'

Jamie leads the way through the middle of the church-yard up to the far corner by the monkey puzzle tree.

'Here he is.'

It is one of my two candidates. A simple red granite headstone with a built-in flowerpot. The grave itself, neat and tidy with trimmed edges and no weeds or litter. A bench right by it, shaded by the tree.

'George,' I say, 'George Ward. A good strong name.'

'He was a good strong man. Didn't say much. Just got on with it. Worked on the docks all his life. Loved rugby. That was about it.'

'He must have been proud of you.'

Jamie looks like he hasn't even thought about it. 'I think he was. Not that he told me, but Mum said he bored everyone in the pub with stories of me climbing frozen waterfalls.'

'How on earth do you climb a frozen waterfall?'

'Ice axes and crampons.' Jamie mimes it, arms slicing through the air showing how to hack into the ice. His sweater rises to show an inch or so of skin.

I try to imagine Tim or even Stephen scaling ice and just can't. 'It never even occurred to me a waterfall might freeze.'

He nods. 'They do in the Arctic.'

'Tell me more about George Ward. Was he a believer?'

'No, but he wanted to be buried here. Kept saying it when he was dying. Checking. "I'm going by the sea, aren't I? I need to be by the sea. You are putting me by the sea?"'

I can hear the Cornish accent in Jamie's voice when he imitates his dad.

'When he was diagnosed, he said he wanted to die at home and be buried here. And he got both those things.'

'Were you with him?'

Jamie rests his hand on the top of the headstone. 'Me; Mum; my sister, Lisa. Carers on a rota. I could have done without Lisa. She had this dream-catcher over his bed, all these crystals. She was putting on this awful voice.

Spiritual and soppy: "Soon you'll be with your mum and dad and Auntie Pam."'

He grins at me. 'And I can see Dad thinking, *I don't believe in any of that, and if I did, I wouldn't be looking forward to hanging around with fucking Pam.*'

I giggle.

'This one night, she'd convinced herself he was about to die. She made us hold hands and close our eyes. Dad was out of it, but she was bossing me and Mum around. So I'm standing there listening to her drone on about angels, and I look down and Dad's staring right at me. And he rolled his eyes, and I burst out laughing. Lisa told me off, said I wasn't taking it seriously enough. Dad had shut his eyes again, so I didn't grass him up. He didn't say much more. He died two days later.'

'Lovely to end on a laugh.'

'Just before he went, he said, "Wass the hold-up?" And then it was like an electric current had been cut.' Jamie makes a chopping gesture with his hand. 'He was gone.'

'You don't believe in an afterlife, then.'

Jamie shakes his head. 'We're here and then we're not. That's it.'

The wind gusts through the trees.

Jamie looks up at the sky. 'It's going to rain.'

'How do you know?'

'Wind on a calm day.' He points. 'And the sky is darkening in the east. Come on.'

We set off back towards the lychgate.

'What is there to do on a rainy afternoon in St Brida? Shall we go out for lunch somewhere?'

I feel a thrill at being asked and then bump back down to earth. I can't even imagine how Doreen and Barbara would react if they spotted me going into a restaurant with the sort of man who climbs up frozen waterfalls. 'I was going to have beans on toast.'

'It'll keep, won't it?'

Vicar's wife lunches with unidentified man. Vicar's wife forgets herself. Vicar's wife is all fur coat and no knickers.

'I'm not sure I should.'

'Why not?'

'I don't think the parishioners would approve.' How tedious I must sound, how provincial and old-fashioned. I try to think of something to say that makes it clear that whilst I might be surrounded by censorious women, I am cosmopolitan and capable of having friends of the opposite sex without being discombobulated. 'You can share my beans on toast if you like.'

A drop of rain lands on my nose.

'We'd better speed up,' he says. 'It's about to tip it down.'

We run up the path and get to the vicarage seconds before the downpour. I offer him a cup of tea, fill the kettle, watch the rain lash against the window. I can't quite believe he is here. I try it out in my head. *Jamie Ward is in my kitchen. Jamie Ward is sitting at my break-fast bar.* He doesn't go with the lino.

I open the tin, decant the beans into a pan, put bread in the toaster. I warn him the beans are not a good brand, that Stephen is revolted by the low-rent nature of my store cupboard. 'I'll jazz them up with some grated cheese.'

He holds out his hand for the grater. 'Let me.'

Jamie Ward is grating cheese in my kitchen.

'Are you happy eating here? The dining room is full of jumble.'

'I'm happy with anything.' He puts the grater down. 'But why have you got jumble in your dining room?'

'It was there when we moved in. Father Robert didn't care about privacy, so people use the vicarage as a dumping ground.'

'You shouldn't put up with that.'

He's right, of course. 'I'm a bit of a pushover.'

I put down the plates and sit opposite him. There's not enough space, really, for grown-up strangers to eat together. We're too close. It feels more intimate than a restaurant, where there would be some distance between us and a waiter to take our orders.

'Smells good. I haven't had beans on toast for ages.'

I've never been less hungry. I push a few beans around with my fork. 'It's a bit different from the last meal we ate together.'

He looks at me. 'I don't want to be disrespectful about your brother and his wife. They seem like nice people.'

He's seeking permission, I think. I give it to him. 'As soon as the door shut that night, Stephen said it had been a fucking awful evening, and that you must have been bored off your head.'

'I wasn't bored.'

I do another bit of bean pushing. 'How is Suzannah?'

'I haven't seen her since.'

I try not to sound delighted. 'Aren't you her boy-friend?'

'That sounds very teenage. We went out a few times, that's all.'

'I did think—' I stop.

'Go on, say whatever you like.'

I hesitate but decide to go for it. 'You didn't look like you fitted together.'

He nods. 'You're dead right. When I met her, I'd just got back from the middle of nowhere. Boiling hot. Nothing to look at but sand. She didn't feel like the worst idea in the world. That night, I saw straight away I needed to call it a day. But you knew that.'

I frown. 'What do you mean?'

'You've got a very expressive face.'

I'm taken aback. 'I thought I was highly skilled at hiding my feelings.'

He grins. 'You might as well have been leaning across the table and giving me what for. *Why are you messing around with this woman? She's not at all up your street.*'

I'm impressed and then remember some of my other thoughts that night. 'So you're a mind reader. That's terrifying. Did you know everything I was thinking?'

He shakes his head. 'I'm sure most of your secrets are safe.'

I wonder if this is true. I watch him eating his beans. He's giving me a bit of privacy to recover myself. I force down a bit of toast.

Jamie puts his cutlery down. 'You're a mind reader, too. You had them all clocked and sorted, didn't you?'

I can't eat any more. I stand up, put my plate next to the sink, turn to face him. 'I've always been a people watcher. I've never thought of it as mind reading before.'

'Try it. Tell me what I was thinking.'

I feel a shiver of excitement. 'I found you hard to read, actually. But you didn't enjoy Suzannah trying to own you, especially when she said about you being on call and having two phones. You liked Sarah and Stephen and you didn't mind Juliet, despite her silly question, or Liam, actually. You just didn't want to do tricks for him. How am I doing?'

He grins. 'Top marks.'

And I think you liked me, I add in my head, looking into his eyes. *I can't say that out loud, but I think you liked me. We both wanted everyone else to disappear so we could talk to each other.*

He smiles at me. It's knowing, but kind. He might be agreeing with me. It feels safer to go back to actual words. 'I am having fun,' I say. 'I haven't been this honest for years.'

'The older I get,' Jamie says, 'the less I can put up with anything else. I don't blame Suzannah for wanting a more serious relationship than I was offering, but I couldn't deal with her not saying it.'

'Didn't she?'

'She said she wanted something light and breezy. But really she wanted a partner. And I'm not marriage material.'

'I know,' I say. 'You've never even had a pet.'

He laughs. 'I did almost get married once, before I knew any better. But I'm a lone wolf, really. A solo traveller.'

'You don't get lonely?'

He nods. 'I do. Which explains Suzannah. I love women. I like sex. But I can't stand obligation. I like the curiosity stage. But I've seen all around me how it becomes about picking up the kids and paying the bills and "why can't you be exactly the way I want you to be". It's not for me.'

'Maybe that's what real love is.'

'Doing the daily grind and not complaining about it? Maybe. Love is a form of madness, isn't it? People fall in love so hard they commit to doing a whole load of boring shit for the next forty years.'

I twist my rings around. 'If you get fed up of being on call for rich people, you could get a job writing wedding speeches.'

He grins, 'It's hard to stay honest too. The longer a relationship lasts, the more compromised it gets. Have you noticed that? You strike me as someone who says what they think.'

'Do I?' It occurs to me that one of the dismal things about my situation is that I'm forced to dissemble, because to be truthful would be rude. 'I'd like to be. Church life makes it tricky to be truthful.'

'Isn't it one of the commandments?'

'Thou shalt not lie. But I bet Moses didn't have to deal with people asking if he'd enjoyed the service.'

'How would you answer that truthfully?'

'Did I enjoy the service? No, I've heard it all before.' I clasp my hand over my mouth. 'That did feel exhilarating. But I'll get in trouble if I say it in the wild. Imagine the headline. *I'm bored of church*, says vicar's wife, 44, Cornwall.'

'It's good to know what you think. And what you want. Being able to say it is another step.' Jamie stands. 'I'll wash up.'

'Let me.'

'No,' he says, pushing up his sleeves. 'You cooked. I'll clear up.'

I've never experienced the kitchen like this before. I'm always the one at the sink or the cooker. This is the first time I've been allowed to sit at the breakfast bar and do nothing but watch. And he's so worth watching. Even doing such a mundane thing, he looks like he's doing it in the optimal way.

When Jamie looks in the larder, he tells me that most damp in Cornwall is about ventilation. The air needs to circulate. I should leave the door open, not put anything against the walls. A de-humidifier would help.

'What next?' he says, when everything has been cleared away. 'Shall we fix your jumble problem? There must be somewhere else it can go. What about the church hall? Who has keys? Do you?'

I shake my head. 'They might be in the key box in the vestry. Or Derek, our churchwarden, might have them. Maybe Barbara.'

'So call or text. Say you want to relocate the jumble and is the church hall a good place? You've got a friend here who will help you carry it across.'

'I can't do that.'

'Why not?'

'They might not like it.'

'Tough.'

'I don't want to upset them.'

'You care too much about what other people think.'

'I know.'

'Don't you want to stop?'

I sigh. 'It's complicated. I can't just please myself. And I don't even know what I want. Let alone be able to say it.'

'Try it. Say, "I want . . ." and see what happens next.'

I look at him, standing in front of the sink. Behind him I can see my laundry hanging on the line, even wetter than when I pegged it out. 'Can I?'

'Go for it. Empty your mind. See what bubbles up.'

I put my hand on the breakfast bar and close my eyes. I'm very aware of Jamie, can feel the warmth of him and his encouragement. *I want, I want, I want. What do I really want?* I want him to touch me, but I can't say that. I might even want him to kiss me, and I really can't say that.

'I want to be able to tell the truth.'

'Good. And?'

I want, I want, I want. I feel like my head might explode. The words burst out of me: 'I want my dad not to be dead.'

His voice is steady. 'Of course you do.'

'And I want Sam to be OK.' I open my eyes. 'For him, and so that I can stop worrying about him.'

Jamie fills a glass of water from the tap and gives it to me. I drink it down.

'Why do you worry about Sam?'

'I try not to. But take your pick. That he's lonely because he doesn't have any siblings or even a pet, and we keep uprooting him. He spends most of his time with middle-aged church people and only knows about death and graves and fungal infections and God.' It doesn't feel right to tell Jamie that I don't like the way Tim speaks to him, or how our home life is joyless, or that I've no idea whether Sam sees me as I really am or just experiences the maternal edit of the Vicar's Wife persona. 'I'm scared about him going up to big school. He can't write legibly or sit still. I worry school won't cope with him and he won't cope with school.' I'm swamped with it, suddenly: the fear that my delightful, eccentric boy will be treated badly by a cruel world. 'You know about boys, don't you? From the army. What would you advise me?'

'May I?' Jamie picks up the kettle. That doesn't happen ever. No one other than me puts the kettle on in this kitchen.

'It sounds to me like you're giving yourself a hard time over Sam. Billy says boys are like dogs. They need to be well loved, well fed, well exercised, and everything else will sort itself out. You're probably doing all right on those fronts.'

I am, I think, *I am*. It's very calming to realise it.

'After that, find something he's good at and encourage him to do it. It can be anything. What does he like?'

'Loves animals. He wants a dog, but Tim's not keen. He's good at technology. That's the only thing he gets decent marks for at school. He wants a phone.'

'Most kids his age have one, don't they?'

'He says so.'

'It's hard to be different as a kid. He's probably un-usual enough already. I'd get him one.'

'Tim doesn't approve. He doesn't even like Sam using the computer, says technology is one of the big evils of modern life.'

'He could be right, but modern life is where Sam has to live. Explain to him it's important that Sam knows he's good at something.'

'As simple as that?'

'Simple but not easy, maybe. Like lots of things in life.' He puts a cup of tea in front of me. 'I'd better go. I promised to help Betsy with some sheep-related task.'

I feel a stab of disappointment. Of course he has to go. 'Thank you for an interesting afternoon.'

'Have lunch with me tomorrow? I'm seeing my client in the morning. I could pick you up afterwards.'

'I can't.'

'Why not?'

'All the same reasons. And Stephen and Sarah. It's their last full day. I wouldn't be able to anyway because of Sam.'

He smiles at me. 'I'll owe you, then. I'll be down here again.'

'In return for your baked beans? From Iceland?'

'Maybe I'd just like to have lunch with you.'

We look at each other. I can't work him out. He can't be interested in me in that way, surely. He must have scores of glamorous women throwing themselves at him. I decide to try a bit more honesty. 'Are you flirting with me?'

'What do you think?'

'I don't know. I have to ask because I have literally forgotten how it works.'

'Don't people flirt with you? Doesn't Derek the churchwarden give you the eye?'

'He's always telling me I should get a slow cooker. They are very economical, he says, because you can use cheaper cuts of meat. That's not flirting, is it?'

Jamie shakes his head.

'Then I can safely say I haven't been flirted with for years.'

The corner of his mouth twitches. 'Would you like me to be flirting with you?'

'I'm not sure I should.'

'But would you?'

My lips prickle. 'I think I would. Shame on me.'

'It's not a matter of shame. Or it shouldn't be. It's just showing appreciation.'

'Is it?' I can't imagine that would work as a line of defence if any of the church ladies could see me now.

'I like you. I like talking to you.'

I feel my cheeks go red. 'Is that flirting?'

'I don't know. I'm not an expert flirter.' He looks down at me and smiles. 'But if it is, if I am, it's nothing to worry about.'

He gives me his number in case I change my mind about lunch, and I stand at the door and watch him walk across the car park, relaxed and alert at the same time. I remember a French expression from school; he is at ease in his own skin. He knows what he wants and how to get it. And he wanted to spend this time with me. Because he likes talking to me. Jamie Ward likes talking to me.

Sixteen

The children want to tell me all about the seals when they arrive home, and the longer I don't mention Jamie, the easier it is not to. I'd prefer to hug the memory of this afternoon to myself and don't want knowing looks or teasing from Sarah.

Stephen says they fancy spending their last day down at the geothermal pool in Penzance. They'll take Sam, as long as I don't mind being left alone again. He might get a people carrier before they come to Cornwall again, he says, as he doesn't like having to leave me behind.

Later, as Sam and I watch another of his hobbit films, I fiddle with my phone. Should I? Or not? Is this temptation? I type out words and delete them. I type out slightly different words and delete them again. *Actually, I could come for lunch tomorrow . . . Turns out everyone else is going to Penzance . . . Are you still up for lunch? If so . . .*

I can't get the words right. Is that because it would be wrong? I think about Tim on his pilgrimage, communing with God. I try a little prayer: *Dear God, am I a bad person if I go out for lunch with an interesting man? He cheers me up. He's energetic and makes me think I could be too. What if I ask him more about Sam and how to manage boys? Or to explain about the damp again. It can't be sinful, can it, if we're discussing the importance of ventilation?*

God doesn't reply, but I can hear my mother's voice. *You're just fooling yourself. You've always been flighty. Don't play with fire. Count your blessings. Tim is a good man. I can't even tell you what I had to put up with from your father. At least you always know where your husband is. Don't rock the boat.*

'What are you doing with your phone, Mum?'

'I'm dithering over whether to send a text.'

'Why?'

'I can't decide if I should meet up with this friend.'

'Do it,' Sam says, not taking his eyes from the screen, where an elf is fitting an arrow into his crossbow. 'You're always saying we need to get out of the house. You should have a nice bit of fresh air.'

'Good advice.' It would be so easy to send the text, even to convince myself it's a sign. But I don't. I'm not brave enough. Or bad enough. Or foolish enough. I'm too cowardly to rock the boat.

Stephen and Sarah call in on their way back to London to say goodbye.

'I wish we didn't have to go,' Stephen says. 'Looked in the estate agents' windows this morning, didn't we, girls? Thought about what it would be like to live down here.'

'Not a good idea,' says Sam.

'Isn't it?' Bella asks, sadly. 'I thought you'd like it if we lived nearby.'

'I would,' Sam says, 'but it's not sensible for you, Bella. Irreversible climate change. You don't want to live near the sea.'

'Why not?'

'It's going to flood the land,' says Sam. 'We're all going to drown.'

Bella's lip wobbles.

Stephen intervenes. 'I don't think we need to worry about that yet.'

'Yes, we do,' Alice chimes in. 'If we don't do anything in the next thirteen years, it will be too late.'

'Why thirteen years?' Sarah asks.

'That's what they said at school.'

'Well,' says Sarah, firmly, 'I believe in your generation. That you'll find a way to fix things. That you'll work out how to make technology do good things. That you'll discover how to put science in the service of humanity. I believe in you, Sam, and you, Alice, and in you, Bella.'

Stephen looks relieved.

Sam is sceptical. 'In thirteen years I'll be twenty-three,' he says. 'I don't think I can learn enough to fix everything by then.'

Sarah takes the kids into the garden for a last go at falling out of the camellia.

Stephen heaves a cardboard box onto the counter. 'Here you go. Boring leftovers like butter and cheese, but there's a good bottle of Scotch and we hardly touched the gin.'

'I promise I won't drink it all at once.'

'Why don't you and Sam come up for half-term? Bella wants to go to Harry Potter World for her birthday. Sam would enjoy that, wouldn't he?'

I hesitate. I don't know what Tim will think about being left to fend for himself, or whether he'll approve of Harry Potter World.

'I'd really like to have something in the diary,' Stephen says, 'with you. Before my birthday. Just in case. You know, a last waltz.'

At last I understand. 'Let's do it.'

'And can I carry on the Sunday-night thing? It helps.'

'Of course.'

As Stephen and I look at each other, a tear escapes down my cheek.

'Cut it out, Sis,' he says, 'we haven't got time for a floor session.'

Sam and I stand by their car as they load in.

'It's been the best holiday,' says Alice, reaching for my hand.

'We'll miss you,' I say, giving her a squeeze.

'Why don't you come and live with us?' Bella asks.

'That's so sweet.' I put my other arm around her.

'You could have the loft bedroom. And Sam can share with me.'

'Don't be silly, Bella,' says Alice. 'Sam's got a dad, hasn't he? Uncle Tim needs to stay here to be the vicar.'

We watch the car turn out of the car park, the girls waving their arms out of the windows until the last possible moment.

'I wish we could go and live with them,' Sam says. 'Can we?'

I look down at his eager face. 'As Alice says, we need to be here for Dad's job. Stephen suggested we go there for a holiday. Would that be nice?'

'Yes,' says Sam. 'When can we go? Tomorrow?'

My heart breaks a little. 'No, sweetheart. Half-term. For Bella's birthday.'

'That's ages away.'

'It will come around quicker than we think.' I cringe at how silly I sound. 'Dad is coming home tomorrow.'

Sam's face doesn't fall, exactly. But he doesn't look excited either.

I put my arm around his shoulder. 'Dad will have missed us.'

'Will he?'

'I'm sure he will,' I say, ignoring a buzz from my internal lie detector. 'He'll be glad to be home.'

That night, as I tuck Sam in, he looks up at me. 'They're different from us, aren't they? Uncle Stephen and that lot. They eat different food, and they go out to places, and they laugh all the time.'

'Stephen always liked making jokes.'

'Dad doesn't like jokes, does he?'

I can't deny it. 'Not much.'

'Is it to do with not believing in God?'

'What, the jokes?'

'All of it. How different they are.'

'I don't know.' I want to offer him something but don't know what. 'It's good that people are different, isn't it? Life would be boring if we were all the same.'

He shakes his head. 'Not true, Mum. It would be great if we were more the same. No arguments. No wars. We could do something about climate change if we weren't always falling out with each other.'

And I look at Sam's earnest face, framed by his new haircut. How astonishing that this boy was once a baby inside me and now he is a whole human being with ideas and opinions. It's a miracle.

Seventeen

When Tim comes back from the pilgrimage, he says he needs to learn to put his own oxygen mask on first. I think this is code for him being even less involved on the domestic front, but then he suggests we take advantage of the weather and Bryony taking the afternoon weddings, and go to the beach. I wonder if someone on the pilgrimage has told him he should be a bit kinder to his family, but still, it's good he's making an effort. I can't remember when we last did something together that wasn't church-related. I make some cheese-and-pickle rolls and we get in the car. It is baking hot and there's a lot of traffic.

'I don't think the aircon works, Dad,' Sam says, from the back seat.

'Just be patient, please. No, don't put the windows down. Give it a chance to kick in.'

We are blasted by hot air all the way, and then the car park by the beach is full.

'Can't we just go in there?' Sam says, pointing to an overflow area, empty apart from three cars.

Tim refers to the notice. 'It's coaches only.'

'But there are cars there.'

'There shouldn't be. They're breaking the rules.'

I close my eyes and tell God that if an apocalypse is on the way, I'd be grateful if it could start right now.

Luckily someone leaves, and Tim drives into the empty space. Then Sam is hopping about, yelping that the tarmac hurts his feet. Tim asks why he hasn't got any shoes on and I say I told him not to bother as I knew we'd be right next to the beach. But really I didn't tell him, I didn't give him permission. I let him get in the car unshod because I remembered a long-ago trip to Ireland with Dad when we hardly had shoes on all summer. Ever since then I've connected being barefoot with a carefree happiness that I never get to experience, and I wanted Sam to know that feeling. I do think Sam is making a bit of a fuss, but when I give him my flip-flops I too have to hop from foot to foot.

The beach is crowded. We find a little space and I put a towel down, but I've forgotten to bring sun cream. When Tim and Sam go for a swim, I realise the tune I'm humming under my breath is a song Dad used to sing about the lads around the boiler making hot asphalt. *We laid it in the hollows and we laid it in the flat, and if it doesn't last for ever sure I swear I'll eat my hat*. I can't remember much more. Tim comes back in a slightly better mood and I get out our lunch. But the people next to us start smoking and playing music, and Sam drops his roll in the sand, so we call it a day and trudge back to the car.

'Look,' says Tim, rather smugly, pointing towards the 'coaches only' area and the yellow penalty notices stuck onto the windscreens of the three rule-breaking cars. And I try to remember that German word for taking pleasure in someone else's misfortune, and then we get back into the boiling car. Tim is cross at the way the other drivers navigate the traffic-calming measures up the hill, saying one man is an idiot for not understanding it is his right of way.

Sam says, 'You're being a bit unkind, Dad. Maybe it's an emergency and he's just found out someone is in hospital.'

I think this is exactly the sort of reflection Tim will welcome, but he frowns and says nothing until Sam sticks his head out of the back window, and then Tim says, 'Don't do that, you look like a dog.'

Sam's birthday is in the last week of the school holidays. I try to convince Tim to let him have a phone, but he isn't having any of it. I buy Sam some sweets, a new pack of cards, and strike lucky with an ornate Lord of the Rings chess set I find in the charity shop.

The day falls on a Sunday and Tim is taking three services, including early morning holy communion over at St Anta. Sam and I have a good couple of hours without him, opening a box from Stephen and Sarah which includes some Lego mini figures, a bonsai tree growing kit, and pictures from the girls. Bella's is a jolly painting of the lighthouse with circling seagulls. Alice has created a rather disturbing dystopian vision where the lychgate burns against the backdrop of a black sea. Sam sticks them both up on his bedroom wall.

After church, Sam and I try to set up a game of chess, but we're missing a white castle and a black bishop.

I look in the box again to no avail. 'I'm so sorry.'

'Don't worry, Mum. I don't mind. Uncle Stephen gave me loads of stuff anyway.'

What a good attitude, I think, and I'm about to tell Sam what a kind and forgiving eleven-year-old he is, when Tim embarks on a sermon-style rant about the horrors of twenty-first-century life and how we've become so dominated by consumerism and capitalism that we can no longer connect to what truly matters. Then he goes off into his study. I try to form the words to say he's probably a bit tired, but they stick in my throat. 'I don't know why Dad reacted like that,' I say. 'But it's not your fault.'

This feels momentous to me, but Sam just nods calmy and suggests we improvise so we use a Lego Stormtrooper as the castle and Darth Vader as the bishop.

We play in silence for a while and then Sam says, 'Do you remember when Uncle Stephen gave me that garage and Dad made me hand it over to the refuge?'

'Did he make you? I thought you wanted to.'

Sam moves Darth Vader three squares. 'He said that thing about much being expected from those to whom much is given.'

'Oh,' I say.

'Checkmate.'

'Is it? Well done. I didn't see that coming.'

'Sorry about the missing pieces,' I say again as we pack away. 'It was a risky thing to buy second-hand. We could choose a new one together.'

'Don't worry, Mum. It's fun using the Lego. And whenever I have something good, Dad stresses out until I give it away, so there's not much point anyway.'

I go into the kitchen and peel onions.

Since then, I have been even less able than before to put up with what I have started in my head to call The Tim Situation. I can no longer ignore the unpalatable fact that my husband does not care about me outside of my function as a housekeeper, child wrangler, and recipient of complaints about our son or the congregation. Since that conversation about honesty with Jamie, I have become terribly aware of how often I lie, either by omission or directly, because to tell the truth would get me or Sam into some sort of trouble.

I wish I had gone out for lunch with Jamie and given myself the treat of being with a man who was a tiny bit interested in me and my life. I endlessly replay our interactions; on the Tube, at the station, in the street, at Stephen's, in the churchyard, over the beans on toast. When he handed me the glass of water; the way he smiled when I asked if he was flirting with me. I marvel at how it felt to be with someone who cared about my safety, laughed at my jokes, and would do the washing-up. I can't picture his face. He's a blur. But I remember the smell of him. And the way he spoke, warmly but with few unnecessary words. The curve of his mouth and the shape of the scar on his cheek. Every time someone knocks at the door, I hope it is him. When my phone beeps, I hope it is him. Sometimes I consider taking the initiative, but when I try to manufacture a reason for getting in touch I can't come up with anything credible, which proves how little we have in common. What could I say? Give him an update on the jumble? No progress. Tell him I tried with the phone? No dice. And then I worry that I am making it all up, that my life is so small and sad that a tiny bit of attention, a sliver of conversation, has made me fantasise something out of almost thin air.

But he did say he wanted to have lunch with me, I think desperately. *He did say he liked talking to me.* And the whole thing is so tragic, so feeble, that I just want to bang my head against the breakfast bar again and again.

Cornwall,
September 2019

Eighteen

The woman in the school-uniform shop tells me they all lose their ties at the beginning because the clip-ons fall off too easily. I'm the fourth mum in that morning buying a replacement. 'There you go, my lover,' she says as she hands me the bag, and I could cry with gratitude at this tiny bit of kindness. In the library, I don't feel capable of anything new so pick up a clutch of Agatha Christies I've read before. I could ask about a job, I think, but there is nobody at the desk so I use the machine to take out my books and leave without speaking to anyone. In Iceland, I use the self-checkout to stock up on biscuit supplies for our visitors, who always want a snack alongside their pastoral care. Bourbons, custard creams, digestives. It looks a bit dull, so I chuck in a couple of packets of party rings. And a curious-looking sweet for Sam: a straw with blue balls in it and complicated instructions. *Sam will enjoy working it out*, I think, but trudging back up the hill, the carrier-bag handles cutting into my hands, I realise it must be very environmentally bad, this sweet: single-use plastic and completely pointless.

As I open the church gate, I see someone sitting on my bench. A man. The sun is in my eyes. Can it be? My heart does a little jump. He stands.

'You're here.' I know I've given myself away. I don't sound like a woman who has not been thinking about him.

He reaches out for the carrier bags. 'Let me take those.'

I rub my hands. There are red creases across my palms.

We stand and look at each other. Some men might look less handsome once accessorised with carrier bags from Iceland, but not him.

'I've a message. Betsy says she's been meaning to invite you for supper for ages and sends me to ask if, on the off chance, you are free tonight, while I'm here.'

'Tonight?'

'Yes. All of you, of course.'

I can't imagine Sam up at Boscawen Hall – or rather, I can't imagine Tim coping with him not using his knife and fork properly and dropping things.

'Maybe not Sam. I can probably get one of the church ladies to babysit. They're always offering.'

'Excellent. And how has it been for Sam? With school?'

I feel a glow at his concern. 'The first few days he came home looking shell-shocked. But he's settled down. He doesn't say much, but he likes his form tutor.'

'That's good. Are you on your way home? Shall I carry your shopping?'

I feel like a girl again. *Can I walk you home?* That was what the boys used to say after discos in the village hall.

'What's funny?' Jamie asks.

'I've just remembered something.'

'Go on.'

And it's so good to be chatting to him again and I can feel myself unfurling like a flower lifting to the sun, but then Barbara appears on the path ahead with her hessian bag, and I'm not at all keen on her observing Jamie and me through her beady eyes.

I tackle it head-on. 'Barbara, come and meet Jamie. He's a friend of my brother.'

'No need to tell me who he is. I went to school with his father. I knew him when he was in his mummy's tummy.'

She pats his arm and looks like she might pinch his cheek.

'You were a fine baby,' she says. 'A good set of lungs. I last saw you at your dad's funeral. How long ago was that, now?'

'Six years.'

'Very sudden, wasn't it?'

'It was male pride and stupidity, Barbara. He wouldn't go to the doctor's. By the time he did, it was too late.'

'He was a bit stubborn,' she says, fondly. 'Good company, mind. Always one for a joke.'

Jamie smiles down at her.

'I keep his grave tidy. He's not far from my parents. And none of you live nearby, do you? So I give it a little spruce-up every so often.'

'That is really kind of you.' Jamie sounds like he means it. 'Mum asked me to get some flowers while I'm down here. What would you advise?'

'You get a lot for your money with pinks,' Barbara says. 'Or stocks are in season. Nice colours and smell lovely. Roses always look good on a grave. They last well and the rabbits don't eat them. Cut them short, mind. Or the wind will get them.'

I have a thought. 'Do say no, Barbara, if it's not convenient, but you couldn't come and watch Sam tonight, could you? So Tim and I can have supper with Jamie. Betsy's invited us up.'

'I could.' She beams. 'I'm very fond of Sam. Even though he keeps beating me at euchre.'

It is only when Sam arrives home that I realise I've not spent all day fretting about him. He's not forthcoming about school but is happy with the arrangement for the evening.

'I like Barbara,' he says, 'though not her apple pie. I don't have to eat any if she brings one, do I?'

'We can say you're full and have cleaned your teeth,' I say. 'And if you make sure you are and you have, it won't be a lie.'

Later, I let Sam play with my phone as I get changed. I wear Sarah's black dress and button my green cardigan over the top. I wish I owned a bit of make-up. Maybe I should buy some mascara. I liked the way my eyes looked when the girls did me up. The perfume Sarah

gave me is on the windowsill. At least I can smell beautiful. I spray it into the air and walk forwards.

Tim comes in. 'What on earth are you doing?'

'It's how you're supposed to do perfume. Not direct
on the skin. You squirt it into the air. Alice and Bella
showed me.'

Tim shakes his head as though he will never cease to
be amazed at the vanity and stupidity of the modern
world. He is still wearing his dog collar.

'Aren't you getting changed?'

He frowns. 'Do I have to?'

'You could have a night off from vicaring. Just be a
person.'

'They might expect it.'

'They're not inviting you as the vicar.' I can hear the
sharpness in my voice and aim for a more neutral tone.
'They've asked us because Jamie is friends with Stephen.'

'What's one of Stephen's friends doing down here?'

I fiddle with the perfume. There's no warmth in Tim's
tone, no curiosity. No sense that there might be enjoyment or interest to be had from anything connected to
Stephen. 'He was born here. Barbara knows him. His
dad is buried in our churchyard. He's coming down a lot
at the moment because a client is staying here. He looks
after wealthy people. Their security.'

'Like a bodyguard?'

'I don't think he does the actual guarding. More like
a consultant. He gets paid a retainer to be available to
solve any problems.'

Tim looks like he is about to quote that bit from the Bible about rich people not getting into heaven, but his phone rings.

I can hear it's Doreen, though I can't make out the words. Tim offers to go round. She gabbles away again and when he says, 'That's what I'm here for,' I experience a surge of rage. I put the perfume down. If I were the violent type, I might enjoy throwing it at his head.

'Doreen is in a terrible state,' he says.

Doreen gets in a state on a regular basis, usually over her son's marital problems or an argument with Barbara or Lynn. She has premonitions, she says, where she senses disaster ahead. Twice now Tim has been summoned out of hours because she's changed her mind about her funeral hymns and can't rest until he's been fully and officially updated.

'You didn't really want to go out, did you?'

I don't reply to Tim because it isn't a real question. I pick up my hairbrush and pull out my ponytail.

'You'll let them know?'

'Yes.'

'At least I don't have to get changed,' Tim says, as he leaves the room.

I stand in the window and watch him walk to the car. He's got a spring in his step now, so much more at ease in his dog collar than without it. I wonder what would have happened if Doreen had phoned before I'd said that tonight was purely social and not even about him. I bet he wouldn't have cancelled Billy and Betsy – or not so easily – if he thought he was expected as the vicar.

Perhaps that's the problem. He doesn't exist as a human being any more, only as God's representative on earth. He's like Jamie, ready to jump into action at short notice. Except he's on a retainer with God and gets little in the way of earthly rewards.

I call Jamie and explain.

'You can come, though, surely?'

'I could, I suppose. I haven't cancelled Barbara yet.'

'I'll drive down and pick you up.'

'I can walk.'

'It's no bother.'

I feel a flip in my tummy. Is this wise? Should I do this?

'OK.'

When I get downstairs, Barbara is in the kitchen. Usually I'm aggravated by the way she knocks and walks in, but tonight I feel well disposed towards her.

Sam comes in wearing his pyjamas. 'Hello, Barbara, I'm full and I've cleaned my teeth.'

'You are a good boy.'

I hear a car on the gravel outside.

I kiss Sam goodnight, enjoying the feel of his smooth skin against mine.

And then I am out of the door. Jamie is standing by his car.

He kisses my cheek. 'Nice perfume.'

He smells extremely good. He opens the door and I get into his car.

Nineteen

Boscawen Hall has an air of faded grandeur. I follow Jamie into the entrance hall, which has a high ceiling and lots of portraits on the walls. I've never been in somewhere so big that is an actual home. I think of my dad and his desire for me to know quality people. We walk through large double doors into the kitchen, where Betsy is peering into a casserole dish on the Aga.

'I'm experimenting with pearl barley. It's meant to be good for you. But it's sucking up all the liquid.' She sloshes in some wine from an open bottle. 'I've poured most of this in already.'

I apologise for Tim's absence, citing a parishioner in crisis.

'That's a shame,' Betsy says. 'But everyone is talking about how helpful and caring he is.'

'That's nice to know,' I say. 'He does work hard.'

I sit at the kitchen table as Jamie makes drinks and Betsy slices a baguette, then washes kale that she grew herself in the kitchen garden.

'Father Robert was a bit past it by the end,' Betsy says as she shakes the colander over the sink. 'Wedding guests were beginning to comment. He was never a well-dressed man but he'd started to look downright scruffy.'

Billy comes in, kisses me on the cheek, claps Jamie on the shoulder and gestures to the drinks tray. 'Give me whatever's going.'

'Tim's not coming,' Betsy tells him. 'A parish emergency to deal with. I was just saying how much everyone is appreciating his dedication and commitment.'

'Absolutely,' Billy says, peering into the casserole dish. 'A big improvement on poor old Father Robert. A lovely man but he should have retired earlier. He nearly flaked out the last time he came up to a reception, couldn't catch his breath.'

'We did want to ask Tim something,' Betsy says. 'Can we run it by you?'

I nod and she explains that the brother of a bride getting married in December works in special effects in films and wants to organise a surprise snowfall for when his sister comes out of the church. A white wedding. 'It should be fun. A little miracle, though made by man rather than God. If Tim isn't keen we can work out how to do something here, but the ideal would be to set it up so she walks out of the church into it. Just like at the end of a romcom.'

'Sounds lovely.' I remember the lesbian wedding that wasn't a wedding. 'It won't get Tim into trouble if it goes viral, will it?'

'Can't think why. *Vicar breaks laws of nature*? No,

I think it's very much a feel-good festive story. He's a professional, so he's got all the insurance in case anyone slips on the snow.'

Jamie is different here than he was in London; chattier, and more relaxed. He looks at home, slicing lemons, getting ice from the freezer, lifting the casserole dish over to the table, passing round the bread.

After asking me about Sam and telling me about her grown-up sons, Betsy talks about how busy life is: nonstop weddings all summer, a yoga retreat next week, creative writing the week after. At least the yogis go to bed early, she says. The writers stay up all night boozing and yakking, and Betsy can hear them from the bedroom. 'Billy sleeps through it all.'

'I don't mind the writers,' Billy says. 'I'd rather a few tipsy humans than the racket the sheep make during lambing.'

Betsy points a finger at him. 'Leave my sheep alone.' She turns to me. 'Billy thinks they're too much work and we should focus on the hospitality. Luckily the accountant says we need them to retain our agricultural status.'

'Betsy prefers the sheep to the guests,' Billy explains. 'I'm the other way around.'

'He likes showing off how well he deals with dreadful people,' Betsy says. 'All those awful brides and their mothers. They're so rude to me, then they roll over for Billy. Honestly, they'd let him tickle their tummies. It's obscene.'

'He's a charmer,' Jamie chips in. 'Saved my life once by persuading an angry man he'd have more fun if he didn't shoot us. We had a friendly game of cards instead. He'd probably have let Billy tickle his tummy, too.'

Billy laughs. 'Some of us can't rely on our physical prowess so we have to cultivate other skills.' He winks at me. 'You know he got the fastest ever time on the Tarzan assault course?'

It feels like I am on an accidental double date. This was what Suzannah wanted: to sit in my chair, to meet Jamie's friends, to learn more about him. He is attentive, bringing me into the conversation, quick to notice if my water or wine glass needs topping up. Just being polite, I'm sure, but I'm so unused to being cared for that it feels romantic. Every so often I remind myself that I'm not Jamie's girlfriend, I'm the wife of the hardworking vicar called away on the business of the parish. But mostly I just have a good time, giggling when Billy teases Betsy over the odd stickiness of her pearl barley experiment, feeling the same poignant envy of their mutual fondness that I did watching Liam and Juliet.

We talk more about the peculiarities of weddings. Aggressive mothers, drunk fathers, teenage offspring from a previous marriage who sob audibly through the speeches or refuse to come out of the toilets. Betsy says the more demanding the clients, the more likely the wedding won't happen at all, though she never finds out the real reason, as everyone who cancels blames it on a bereavement. 'It can't always be true, can it? That the bride's beloved grandfather has popped his clogs?'

I say it's often something about the wedding itself that breaks a couple up. Tim once had one called off because the groom overheard his bride say, 'I don't want to wear some piece of shit his great-grandmother owned,' about the family-heirloom ring he was about to bestow on her. One man went off his wife-to-be because she was too greedy over the gift list, and another became overwhelmingly depressed by the need for the flowers in the bridesmaids' bouquets to colour-match the silk handkerchiefs in the ushers' breast pockets.

Billy says to Jamie, 'Didn't you nearly get married once?'

He shudders. 'I was twenty-three and knew no better. But it's like Ann says. She wanted me to have her brother as my best man. I couldn't stand him. But she was intent on getting her way. And I thought, why am I tying myself to someone who wants me to do something I don't want? So we split up. And I'm still glad about it. I've had a few lucky escapes in my life, but that's number one.'

After tiny chocolate puddings and mint tea, and lots more chat about sheep and how intelligent they are, I catch sight of the time and say I must go. Jamie offers to walk me home.

'Here.' Betsy gives him a torch. 'It's pitch black all the way when there's no moon. And would you like some kale? I've got so much.'

We leave in a flurry of hugs and appreciation, Jamie carrying both the torch and the kale.

I enjoy the cool air on my cheeks.

'Glad you came?' Jamie asks.

'Very much so,' I say. 'I was a bit overwhelmed at first. The size of the place. I don't know anyone with portraits of their ancestors on the walls. But I did enjoy myself. I love laughing and I don't get to do it that often.'

'How come?'

It doesn't feel fair to tell him that not only does Tim have no sense of humour, but he doesn't approve of me having one. Yet again, I compromise. 'Tim is a serious person. Sam has a funny way of seeing the world. Church *is* funny, that's the thing, but church people don't see it or appreciate being laughed at.'

We walk on into the beam of the torchlight, the night silent apart from the sound of our footsteps and the rustle of the bag of kale.

'Are you busy tomorrow?' Jamie asks.

'Not really. My domestic routines. Tim's out early to go to St Anta. He's running a quiet day. When he explained it, Sam said, "What, so everyone just sits around not talking and thinking about God?"'

Jamie laughs.

'I know! I thought it was funny. Tim didn't. Anyway, that's tomorrow. I'll get Sam off to school. Clean stuff. Cook stuff. Aren't you leaving?'

'Change of plan. My client wants me to stick around. I don't know how long for.'

I stumble on the path, and he reaches out. When he takes his hand away, I want to ask him to put it back.

'You never told me the funny thing,' he says.

'What?'

'Earlier. You were going to tell me something and then Barbara appeared.'

'Oh yes. It felt a bit naughty for the churchyard in daylight anyway.'

'Go on, then. Take advantage of the cover of darkness.'

It does feel luxurious and intimate to be surrounded by all this black but with someone I like and trust. 'When I was young – fifteen – I went to these discos in the village hall. At the end of the night, boys would ask to walk you home. But what it really meant was that they'd try to get off with you in an alleyway. My friend Kitty had this theory about when you should let them get anywhere. That's what she called it. "Don't let them get anywhere until you're nearly home," she'd say. "Or they might not walk you the rest of the way."'

'A keen strategist.'

'It was all a battle. Or a transaction, at least. The boys were always trying to get somewhere. The girls just wanted to be walked all the way home. I don't know why I thought about that today.'

I do, of course. Because being with Jamie makes me feel like a teenager and I both hope and fear he will try to get somewhere. And maybe because I was noting that he was going to carry my shopping home for me with no guarantees, which would have been a good coup back in the day.

'I was reading all these books where boys would give girls apples and escort them home from school carrying their satchels. But in my real life it was all about the precise moment when you should let yourself be fingered. Too early and he'd go off you. Too late and he might lose interest. It was a narrow window.'

'Did you successfully find the window?'

'Not really. And then Dad died and we moved to live with my grandparents, and there was no village hall.'

'I'm sorry.' His voice is warm in the darkness. 'About your dad. Not about your removal from the village hall disco scene, which doesn't sound like a loss.'

'I had bigger fish to fry then. Actually, chips were another big part of it. There was a chippy next to the village hall. So whether he would buy you your own tray of chips was another factor.'

'Presumably the fingering came after the chip eating.'

'Yes, you'd sit on the wall for the chip bit. That was all a bit performative. Who was sitting on the wall with who. And then walk home afterwards. Was it like that here?'

'Don't hate me, but I did quite often get somewhere around the back of the church hall.'

I go for mock outrage, 'Our church hall?'

'After the youth club. The set-up was pretty much as you've described. No nearby chippy though.'

'And did you walk your girls home afterwards?'

'Always.'

We've reached the vicarage.

'Thank you,' I say. I consider adding something about him walking me home for no reward but can't corral my words into a sentence that doesn't sound too sexual.

'It was a pleasure.' As Jamie hands me the bag of kale, our fingers brush. 'I'd have happily carried your satchel, if required.'

I hope it is too dark for him to see me blush.

'I might call around tomorrow morning if this little idea I've got comes off.'

'Intriguing.'

'Shall I offer to see Barbara home?' he asks. 'I promise I won't try to get anywhere with her behind the church hall.'

Twenty

Sam has not long left for school when I hear a knock on the door. I can tell even from the tone it is him.

Jamie holds up a key and for a moment I panic, thinking I have led him to believe I am in the market for a quick bunk-up. Then I see that the keyring is a heavy wooden angel.

'We're transferring all the jumble to the church hall. Fully authorised by Barbara. She agrees that what might have been suitable in Father Robert's day needs a re-think now there is a family in the vicarage.'

I'm amazed. 'Really?'

'She offered to help with the carrying, but I said we could do it. So she's trusted me with the key, which I promised I would return to the hook in the vestry.'

'You are a miracle worker.' I want to hug him but restrain myself. If I start touching him, I might not be able to stop.

'I have my moments. Shall we crack on?'

*

It is fun – there is no other word for it – making multiple trips over to the church hall carrying all the smelly bags. We take all the boxes of service leaflets too. After the last lot, we lock the hall and walk back to the church.

When we reach the vestry, I pull aside the red curtain and point Jamie towards the key box.

'Mission accomplished.' Jamie smiles at me and I have a sudden image of us having sex right there, me sitting on all the embroidered robes, him standing in front of me. I feel like the breath has been squeezed out of my body.

'Do you know what I think we should do?' he asks.

My heart is racing. 'What?'

'Give your dining room a clean. And then get some chips and eat them at Gull Point.'

At the chippy on the high street I try to pay, but Jamie won't let me.

'And shall we share some fish?' he asks. 'Or you can have a whole one to yourself. I'm not trying to put you on short rations.'

'Very flash. But I'm happy with half.'

'Mushy peas?'

'Yes, please.'

'Curry sauce, pickled egg, ketchup?'

'No way, but don't let me stop you.'

'I wouldn't have judged, but I would eat my own eyes before letting any of those things near my chips.'

When the server asks if we want salt and vinegar, we both say 'lots' at the same time and then grin at each other.

Jamie carries the bag as we walk on through town. He points out a clothes shop that used to sell snuff and knives, and the optician's that was once an ice-cream parlour.

'That's where my parents met. Mum was on a day trip down from Devon. Dad was behind her in the queue.'

'Were they happy?'

'Not really. He was a man of few words. Mum was bored. She left him when I turned sixteen.'

'On your actual birthday?'

'The day after. She said she was going to stay with Auntie Pam for a bit. But I knew she wasn't planning on coming back. And then I had to cope with the old man. He hadn't paid her a lot of attention, but he missed her when she was gone.'

'Was there somebody else?'

'For a while. But it didn't work out. And then Mum came home. She was grateful, I think, that he took her back. But they never seemed to like each other much, even then.'

'Barbara sounded fond of him.'

'She did, didn't she? Like she was always creasing up at his jokes. I don't remember him laughing much. Maybe marriage changed him for the worse. It does that a lot. Or having kids does. How to turn love into contempt in three easy steps. Get married. Have a kid. Have another one.'

I look across at him. 'That's very cynical.'

He shrugs. 'It's just what I see. Not always. But a lot.'

*

At Gull Point, there are a few people milling around and a little queue for the ice-cream van. We find a bench facing out to sea. Jamie hands me my box of chips and divides up the fish.

'Food of the gods,' he says.

As soon as I taste salt and vinegar and fat, I am transported. 'My dad once went to the chippy to fetch Stephen's birthday tea and didn't come back for a week.'

'What happened?'

'He met a mate in the queue who was on his way back to Ireland. So he went along. He paid a boy to bring round our fish and chips.' I can picture it all. 'Mum was furious, interrogating the boy. He didn't know anything. He'd just been given a fiver to deliver the food. I was unwrapping the newspaper and dishing it up onto plates because Mum thought it was common to eat from the paper. Stephen started crying. Mum was shouting at the boy, "Five pounds! He gave you five pounds! But where was he going?" And the boy was in tears too by now: "I don't know, missus, I don't know anything."'

'You were sorry for him.'

'I was. It felt unfair. One minute he's getting an easy fiver and the next he's being yelled at. I just wanted Mum to stop shouting. From quite a young age I could see that Dad wasn't easy but that she always made things worse.'

'Did they never get on?'

'Not that I remember. There was this famous story of love at first sight. Dad looked at Mum across a crowded room in a pub in Liverpool, and that was it. But she was full of regret and resentment.'

He nods, picks up another chip. 'Tell me more.'

So I tell him about my father. How much fun he was. Loud and boisterous, even when sober, with a great, ringing laugh. Always singing. He liked Irish songs and English telly. He loved *Only Fools and Horses*, was always saying, 'This time next year, I'll be a millionaire.' He'd literally throw money around, coming home with a wedge of cash and chucking it up in the air, and Stephen and I would jump around catching and giving the notes back to him, and when the wedge was intact again he would peel a note for each of us off the top and say, 'Have a drink on me.'

He taught us to play cards – often for real money – and would tell me off if I wasn't bold enough, if I said stick when he thought I should twist. Pontoon, blackjack, poker. Stephen and I learnt to keep our faces expressionless when we picked up a pocket pair or had a full house from the flop.

He had a knack of finding a party, a bit of craic. That's what he was always after. I didn't know it was an Irish word until I saw it written down long after he died. I always imagined it like a whipcrack. 'How's the craic?' he'd say. And when Stephen or I made him laugh, he'd be delighted: 'You've got the craic, all right. You'll never want for friends if you've got a bit of craic about you.' When Mum was angry at him for being late home from the pub, he'd say, 'But the craic was good,' as if that explained everything. When she said he should come straight home after work, he'd say, 'For Christ's sake, I need something to get the taste of mud and grit out of my mouth.'

When we were younger he'd bring his friends home, wake us up, and get me to sing and Stephen to ride the dog. But Mum hated his friends and the way their dirty boots left dust all over the house. They were mainly Irish and she hated Ireland by then; him talking about it or wanting to go there. She was always shushing him. So he stopped coming home. I missed him and I knew it was her fault. It wasn't Stephen and me he was trying to escape by always being in the pub. Dad went where the craic was, and that wasn't in our house.

I tell Jamie that this general unreliability, this habit of popping out for a quick pint and disappearing for a couple of days, meant we'd got used to his absences. And so we were not worried that last time he didn't come home. Though there were signs that things had gone adrift. He'd not been throwing money around for a while. He kept telling me what a good girl I was, how good I was at looking after my little brother. 'I wish I'd had a sister like you,' he'd say. 'I'd have turned out different if I'd had a sister like you.'

So that morning when the policeman came to the door, it was a terrible shock. We thought he'd been off having fun somewhere. And he hadn't. He'd got drunk one last time and then – what? Did he jump? Fall?

'Mum was convinced it was an accident. Needed it to be an accident. She wanted a funeral in the church and thought he couldn't have that if he'd meant to do it.'

The big black car. It was raining. I had my period, and it seemed especially unfair that as well as everything else I had to cope with that. Stephen was sitting next to me. 'I hadn't cried until then. The policeman told me to be a brave girl and I'd been looking after Stephen. It was only when the hearse arrived that I really believed it. So I started to cry. And Mum said, "Don't cry. You'll upset everyone."'

I give a sorry little laugh. 'Imagine, that she would say that. The funeral is a blur. I remember Dad's friends carrying the coffin. It had funny shiny handles. Then a wake at the pub. The same one he'd been drinking in the night he died. They all said he'd left on good form. Everyone wanted to believe it was an accident. The men all drank Guinness or whiskey, and the women were mainly having tea, except my friend Kitty's mother who was glugging wine and weeping. People kept telling Stephen he was the man of the house now, and the same people kept telling me I needed to look after my little brother. And I heard—'

I stop.

'Go on.'

'I can't.'

'It might make you feel better. We had a chaplain who encouraged us to talk. He said it was our secrets that make us sick. Have a couple of breaths.'

I feel a churn in my stomach. I look out to sea and take a deep breath. 'I heard one of Dad's friends – Tommy

Mac, Dad called him. Dad always called people by both their names. Tommy Mac and Jimmy Murphy and Bobby Rooney and Mick Doyle. They were standing in a group by the bar.'

I stop again. I feel trembly.

'You can do it,' Jamie says.

'I heard Tommy say, "Trust your woman to put on a good show, but there was nothing left of him to put in that box, I heard. He was torn to pieces by that big old train." And then Jimmy saw me listening and nudged him, and they started singing not long after. I wanted to ask Stephen if he thought it was true, that Dad was still in bits all over the railway, but I didn't want to upset him. Everyone said I had to look after him, so I said nothing.'

'And you've worried about it all these years.'

'Dreams. Where he visits me with bits missing. Only half his head. An eye hanging out.' I shudder. 'I suppose you've seen it. Bodies destroyed.'

Jamie nods. 'You get used to it, and then you get disgusted at yourself for being used to it.'

'They wanted me to sing "Danny Boy", his friends. I tried, but I couldn't get through the second verse. It's so sad and all about graves. I broke down. Mum was cross because she hated all that, anyway, the singing. Then they were halfway through this song called "The Parting Glass".' I look at Jamie to see if he knows it and he shakes his head. 'It's sung at wakes. It's from the point of view—' My voice falters. 'Of the dead person.'

Jamie stretches his arm along the back of the bench and I lean against it. I feel a bit sick, but I want to carry on now. I want to tell it all. 'Stephen had disappeared. I found him outside the back door of the pub, throwing up. Tommy had been giving him whiskey. He was only fourteen. And I was patting his back, there in the freezing cold, steam rising off his sick on the floor. I could hear the refrain of the song: *Good night, and joy be to you all*. That's supposed to be the dead person wishing you well as they go on their way. And I thought, if Dad was here, then Stephen wouldn't be like this, because Dad wasn't unreliable in that way. He always had an eye to us. He'd never have let Tommy feed Stephen a load of whiskey.'

I'm still leaning against Jamie's arm. I look at him. 'And I fully got it, in that moment. Dad had loved us and he was gone. We'd have to get by without him.'

I close my eyes. 'A few days later, we found out we didn't even own our house because Dad had borrowed against it. We went to live with Mum's parents. She hated that because they'd been proved right about him.' I don't want to carry on now, not into the last shameful bit. He'd hate this, Dad would. He'd hate people knowing.

'Shall I put my arm all the way around you?'

I nod. Jamie's hand is warm on my upper arm. I lean my head against his shoulder. 'I've never told anyone this bit.'

He presses his hand more firmly against my arm. 'Think of it like the last bit of shrapnel. You've done a great job cleaning the wound. But if you leave splinters behind it won't heal and you'll need to open it up again.'

I take a deep breath. I can't look up. I'll have to say it into his shirt. 'They even had to pay the undertakers. My grandparents who'd never liked him. Mum had ordered the fancy coffin before she knew we were poor.' And I'm crying now against his chest. 'They had to pay for the ridiculous handles. And they settled the bill for the wake. All that whisky Stephen threw up. Other things. My grandfather kept writing cheques with pursed up lips.' I can taste the humiliation of it down through the years. I swallow. 'They paid for our uniforms for the new school. Stephen got a job in a restaurant because he couldn't stand taking pocket money from our grandfather, the way he used to put the money into our hand. It was all awful. But we got through it somehow.'

'And Stephen kept working and earning.'

I nod. 'I used to call him Scarlet O'Hara because he never wants to be poor or hungry again. Not that he accepts there's a link.'

Jamie takes his arm away and I straighten up. I feel better but a bit shy.

'And you chose a husband who was the opposite of your dad.'

I look out to sea. 'I never thought about it like that. But yes, I wanted someone respectable. Though now I think I might have been better off with someone cheerful. He was very cheerful, my dad, until he wasn't. It was a happy childhood in lots of ways. Not stable, but happy. Until it wasn't.'

We don't talk much as we walk back through town, but it is a friendly, thoughtful silence.

'Thank you,' I say, when we reach the lychgate. 'For everything. The jumble solution, the chips, being a handkerchief. You're a good listener.'

'I like listening to you.'

For a moment, I think I might cry again. This beautiful man likes listening to me. I can't find any words.

'If I'm still here tomorrow, will you walk up to the florist with me?'

'I'm no good at flowers. You might be better off with Barbara.'

He laughs. 'I'm fully briefed. And I'd prefer your company.'

'In that case,' I say, 'it's a date.'

Our eyes meet. I feel my cheeks flush. I don't look away.

For the first time ever, I serve a meal in our dining room. It's cottage pie, and I've stretched the mince by adding in a couple of handfuls of frozen peas.

Tim says grace then tucks in.

'Why are we in here?' Sam asks.

'I thought we'd celebrate getting rid of the jumble.'

Tim looks around. He hadn't noticed. 'Where is it?'

'The church hall.'

'Why?'

There are times when I think Tim might be from a different planet. Surely most people would not need it explaining. 'Because I don't want a dining room full of stale jumble.'

He looks pained at this evidence of my superficiality. 'Is there room in the church hall?'

I know what he's really worried about. 'Barbara agreed it.'

Relieved I haven't caused a scandal, he goes back to shovelling in his pie.

Sam wrinkles his nose. 'Still smells in here, Mum.'

Twenty-One

'Roses look good on a grave,' Jamie says the next day, as we stand before the buckets full of flowers.

'And the rabbits don't eat them. Though you get more for your money with pinks.'

'What do you really think?'

'The white roses are stunning. And Barbara might say that a bunch of those yellow freesias would create a nice bit of contrast.'

Jamie also wants to get something for Barbara, to thank her for all the sprucing up. Would she like flowers or a plant?

'I think she'd prefer something that will last. She'll like showing it off to anyone who comes round. *I knew him in his pram, you know. He had a fine set of lungs on him.*' And I'm surprised by a wave of fondness for Barbara, can imagine her talking about Sam in years to come. *I met him when he was ten. I taught him to play euchre. He was always an interesting boy.*

We consider the orchids, but settle on a pot plant called Angel's Wings because of the appropriately religious name.

As Jamie pays, I notice the florist glancing between us. She's trying to work out what we are to each other. *You and me both*, I think.

Fetching the flower scissors from the vestry, I spot a bit of Lynn's contraband Oasis hiding in the back of the cupboard and show it to Jamie. 'When it's wet, it goes all spongy. Sam loved sticking his fingers in it when he was little. He always had green gunk under his nails.'

Up at the grave, Jamie takes the metal vase and fills it with water from the outside tap. I unwrap the flowers and lay them out on the grass. The rose stems are much longer than the freesias.

'Do you think they all need to be trimmed to the same length?'

Jamie kneels down next to me and tests a rose in the vase. 'That's far too long. I'd say these all want a good twenty centimetres lopping off. I'll do that first.'

He picks up the flower scissors and sets to. *He's good at everything*, I think. *And looks good while doing everything.*

He catches me staring. 'What is it?'

'I'm admiring your flower-arranging skills.'

He carries on snipping. 'Really?'

'I like the way you turn your hand to anything. Washing up, grating cheese. Nothing is beneath you, or women's work. You're doing that with the same attention you'd give to dismantling a bomb.'

He fits the lid to the vase and puts in the first rose. 'I'm practical. Always have been.'

'I'm not.'

'You've got other talents.'

'Have I?' I feel embarrassed. 'I'm not fishing. I just don't think I have. I can't do anything.'

Jamie doesn't take his eyes from the flowers but reaches out and touches my shoulder. It's brief, somewhere between a pat and a press. It feels consoling. I watch him arrange all the roses then dot the freesias amongst them.

He leans back. 'What do you think?'

'Perfect. You could get a job doing that.'

'I reckon less would be more.' He removes a few buds, then gets up and offers me his hand. I feel his strength as he pulls me to my feet. We stand at either side of the grave, looking down at the white and yellow.

'I promised Mum a photo.' He takes a few and shows me.

'I like the one with the monkey puzzle tree in the background.'

He puts his phone back in his pocket. 'Shall we take a seat and admire our work?'

On the bench, I look down through the trees towards the harbour. 'This is a beautiful spot. And she must have loved him, your mum, don't you think? If she wants a photo of his grave?'

Jamie shrugs. 'Probably wants to show it to people. She's fonder of him dead than when he was alive. He can't get on her nerves any more. Would you call that love?'

I look down at my hands in my lap, fiddle with my rings. 'Sam thinks love is a scam.'

'And what do you think?'

'I love him. And Stephen and Sarah and their girls. I loved my dad.' I pause, remembering last night in the dining room, how I had to invoke Barbara's permission to avoid being chastised about the relocation of the jumble. I'm so fed up with trying to be loyal to someone who gives me so little in return. 'Romantic love hasn't worked out for me in the way I hoped it would.'

'Hasn't it?'

I glance at him. He's looking towards the harbour. 'I would now question the wisdom of marrying someone whose main relationship is with God.'

Jamie turns towards me. 'Don't you believe in God, then?'

'Not really. I mean, sometimes I think I do. But honestly – this is embarrassing to admit – I suspect it was just part of deciding to sign up for Tim. I went all in.' I panic that I'm being too serious and revealing and try to reverse out. 'Women do it, don't they? Take on the interests of the men in their life. Like Sarah started watching football when she met Stephen. I still don't believe she really likes it.'

'Not just women.'

I look at him. He exudes self-reliance. 'I can't see you doing that.'

'It's been known. I got into art because of a woman.'

'Really? This wasn't your bride.'

He laughs. 'No, years later. She taught me about pictures. We used to meet in the National Gallery. She liked educating me.'

I'd like to look at art with you, I think. *Or just look at you looking at art.*

'What happened?'

'It was never going to last. She was married.'

'Married?' It comes out shriller than I intended.

Jamie looks at me. 'Are you shocked?'

'A bit.' I feel silly. 'I shouldn't be, I suppose. No reason why you should care about marriage vows.'

'I don't care about them. It's not the business of church or state who anyone wants to sleep with.'

I look up at the sky through the branches of the monkey puzzle tree. 'I'm waiting to see if you get struck down.'

Jamie grins. 'How long do you think it will take?'

'Not long. You could pass the time by telling me about your art teacher.'

'I will one day, if you like. But not now, because we were talking about you and I'm not going to let you wriggle out of that point you were trying to make.'

I make a face at him.

'I'm confused,' he says. 'I thought you'd chosen this life because you believe in God. That made a certain amount of sense.'

I shake my head slowly.

'If you don't, then I don't get it. How did you end up here?'

I sigh. 'It's a long story.'

'We've got plenty of time.'

And then his phone rings. The other one.

I take all the flower rubbish to the bin and wash my hands under the tap. When the call is over, Jamie walks towards me with a quick, urgent step. 'I've got to get back to London. I need to be on a flight tonight.'

I don't ask where he's going, or for how long, or if it will be dangerous. I don't have the right to any of that knowledge. As we look at each other, I feel like he is telling me he doesn't want to go. I don't want him to go.

'Any frozen waterfalls to climb up?'

'Sadly not. I don't mind the cold, as far as extreme territories go.'

I remember what he said about meeting Suzannah after looking at sand in the middle of nowhere. I try to formulate a joke, something like, *Don't go away for too long and come back lonely and hook up with some other unsuitable woman who is not up your street*, but I can't do it.

Jamie holds out the leftover flowers. 'Something for your kitchen windowsill?'

As I take them, our fingers touch and it feels like an electric shock.

We walk back towards the church. 'I can give Barbara her plant, if that would be helpful.'

He nods. 'Thank you. And for keeping me company these last couple of days.'

'Ditto. And for sorting out the jumble.'

'I never did take you out for lunch.'

We are awkward and stilted now, cut off mid-conversation with no legitimate avenue to ever pursue it. He could be gone for months. He said he'd tell me the story of the art woman, but he's hardly going to text me instalments.

'I liked my bag of chips,' I say. 'We'll always have Gull Point.'

And I remember how it felt to cry against his shirt and for a moment I think, *Fuck it, what if I just throw myself into his arms?* But we are at the church door. I should return the flower scissors and retrieve Barbara's plant before Doreen finds it and makes it the centrepiece of some ghastly arrangement.

'I'll leave you here.' I can hear the flatness in my voice, the horrible anticlimax of it all. Real life digging its claws back into me after this too-short respite.

'You know' – Jamie looks down at me – 'they made fine children, your parents. Maybe it was biological, in that pub in Liverpool. They knew what a good match they were. Whatever else happened later, it's good that you exist, isn't it? You and Stephen. Especially you.'

He moves and I think he is going to embrace me, but then I hear the clang of the front gate and see a flash of pink, and Doreen is bustling up the path.

'Make your escape,' I say, 'go on.'

And he gives me a last smile, and I can't even watch him walk away but must assume my Vicar's Wife expression, as Doreen tells me that she's just been to the chemist to book a flu jab. It will be winter before we know it, so best to get in early and beat the rush. She lowers her voice. 'I saw Ken on the pier on my way back. Just sitting there staring at the boats. I said he should get that scaly growth on his nose checked out by the doctor. It doesn't look good to me.'

London, October 2019

Twenty-Two

Becky rests her hands on the back of the black leather chair and looks at me in the mirror. 'And what are we thinking today?'

I'm in a ridiculously posh hair salon in central London. I've never been anywhere so shiny. It's all chrome and glass, and the hair stylists wear black and glide around at top speed.

It's the last day of our trip to London. Sam is at Harry Potter World celebrating Bella's birthday. Both Stephen and Sarah tried to give me their place in the car, but I held firm. Eventually I said to Stephen, 'Do you remember when you told me to stop arguing about going to that steak restaurant? Or wanted me to get the point about why us coming London before your birthday was important? This is like that. If you make me spell it out, say how much I love to see Sam welcomed into your family, how moved I am that he looks so happy going swimming with you, or cooking with Sarah, or getting into the back seat with the girls—'

I started crying anyway, so I didn't have to finish my sentence with 'you'll make me cry'.

Stephen patted me on the back. 'Point taken.'

Sarah came up with various schemes for my amusement. I could take her membership card for Kew Gardens or the Tate, or why not see a matinee?

'You don't need to find me an activity,' I said. 'I'll enjoy some time alone reading or exploring Chiswick.' Later she presented the haircut plan as if I'd be doing her a favour. She'd booked for the wrong day and didn't want to inconvenience the magnificent Becky by cancelling at short notice. 'Please take the appointment. I know it's a bit shallow, but it always lifts my spirits to be smartened up by someone else.'

I reached my hand around to the back of my head. 'I've been cutting my own hair for years. Can't remember what it feels like to have someone else do it.'

'How do you even do that?'

'Wash it, tie it back, lop an inch or so off the bottom.'

'Don't tell Becky. She's a bit stern about DIY stuff. Told me off when I admitted to plucking out my greys with a pair of tweezers.'

'You haven't got any.'

Sarah tossed her hair. 'I've got loads hidden under all these highlights. Go on – you'll enjoy it, I promise.'

Now, looking at Becky, very aware of how unkempt and uncool I am compared to every other person in this room, I'm regretting it. It's too much of a leap to go from my own kitchen scissors to this place. The phrase 'fish out of water' is echoing in my head, and I can't imagine how Tim or Barbara or Doreen would react to all this glossiness and glamour. I'm not enjoying having to confront myself in the mirror either and feel dangerously close to tears. Maybe I should focus on getting out of here as soon as possible.

'Just a trim,' I say.

When Becky touches my hair, running her fingers through it, there is something soothing about it, and her expression as she glances between my hair and my face is curious and kind.

'Sarah thinks I should get rid of my ponytail,' I admit, 'but I don't want anything tricky to look after. I haven't even got a hairdryer.'

Becky smiles. 'Let's do low-maintenance, then. Life's too short to waste it on blow-drying, anyway. How about a bob? You've got the right shape face and it's easy to manage. I can blow-dry it smooth and sleek for you today, but the natural look will be great too.'

I'd use less shampoo, I think. 'OK, let's do it.'

'I'll cut a bit of this off before we wash you.'

A flash of metal, and then great chunks of hair fall to the floor. I feel a breeze on the back of my neck.

Becky rests a hand on my shoulder. 'Satisfying, isn't it? Already feeling a bit lighter? I reckon I'd be happy in an army barracks, running the clippers over all those heads and sending them out clean.'

Everything brings me back to Jamie, I think, as I watch Becky at her work and wonder if he ever had all his hair shaved off. I texted him when our half-term trip to London was confirmed, but he replied that he was still out of the country with no idea when he'd be back. Sometimes I try to imagine him against different backdrops – deserts, mountains, oceans – but mainly I flick between nostalgically replaying all our conversations and giving myself pep talks about how I should not allow the pleasure and safety I felt in his company to be ruined by fretting about what it all meant, and whether I'd done anything wrong. *Just be pleased and grateful you've made an interesting friend. You haven't done anything wrong. It's not a sin! Men and women can be friends. And it's not like you'll never see him again. He'll come and stay at Boscawen Hall, and maybe you'll go for a walk, or you'll help him with an errand, or he'll help you with a task. But that's all it can ever be. You're a vicar's wife. There are already three of you in this marriage. There is no room for a fourth. And he's not reliable, remember. Doesn't want to be tied down. He could not have been clearer about that.*

I look in the mirror at the women behind me. One has little foil packets all over her head. The other has an oddly shaped face. Her earlobes are at the same level as her jaw, and her lips look like a letterbox.

Becky catches my eyes and leans down. She whispers, 'We're just around the corner from Harley Street.'

Becky holds up a mirror so I can see my new haircut from all angles.

'You are clever,' I say.

'It's been a pleasure to give you happy hair. I hope you're going to show yourself off. Have you got any exciting plans for the rest of the day?'

I see the despair flash across my face. I want to tell this kind woman, confess to her, that I have no exciting plans and I probably never will. The most I can hope for is to do my duty by my husband and take satisfaction in bringing up my son, while hoovering up a few crumbs of affection and care from my brother and his wife. That's it. That's my lot in life, and I need to be grateful for it.

'I thought I'd go to the National Gallery,' I say. 'Look at some art.'

I sit on the wall and look down to Trafalgar Square and the vast groups of foreign teenagers clustering around the fountains. I close my eyes and wish Jamie were here. I imagine him standing in front of me and picture his face, the way his scar crinkles slightly when he smiles. It feels so real that when I eventually open my eyes, I'm almost disappointed to have failed to conjure him.

My bottom is cold against the concrete. What a fool I am. I'll go into the gallery and warm up. If I had Jamie's address, I could send him a postcard. How about a photo? I stand and take one, then compose a text.

Inspired by you, I am trying to educate myself about art.
No.
Thinking of you.
Weird. I delete the photo. I should go and immerse myself in some learning, take my mind off this absurd crush and stop behaving like a lovestruck teenager.

My phone beeps. There it is. His name on the screen. I fumble as I press on the alert.

Are you still in London?

I feel like I've been injected with a magical drug. I sit up straighter. My heart beats a little faster. I type, *Yes. It's our last day. Sam's at Harry Potter World. I'm at a loose end. Got the day to myself. Currently outside Nat Gallery wondering if I should educate myself about art.*

Too keen? I delete the bit about having a day to myself. That's obvious anyway. I read it again. I press send.

Like to hang out with me instead?

Yes please.

Too desperate? I delete the 'please'.

Yes. I press send.

Twenty-Three

As soon as I spot Jamie leaning against the wall outside Turnham Green station, I know there is little point denying that every single bit of me is delighted to see him. Body, mind, soul. It doesn't matter what words I use; my entire being lifts at the sight of him, and even more so at the way he smiles when he sees me.

He's dressed in jeans and a sweater, as he usually is, but with a woollen scarf in a beautiful shade of deep blue. I wonder if he'll kiss my cheek. He did when he picked me up from the vicarage in his car and I almost swooned at the smell of him. But he just stands in front of me. 'Nice hair.'

'Sarah treated me.'

'Suits you.'

'My neck feels a bit naked.' As I say it, I imagine him kissing my newly available nape. I blush and turn my face away. When I peep at him, he looks amused.

*

Jamie takes me to a cafe on the High Road, and we choose a table outside. It has a red oilskin tablecloth with little white stars.

'Hot chocolate?' he asks. 'Double espresso? Green tea?'

'Surprise me.'

He goes inside, and I watch all the well-dressed people walking by. Everyone is smart, including the children, lots of whom are holding helium balloons. Have they all been to the same party or do the local restaurants hand them out? A little girl with blonde pigtails lets go of hers, and it drifts upwards across the road and into the sky. There's no possibility of catching it. As she starts to wail, arm outstretched, I see the look of frustration on her mother's face. 'It's just a balloon,' she says, but then, as the wailing increases: 'Let's see if they'll give us another one.'

Jamie comes back carrying two green mugs and sits opposite me.

'Turmeric latte.'

The foam has an orange tint. I warm my hands on the cup.

'You're not too cold?'

I shake my head, feeling a little thrill at his concern and how observant he is.

'Here.' He hands me his scarf. 'We don't want your newly naked neck getting chilly.'

I blush, put it on, enjoy the smell and the feel of it against my skin. I try to think of something sensible to say. 'So you've been away?'

'Only got back last night.'

I register that one of his first actions was to contact me. 'Good to be home?'

'Very.' He smiles. 'I'm glad I caught you at a loose end.'

'If Stephen owned a people carrier – as he keeps threatening – I'd have been at Harry Potter World drinking butter beer and hanging around with owls.'

Jamie chinks his mug against mine. 'That would have been my loss.'

The latte is sweet, spiced and warming.

'Where were we?' Jamie says.

I don't know what he means.

'When my phone rang in the churchyard that day, you were about to tell me the story of your life.'

'Ah,' I say. 'We were in the swing of things, then, weren't we? All that honest chat. I'm not sure I can launch straight back into it without a run-up.' Or maybe I just don't want to think about Tim at all. I might prefer to forget he exists for a few hours.

'Good point. What would you like to do? We've got no chores to tackle.'

'You could tell me about the art woman.'

He smiles. 'You want a story from me first? Is this a trade?'

And I realise I don't. In a rare move, I'd rather experience the present than dwell in the past. 'Actually, I don't want to talk about other people. But shall I tell you the short answer to how I ended up where I am?'

'Only if you want to.'

I feel a wave of sadness. 'I was lonely – that's the really short answer. I was lonely, and Tim didn't seem like the worst idea in the world. And unlike you, I didn't quickly clock my mistake and reverse out. I doubled down. And that's where I am now. Over-committed to something that probably wasn't right in the first place.'

He nods. 'Yes, I see all that.'

I look down at the table, connect the stars with my finger. 'And now there is Sam.'

'That's tough.'

'It is.' And it is. But today I am here, I think, with pretty hair, drinking orange foam from a green mug opposite a handsome man who has given me his soft scarf to keep my neck warm. I've jumped tracks, given my proper life the slip, even if only for a few hours.

'You've got an afternoon off,' Jamie says.

'Are you reading my mind again?'

He laughs. 'Do you like burrata?'

'I don't even know what that is.'

'Super luxurious mozzarella. But that doesn't do it justice.' He points. 'They sell it at that shop. Shall we get some? I could make you lunch at my flat.'

I want to go to his flat, of course I do, but I'm not sure I should.

'Or we can go out somewhere,' Jamie says, quickly. 'What do you like? French? Lebanese? Modern British? Burger King? A kebab? There's an Italian ice-cream parlour up the road. We could see how much zabaglione we can eat before we feel sick.'

I giggle. 'You know, Suzannah thought you might be a bigamist. Because you didn't invite her to your flat.'

'That's duplicitous people for you. They think everyone's at it.'

'In the spirit of being fully in the honesty zone,' I say, 'can I ask you a nosy and direct question?'

'Ask me anything,' he grins. 'You know I like it. You don't have to tiptoe around me.'

'Why didn't you? Invite her. And why are you asking me?'

'Good questions.' He does look like he is enjoying himself. 'I didn't ask her because I'm very careful about who I let into my space. I don't like snoops, and she had a bit of that quality about her.' He holds up his hands. 'I know, I know. I shouldn't have carried on going out with her, but it's back to that loneliness thing.'

I put my hands up too. 'I'm not judging.'

'I could see she wasn't discreet either. I don't much like being talked about. All that twee bollocks civilians can do. *Ooh, what muscly arms! Can you run* very *fast? Have you killed* lots *of people?* You were right – I didn't like it when she told everyone about my phone. But it was my fault. I should have known better than to put myself in the power of someone I don't respect.'

'Wow,' I say, 'that's such a good way of putting it.'

He winks. 'Not a bad rule for life.'

My head is spinning. Lightbulbs popping. I am so often in the power of people I don't respect.

'As for inviting you,' he smiles, 'I'd say you're highly trustworthy. I like you. It's as simple as that. When I think of you being in my flat, sitting in my kitchen while I make you something good to eat, it feels right. So you'd be very welcome. That's all. But we don't have to do that. I never want anyone to do stuff they don't want. And especially not you.'

'Why especially?'

He looks across at me. 'You've got plenty of that in your life, haven't you? Your first rule, for an afternoon off, must be to only do what you want.'

I want, I want, I want.

'In that case,' I say, 'I'll choose the burrata option, please.'

Twenty-Four

Jamie's flat is in a mansion block that used to be a school. It says 'Boys' over the door, carved into the concrete.

I shiver as I step over the threshold. Excitement? Guilt? I don't even know any more. I'd like to stop thinking for a bit, to drop into my body, as Bryony likes to say. I walk across the wooden floor, taking in the white walls, high ceilings and enormous windows just above head height. It's so bright and clean. Apart from functional-looking furniture, including a huge grey corner sofa, there is almost nothing in it. No art, photographs, ornaments. None of the usual domestic clutter.

'Betsy helped me house-hunt. She didn't approve that the windows are so high you can't look out. She said this flat would have been the kitchens, designed like that so the servants wouldn't get distracted. What do you think?'

'The poor servants. But I love it. Lots of natural light and no one looking in.' I think of the horrible net curtains at the vicarage. It doesn't matter how much I wash them; they don't lose the tinge of Father Robert's tobacco. If I lived here, I'd never have to wash a net curtain ever again. 'I love that you haven't got loads of stuff. It's only being here that makes me see most rooms are just too full. Though I couldn't do without books. Apart from that, it's perfect.' I stretch out my arms and spin around in a circle. I couldn't do that anywhere in the vicarage. Or at Stephen's.

Jamie is leaning against the door frame. 'I'll get a bookcase if you help me fill it up. I wouldn't know what to choose.'

'You do know the way to my heart,' I say, and worry I sound too serious. I try to think of a way to lighten it, but there is such warmth in Jamie's eyes that I decide not to bother.

I notice two stones on the mantelpiece. 'What are they?'

'My guilty secrets. I don't really approve of taking things from the landscape but I broke my own rules for these two.' He lifts the larger, rounder stone and puts it into my hand. It's dark grey and covered with little pockmarks.

'What is it?'

'Lava rock. Which is gnarly and unforgiving, usually, but this has been wind-blown smooth by sand. Don't you think it's incredible? That it was once liquid and inside a volcano? Then it got spewed out, cooled into rock, and was sandblasted for millenia on a black sand beach on the south coast of Iceland.'

I feel the weight of it, run my fingers over the tiny holes. 'It's beautiful.'

He picks up the other stone. 'Do you know what this is?'

I shake my head. It looks like a big gravel chip from our car park.

'Come with me.'

I put the lava rock down on the mantlepiece and follow Jamie into his kitchen. At the sink, he turns on the tap and holds the stone under the water. Then asks me to hold out my hand.

'Can you see?.'

It's transformed. The surface shimmers like mackerel skin.

'That's amazing.' I tilt it from side to side. Sam would love it. Bryony would be able to get a sermon out of it, equating humans to the stone and God's love to the water. I look up at Jamie's face, can imagine him out in nature, far from anything manmade, communing with the habitat. I hand the stone back to him. 'I loved seeing that. Thank you for showing me your secrets.'

Jamie gestures towards a glass-topped table. I sit and watch him as he unpacks the stuff we just chose at the shop, lining it all up efficiently. He washes his hands, then takes a knife from a block. The light glistens off the edge. No blunt knives here. Jamie takes the packet of burrata, splits the plastic, and drains the milky liquid into the sink. Then he cuts through the green string. He gets two white plates from the cupboard and divides the burrata between them. Then he slices two tomatoes and tears some leaves from the basil plant. He drizzles a few drops of olive oil over the top and twists the salt grinder.

He sits opposite me. I want to weep, it looks so pretty. I lift my fork. 'So creamy.'

We eat slowly and in silence. Every inch of my skin is tingling.

I put down my fork. 'That was the best thing I have ever eaten.'

'I liked making it for you.'

We sit, and it is as if I have twirled a kaleidoscope as other instances of us looking at each other flash into my mind. Were they all leading here?

'You're looking at my mouth,' I say.

'I like looking at your mouth.'

I can hardly breathe.

I don't know how long we sit there. We don't say anything. Not out loud. I imagine running my finger down the middle of his face – over his nose, his lips, his chin, fitting the tip into the groove of his scar. But really what I want is for him to touch me. I want him to touch my mouth, my cheek, lay his fingers against the back of my neck.

After seconds or hours I say, 'Would you like to touch me?'

'I would.'

I put my elbow on the table, hold up my hand and stretch out my fingers. He mirrors the action. His hand is close to mine now. I move my fingers one by one until they are all touching his. We do the same on the other side and it is like electricity flows through us.

After some time, I think I'll die without more. 'Would you like to kiss me?'

Jamie disconnects his hands from mine. He stands but walks away from me and leans against the sink. 'I'm longing to kiss you. I can't even say how much I want to kiss you. But I don't want you to do anything you might regret. I don't want to be a threat or a disturbance to you.'

'I appreciate you saying that.'

I get up and stand in front of him. 'Will you touch my mouth?'

'You're sure?'

'Yes.'

He stretches out his hand and runs the tip of his finger along the edge of my bottom lip.

My whole body gasps.

He traces around my top lip, then puts his finger under my chin and lifts it ever so slightly. 'Can I do that again?'

'Yes.'

The first place his lips meet my skin is on my collar bone. Then the back of my neck. He asks at every stage, 'May I kiss you here? May I touch you here?' When at last he kisses me on my mouth, I think I might explode.

Afterwards we lie tangled up in the sheets. I've never felt like this before. So far from the boys from the village hall, the greedy lovers of my twenties, from poor

Tim and his sanctioned fumbling. Not that I want to think about any of that now. I just want to enjoy being in Jamie's bed with him; the warmth of his body, the feel of the crisp sheet against my skin, the fading light coming in through the high window.

If only I didn't think of Bryony at this moment.

'What's funny?' Jamie looks ready to be amused.

'Our curate does these mindfulness sessions. We cycle through our senses one by one. Imagine if she knew what my senses were up to right now.'

'Do you feel good?'

I curl myself around him, lay my head against his chest. 'I feel completely alive.'

He kisses my forehead. 'So do I.'

I could weep, to feel so cherished. 'When did you know this would happen?'

'I didn't ever know it. I don't take things for granted. It might never have happened.'

'Think it, then.'

'The possibility? When you opened the door at Stephen's. You'd been a stranger on a train until that moment. I liked your face. I didn't think I'd see you again.' He squeezes me. 'And then you were there in the doorway, covered in gold. I was surprised at how pleased I was to see you again.'

'What did you like about my face?'

'You're beautiful, but that's not it. There's so much going on. On the Tube, I felt I was watching a film. And all the action was on your face.'

I close my eyes, stroke his chest, think I might cry. 'It's so incredible to me, the way you notice me.'

'I love noticing you.' He picks up my hand, kisses my palm. 'Shall I notice you some more?'

'Do you know what I like best about sex?' Jamie asks.

I'm lying on my front, and he is running his fingers up and down my spine.

'Tell me.'

'This. Afterwards. Lying around together. Feeling a bit smug. Aren't we clever that we just did that? The intimacy of post-coital chatting.'

'You must be used to having good sex.' I regret the words as soon as they are out of my mouth. Too bitter and revealing. I wish I had stayed in the moment of pleasure.

Jamie gets up. 'All sex should be good. Or you shouldn't have it.'

He leaves the room, and I sit up and pull the duvet over me, thinking of all those magazine articles that say you must always be open for sexual business to keep your husband in a good mood.

Jamie comes back carrying two glasses of water.

'Thank you. You are a great one for keeping me hydrated.'

'If in doubt, have a glass of water.'

'I should start writing you down,' I say, 'make a little manual for myself. The Jamie Ward Guide to Life.'

He sits on the edge of the bed. 'People get in a mess about sex.'

'What do you mean?'

'We treat it seriously but without respect. Sex is no more and no less than one way to know a person. Consenting adults should do what they like. And that includes not having to do it with someone because you once said you would and now you're tied up together. I'd hate to be having sex with someone who didn't want to be there.'

'And what about love? How does that fit in?'

'Love, lust, infatuation, affection. I'm not sure I've ever really known the difference. But it's a good word. When it's about curiosity and playfulness, being interested in someone and wanting good things for them. But it gets all these bolt-ons. I love you, and that means you must do what I say. I love you, and you'd better love me back. I love you, and that means I'm allowed to behave badly and you have to put up with it. It's the obligation I can't stand.'

I get up. 'Speaking of obligation, I don't want to, but I'd better check my phone.'

Sarah sent me a text an hour ago telling me they were home. I reply saying I might be back late; I bumped into an old friend in town and we're catching up. Is that OK?

An immediate beep. *All fine. Sam is cooking dinner.* Love heart emojis interspersed with frying pans.

I send back a row of hearts and feel a whisper of guilt, but probably not as much as I should.

In the bathroom, I look at myself in the mirror. My hair is still smooth and silky. My skin is plumped and pink. I look like I've had a facelift as well as a haircut. *I'm wearing one of Jamie Ward's T-shirts. I've just got out of his bed.* Can I be the same woman who sat in that chair at the salon, scared she might burst into tears? Or perhaps I haven't changed, I've just stumbled across a door into another world.

Jamie is in the kitchen. 'Do you like grapefruit?'

'Love it. But I can't be doing with the faff. All those fiddly segments.'

He takes a grapefruit, cuts it into quarters, then eighths, and then deftly carves the flesh from the skin.

'You're so good at everything,' I say.

'It's not hard. Just treat it like a fish. Fillet it.'

I tell him I'd have even less idea what to do with a fish and he laughs, hands me the bowl, and says maybe we'll go fishing one day and then cook our supper on the beach.

I watch him prepare another grapefruit for himself. It is very relaxing, hypnotic even. He finishes, wipes the blade and sits opposite me. When a bit of grapefruit juice drips down my chin, he leans over and wipes it with his finger.

Then he makes scrambled eggs on sourdough toast, all buttery with flecks of chive. We agree we both like eating breakfast food at any time of the day, and when he clears up – he won't let me help – it turns out he has

275

no dishwasher either. He doesn't want to be spoiled by mod-cons or bogged down by possessions. He likes to travel light, and often the simplest way of doing something is the best. It serves him to live a stripped-back existence. Less to worry about when he goes away. He's not always on call, he tells me; he works for intense periods so he can do what he likes with the rest of his time. He gets restless when he spends too long in civilisation, and needs to sail somewhere or climb something. He's planning a trip to Patagonia. He likes the high latitudes, the extremes, the urgency of the seasons. Yes, things go wrong sometimes. That's all part of it. The worst thing you can ever do is give in to self-pity. 'If I start feeling sorry for myself, I'm fucked.'

I can't bear to even look at a clock. I wish I could press pause on the rest of the world and stay here, enjoying kisses and conversation and delicious tiny meals. But I can't.

Even after texting Sarah for another extension, the time rolls horribly on.

'I don't want you to go,' Jamie says.

'I don't either.'

I get dressed. It is strange putting on my clothes from earlier, as though they belong to a different woman. Jamie gives me the blue scarf. It's dark and cold when we get outside and I feel a bit light-headed. 'It's like I'm re-entering reality.'

He puts his hand on my back. 'You've had a few hours off from ordinary life. It will be good for you.'

'Hope so.'

In the car, Jamie is calm. There's none of that tutting at other drivers or complaining about roadworks that Tim goes in for. I watch his hands move over the steering wheel, thinking how capable he is, how well he manages to move around in the world. He never wastes energy on things he can't control.

'What are we to each other, now?' I ask.

'What would you like us to be?'

'Friends,' I say. 'I'd like you to be my friend.'

'I'm extremely happy to be your friend.'

'And do you think we'll do that again?'

'Would you like to?'

I feel my body lift itself up from the seat. 'Yes.'

Jamie takes his hand from the wheel and puts it on my thigh. 'Then I very much hope so.'

We talk about practicalities, how he can call or message me when Sam is at school, how I might be able to say I am visiting a friend and then meet Jamie at a hotel instead.

For the first time, it feels a bit sordid. I'm not ashamed of what we've done but can see that to keep doing it will involve some subterfuge.

'Promise me something,' I say.

'Anything.'

'I don't want to do anything near Sam or the church. Promise me we won't ever have a quickie in the vestry or get it on in the larder.'

'We won't ever do anything you don't like.'

*

Jamie pulls up around the corner from Magnolia Road. 'I'd better not deliver you to the door,' he says, 'but I don't want you to think I'm trying to get out of taking you all the way home.'

For a moment I don't understand, and then I remember tales from the village disco on the way back from Boscawen Hall. It feels a long time ago. 'You mean you're not going to lose interest now you've got somewhere?'

'Not at all.' He leans forward and kisses my neck. 'I'm extremely keen to get everywhere again.'

I don't want to let him go.

'If you don't stop kissing me like that,' he says, eventually, 'I'll have to take you straight back to bed.'

I stand and watch the lights of the car as he drives off, nestling my face against his scarf. Then I turn around to see Stephen staring at me from the other side of the road.

Twenty-Five

Sam is in bed when Tim comes back from the PCC meeting. Tim sits at the breakfast bar as I make him beans on toast and tells me that Bryony wanted them to open with a mental health check-in, but Doreen wasn't keen. Now he's on a long rant about Derek and a dispute over confidentiality during circle time at the Men's Shed. I must drift off, because the next time I pay attention he's moved on to Barbara and Doreen and the ramifications of the great harvest festival fallout, but I'm not taking in any of the details of who has done what to whom.

I should have tried this years ago. What a thrill, to discover that I can conserve my energy by not actually listening. Tim never wants my input anyway, so it will be enough if I occasionally say, 'How awful,' or 'What a shame.' I stir the beans and consider not bothering with the cheese but decide that's a bit mean. I don't hate Tim or want to deprive him of nourishment. As I grate, I close my eyes and remember Jamie being here.

'Ouch.'

'What's wrong?'

'Just a nick.'

I get a bit of kitchen roll, watch my blood turn the white tissue red. That should be a lesson to me. Next time I want to close my eyes to moon over my lover, I should not do it when my knuckles are near sharp metal. *My lover, my lover.* I still can't really believe it: that when I came back here after half-term, I had become a woman with a lover.

As the train pulled into Truro, I felt awkward at the prospect of seeing Tim for the first time since my infidelity, like I had a scarlet letter scrawled on my forehead. I expected to feel guilty or sad or ashamed of myself, but when Sam and I got off the train he wasn't there. We watched everyone else get picked up, all the happy embraces, and then went outside and sat on a bench. It was cold. I was grateful for Jamie's scarf.

'Do you think Dad has forgotten about us?'

'He's probably just running late. It's good you've got that big Hogwarts hoodie to keep you warm. Shall we play I-Spy?'

'That's so lame, Mum.'

Then Tim arrived, rushing, dog collar on. He didn't apologise, just said he'd been held up because Doreen and Barbara were in dispute over arrangements for the harvest festival.

He took the suitcase. 'What have you done to your hair?'

I was surprised he'd even noticed. I said that Sarah had treated me, aware I was using the same phrasing as with Jamie.

'I liked it long,' Tim said.

Then Sam gave him a little packet of chocolate biscuits he'd saved for him from the train and told him you get given loads of free stuff in First Class.

Tim frowned. 'What on earth were you doing in First Class?'

Sam looked panicked. After a week away from Tim, he'd forgotten that luxury and even enjoyment are wrong.

I jumped in. 'Stephen gave us the tickets as a present.'

Tim sniffed, threw the biscuits into the side pocket of the car, and didn't respond as Sam told him about making cheesecake with Sarah and sharing Stephen's chicken jalfrezi with him, even though it was too hot for everyone else including me.

When we got home, Tim went off to finish his sermon and Sam ran into the garden. I unpacked the suitcase and assessed the situation. The sink was full of dirty dishes, the laundry basket full of clothes and towels; the bathroom smelled, and there was a pile of plates and mugs on Tim's bedside table. I considered how this homecoming would be much more upsetting if I were still a well-behaved and faithful wife. As it was, I could activate my Vicar's Wife persona, press the domestic duties button, and crack on.

In church the next morning, Tim preached about the pitfalls of modern life with all its material temptations.

If we opened ourselves up to God and his love, he said, there would be no need to buy things and we would see tiny miracles everywhere. I looked at him standing there in his robes with the green stole around his neck, and filled up with fury at how he so continually ignores the considerable miracle that is the child we made together. Then he said we must always remember that life is a rehearsal space for the kingdom of heaven.

When the service was over, and everyone was making their way towards the back of the church for coffee and custard creams, Sam asked me what Tim meant. I admitted I wasn't sure – maybe that life is to prepare us for what comes next – but even as I was saying it, I thought how miserable that was, that life had any other purpose than itself. And Sam said, 'Is Earth just a massive malicious test, then? Designed to rat people out who aren't good enough to go to heaven?'

The toaster pops. I butter the slices, pour on the beans, sprinkle cheese over the top, and put the plate in front of Tim. I open the cutlery drawer, pass him a knife and fork, get the salt and pepper from the cupboard, fill a glass with water and put it next to him. I make little robot noises in my head as I do it. Buzzes, clicks. It's quite good fun. I should have thought of this years ago, too.

Tim bows his head. 'Bless us, O Lord, and these thy gifts which we are about to receive from thy bounty. Through Jesus Christ our Lord. Amen.'

I replace my kitchen roll bandage with a waterproof plaster, and wash up the pan and the grater. I remember

Jamie making the burrata, carving the grapefruit, chopping the chives. And cleaning up after all of it. In those few hours I was with him, I didn't so much as rinse a glass. *It's like having a butler,* I said.

I become aware that Tim has stopped eating and is looking at me. 'Are you OK?'

There's no real concern in his voice. He sounds like a line manager checking no one has died before reminding a sales assistant they need to look cheerful behind the till.

'I'm fine,' I say.

'You don't seem yourself lately.'

He's confused because I am malfunctioning. Vicar's Wife 44 has gone offline. It will be inconvenient if he needs to take me to the repair shop to have my settings adjusted.

'You've been strange since you went away at half-term.'

I wonder what would happen if I told the truth. I run it in my head as I watch him fork more beans into his mouth: *I'm having an affair, Tim. I didn't mean to. It was supposed to be a friendship. We mainly talked about dead relatives and damp, so it felt innocent. And even when I asked him to kiss me – I know! Brazen! – I was telling myself it would be like going on a day trip or taking up a new hobby. I hoped it might help me put up with the daily grind, might make my actual life more tolerable. But it has got out of control because I am completely obsessed. I can neither eat nor sleep for thinking of him. I feel absurdly happy and alive when I talk to him but when I lie awake at night I feel foolish and insecure. Sometimes I wish I could turn back the clock and make different choices, but I don't want to do that because it terrifies me how easily I might not have met him and might not know what it's like to be with him, and to feel fully and truly myself. So that's my update, my check-in. That's where I'm at. And Stephen's not talking to me, by the way, because I'm so useless at adultery that he found out straight away and strongly disapproves. So I'm in a bit of a pickle. My current challenge is to work out what lie to tell so I can escape next weekend and get a train to Taunton. And you know what, Tim? I feel bad about deceiving Sam, but I don't feel guilty about you because you've treated me so casually, with such little respect and care, that I truly think you only have yourself to blame.*

Tim pushes the plate away. Not in any useful direction, like towards the sink. Just one of his many signals to me that he is ready for service.

'You're welcome,' I say.

'What?'

'You're welcome.' I put his plate in the sink. 'I used to have this colleague, Belinda. She hissed, *You're welcome*, when customers weren't sufficiently appreciative. I thought I'd try it out.'

Tim is looking at me like he thinks I've gone mad.

'You never say thank you, Tim.'

'Yes, I do.'

'Not to me.'

He stares at me, mouth slightly open.

'You say it to God. You say it to Bryony, Barbara, Doreen, Derek, everyone who comes to church, the postie and the binmen. You must think it's important because you shout at Sam if he forgets or is slow. Though you don't say it to him either.'

'I don't think that's true.'

'It is true, Tim. How many meals is it, do you think? Over the years? How many slices of toast and cups of tea and glasses of water have I delivered to you for no acknowledgement?'

'You're in a very odd mood.' Tim presses his fingers to his temples. 'This isn't like you.'

I lean against the sink. 'You don't know anything about me, Tim. I can't remember the last time you looked at me as though I was a real person. I'm just here to feed and launder you, take messages, look after your child and pretend to enjoy going to church.'

'What is it you mind so much about?' His tone is cross, as though the last thing he needs at this time of night is to deal with another irrational woman.

'Mind? I mind that the house was a complete tip when we moved in and everyone expects me to fix it with no money and my magical woman's touch. I mind that the ceiling fell in on our very first night and no one has yet come around to look at it. I mind that Doreen expects you to jump every time she wants to change her funeral arrangements. I doubt she'll ever die, that woman – she's like a cockroach. And I mind the open-door policy. It's not fair that Sam can't make any noise in his own house. And that I can't curl up with a book in the evening without someone popping in and saying they wish they had time to read.'

'Only me.' Barbara pokes her head around the door. 'Just popping in to— Have I come at a bad moment?'

'We're having a row, actually, Barbara,' I say, 'so it might be better if you come back later.'

'Dearie me,' Barbara says. Her eyes are out on stalks.

'Is that OK? Tim and I need to carry on with our ding-dong now.' I am close to laughter. I look at Tim to see if he thinks it is funny, but he doesn't.

'Ann's idea of a joke, Barbara,' Tim says. 'We're not really arguing. But we do have a few things to talk about, so maybe tomorrow would be best.'

Barbara closes the door behind her.

Tim frowns. 'Should you lose your temper in front of Barbara?'

I don't think it's funny any more. 'Do you know what, Tim? I'm done with caring what Barbara thinks of me.'

'I don't understand why you are so wound up.'

And I can see that he doesn't. We could be speaking different languages for all I'm getting through to him. I try again: 'Because you are in such a bad mood all the time, so exhausted by other people, that by the time you get to us you're running on fumes and sludge. Don't you see it's mad that you're too tired to be nice to the people under your own roof?'

He looks confused. 'Aren't I nice to you?'

How does he not know? I shake my head. 'Not really, no. You complain, criticise, and subject us to a continual agenda of moral improvement. Like that horrendous film. Sam was ten and about to start a new school, and

286

you made us watch a little boy get stabbed to death by bullies because Doreen had recommended it.'

'I didn't know that was going to happen. She said it was about kindness.'

'But he wanted to watch *The Hobbit*! We could have had a nice time with elves. But you had to make a lesson out of it, like you do with everything. And you treat him like he's this terrible materialist. He's a child. He's allowed to be excited if he gets a present; he shouldn't have to give all his stuff away. He can have some fun. My childhood was full of laughter. I want that for Sam.'

'But your dad—'

'I know. But up until then, there was a lot of joy. I miss it. We used to laugh over ordinary things. When do we ever laugh, Tim? Tell me.'

I watch my tears splash down onto the breakfast bar.

'I'm sorry,' he says, oddly formally. 'I'm sorry you're upset. There should be joy in a life with God.'

I feel another surge of anger. 'I've had enough of God, Tim. Of you never taking off that bloody collar. Sundays are awful. All the times that are supposed to be holy and special are horrible because you're so stressed. And all you care about is how I appear to the likes of Doreen and Barbara. You never care about how I feel.'

He looks at me. 'And how do you feel?'

The anger drains out of me, and I am left with a sad weariness. 'That you don't like me very much, Tim. You'd have been better off with a self-sacrificing woman who was more enthusiastic about playing second fiddle

287

to God. Or as a disciple setting out with your one pair of sandals. Or an anchorite. Like Julian of Norwich. Then you wouldn't need to have the distraction of other humans in your house. You could concentrate on the divine.'

I fill the kettle. 'But I'm too tired, Tim. I'm not wound up so much as worn out. I just want to make my hot-water bottle and go to bed under Barbara's dead parents' eiderdown. I just want to go to sleep.'

The next morning after Sam has left for school, Tim comes into the kitchen where I am washing up the breakfast dishes.

'I do like you.'

'What?'

'Last night you said I don't like you. But I do.'

Tim looks distressed. But not angry. It would have meant a lot to me if he'd said this a few weeks ago. What a shame that I didn't come out with all this before. Or couldn't.

And was I being honest last night, really? Everything I said was true, but I was saying it to divert attention from a larger lie. Because what is really wrong with me is that I am completely and ludicrously in love with someone else.

Cornwall, November 2019

Twenty-Six

At the first Mindful Monday in November, eleven of us gather in the church hall and nod along as Bryony says even happy lives are full of pain, uncertainty and effort, and there is ease and comfort in the acceptance of that. Barbara tells us her mother always said the secret to life is learning to take the rough with the smooth. We lie down and do a body scan. I do feel calmer, and wonder if anyone else is using these sessions to navigate the challenges involved in meeting up with their lover. We're breathing light into our sacral chakras when Doreen says it's too cold to be lying around on the floor any longer. As we sit back on our chairs, Bryony talks about the ancient wisdom of winter and how our bodies are instinctively readying themselves for retreat and hibernation.

Mine isn't, I think.

Jamie has found a hotel he thinks I will like not far from Taunton. He will pick me up from the station and has booked a little cabin, which means that I won't have to go through reception. He texts me a link. When I click through, it says, *Our private cabins are a home away from home.*

I hope not, I think, and almost spin into an existential crisis over the realisation that they must use that expression because people like it, which means home must signify all sorts of things for other people that it doesn't for me. Then I remind myself that I wouldn't be having an affair if I was happy at home, so it is pointless to get upset about the conditions that have led to me having opinions about the marketing language used by hotels I might visit illicitly. So I lose myself in the soothing interiors, the enormous bed, imagining us in the copper bathtub on the private terrace, and it is only when Sam comes into the kitchen to ask about the horrible smell that I realise the potatoes have boiled dry.

Tim has been much nicer to me since our row. He has made me a cup of tea on three separate occasions and is gentler with Sam. I feel a bit sorry for him, that his efforts are falling on stony ground.

I know the easiest way to get Tim to sanction time away is to cast myself as the doer of a good deed for a suffering friend. I invent a pal called Caroline – we worked together in Doncaster – but thinking up her dilemma is tricky. Giving her fertility problems or a difficult husband makes me a bit queasy. And there's no way I can give her a child and allow anything bad to happen. I settle on a recently deceased father. I can't bear for him to suffer anything other than a quick and painless death, but they were very close. As I tell Tim about how hard Caroline is finding life without her father, I am moved to tears and I'm not even pretending. Tim pats me on the shoulder, agrees that Sam is responsible enough to be left at home while he takes his weddings, and says he will mention Caroline in his prayers.

I don't feel at all guilty until Saturday morning when I say goodbye to Sam. He's sitting at the breakfast bar in slightly too small pyjamas, playing chess against himself. 'Have a good time with your friend, Mum. I hope you can help her cheer up.'

And it hits me then that I've lied to Sam. Not directly, but because I've lied to Tim, Sam is also being deceived. For eleven years I've done my absolute best to be as truthful with him as I can, and now I've chucked all that in with hardly a second thought. I put an arm around him, but he wriggles away.

He moves the black queen over to the other side of the board. 'Do you think I should try not to love you so much?'

'No!' It comes out like a cry. 'Why would you even want to?'

He looks up at me. 'So I won't be too upset when you die.'

'Sweetheart.' I reach for him again, and this time he folds into me. 'I'm not sure it works like that. And I'd be so sad if I felt less loved by you. Come on, give me a proper hug. It needs to last me until tomorrow night, so let's make it a good one.'

And I feel all the usual joy of holding my boy, rubbing my cheek against his – but it is hard to ignore the knowledge that I should be sitting down at the other side of the breakfast bar to play chess with him, not skipping off to cavort with my lover in a copper bathtub. But I do ignore it. I kiss Sam on the top of his head and walk out of the door.

For the first time ever, I'm not interested in the other people on the train or in what I can see out of the window. I don't look around, or eavesdrop, or catch anyone's eye. I don't want to draw attention to myself. I feel like my whole body is signalling that I am on my way to meet my lover. I might as well be a cartoon character exuding little pink love hearts. I stare out of the window and remember being in Jamie's flat, when he held that stone under the tap, his voice full of excitement and pleasure as he showed me how it transformed.

We have not long left Plymouth when my phone rings: Tim. I expect him to ask where Sam's coat is, or what he should give him for lunch, but his tone is sombre. Father Robert is dying. Tim has just spoken to the district nurse. His illness accelerated very rapidly and now he's got a chest infection. He's on antibiotics. They won't cure him, just buy him a bit more time. But it's a matter of days.

I make consoling noises.

'He wants me to go to him.'

The signal drops out for a few seconds, and then I hear him say something about next of kin and being the executor, about his afternoon wedding, and that Barbara will mind Sam until I get home.

'Sorry? I didn't hear that last bit.'

'I want to get on the road as soon as I can. I'd better get on with this wedding. Will you let Barbara know what time you'll be back?'

I hang up the phone without replying. Let him think I've gone into a tunnel. I flop forward, rest my head against the back of the seat in front. I could scream. Tim didn't ask me to abandon my plans, just assumed that I would. He's forgotten all about poor Caroline needing to be comforted in her grief. Could I call back and suggest he waits until tomorrow morning? That we split the difference? He sets off later than he wants, and I come back earlier than I want. But I know I can't. I doubt I could if Caroline were real, and I certainly can't when she isn't.

I remember Mrs Holt's collapse, how none of Doreen's emergencies ever turn out to be real. *Father Robert better be dying*, I think. If I go home and he doesn't die, I am going to be monumentally fucked off.

I want so much to be with Jamie. I want to see the warmth in his eyes as he looks at me. I want to look at him and touch him and laugh with him and kiss him. I want to lie in his arms. Could I wait until Tim is on the road and then ask Barbara to have Sam overnight? And that's when I know I have gone mad. *Not good*, I think, pressing my forehead into the seat in front. Not good to be so desperate to spend the night with my lover that I'd shack my son up with a woman who likes a breakfast whiskey and her antisocial, accident-prone husband who I have never actually met.

I cry all the way to Totnes, then get off the train and cross over to the other platform. Homeward bound. I walk to the far end because I don't want to be near other people. My suitcase feels heavy. And so does my heart.

I text Jamie. I don't call because I don't trust my voice not to betray the depths of my unhappiness. I try to sound casual, not that I am weeping hot tears of frustration on the cold platform. It starts to rain, but I don't want to walk back to the shelters and huddle under them with all the clusters of travellers. My phone beeps. Jamie. A sad-face emoji. I don't know what I wanted but it wasn't that.

I wonder what he'll do now, with his unexpectedly free Saturday night. He'll have set off already. Will he turn around at the next junction? Maybe he will carry on and stay at the hotel alone, splashing around in the copper bathtub on his home-from-home private terrace.

The rain drips from my hood onto my face. The train is announced. My train. We are told to stand back behind the yellow lines. I look down to see two thick lines under my feet. I am too close. There is another announcement. Not pre-recorded this time. The voice sounds like it belongs to a real person somewhere behind the scenes who is looking at me, who is not far off from saying, *Hey you, yes you, get back behind the lines*. I don't move. The tannoy crackles again and I step away, walk all the way back towards the railings. With every stride I am signalling to my unknown audience that they do not need to worry, that I may be crying in the rain, but I am not going to do anything drastic. The train is approaching.

If I were Anna Karenina, I might throw myself under it. But because I am me, I get on and head home.

I sit across the aisle from a boy who is laughing and snorting and banging the table. His mother looks tired. The man in the seat next to me coughs. A couple get on with a toddler in a buggy. She's got a dummy in her mouth and clutches a phone playing cartoons with tinny music on a loop.

The boy is slapping the window and shouting. Some people avert their eyes as they go by; others smile and say, 'I wish I could have that much fun.' The mother smiles back, and I think how her life must be full of trying to ignore people who avoid them and having to be grateful to people who are nice to them, and I hate myself for thinking my life is difficult. My head aches. The man next to me coughs again, gets out his phone and starts watching a film. Men are shooting each other. He has no earphones, and I wonder when that became a thing, that everyone felt free to impose their entertainment on each other.

I think of Jamie and Tim driving on the same motorway, and of Sam at home with Barbara, and I hate myself again for not wanting to be on this train on my way back to my real life, and for being in this situation, for having acted in a way that means I can never be happy because I am always either miserable where I am supposed to be, or happy where I am not supposed to be, or shuttling uncomfortably between the two. And while I am a bad mother, I am not a bad enough mother to think, *Fuck it,*

I'll abandon my child and follow my lover around until he gets bored of me. Perhaps it would help to be a better person or a worse person, not the precise calibration of person I am.

I watch the woman and the boy in the reflection of the window. She wipes his nose.

He burps. 'Pardon you,' she says.

He wants to be cuddled. He puts his hands together and under his cheek.

'You're tired,' she says. 'Not much longer now.' He puts his head down on the table and she strokes his hair. I wonder how old he is. A couple of years older than Sam, maybe. Sam's years of wanting to be cuddled are coming to an end. Maybe that's why I have found a lover. Because I can't bear the thought of not being touched.

When Tim and I walked along the canal all those years ago, he seemed so wise. *We will do better*, he said, and for almost the first time ever I thought that maybe I could do better, could be better, that I didn't have to be stuck forever wanting my dad to walk through the front door but hearing the knock instead, seeing all the black of the police uniform through the dappled glass of the door. Tim offered me another life. The mystery is how far it has diverged from what I thought it would be like.

Maybe I am not a good person. Is it as simple as that? I'm too selfish to spend vast swathes of my life making refreshments for church functions and never having any fun. I don't want a partner who cares only about unfortunate strangers, who folds Sam and me underneath his hair shirt. I don't want to be married to someone who is nicer to Doreen than he is to me. I wish I'd chosen someone who would put me first. Is that what I'm looking for? Or chasing something that doesn't exist?

The boy is asleep now, leaning on his mother's shoulder. On my neighbour's phone screen, the men are punching each other. One of them pulls out a gun. The other begs him not to shoot. I close my eyes and try to ignore his pleas for mercy.

Twenty-Seven

When I get home, Barbara and Sam are playing euchre in the kitchen. Sam is wearing his Hogwarts hoodie and looks cosy and happy. 'Sorry you didn't get to see your friend, Mum.'

Barbara tries to interrogate me over the precise nature of Father Robert's illness, sharing her theory that he was probably ill before he left and that's why he made the mistake with the grave and stopped looking after himself. He always had bits of blood-stained tissue stuck to his face, she says, and would sit in the lychgate huffing and puffing.

'I don't know anything,' I say. 'Tim didn't say much on the phone, and I couldn't hear him well.'

Barbara keeps talking, and I keep making non-committal noises. Eventually she gets her coat. 'Best get back to Ken. He's a bit low, tummy playing up, and he doesn't like November. Too grey and wet, he says. It was our wedding anniversary yesterday. Forty-nine years. He said he doesn't need a medal, but he does need earplugs.' She bursts into laughter and whisks out of the door.

Sam and I sit on the sofa with one of his hobbit films. I keep thinking about what I would be doing in the other universe, in the one where I got off the train and into Jamie's car. I look at the hotel on my phone again, at that copper tub. Maybe it would have been too cold for it anyway. I read the dinner menu, can almost taste the crab linguine. I try to guess what Jamie would have ordered. Tim would choose something cheap and filling – pasta arrabbiata, probably. Stephen would have three courses, including the rib-eye, and not mind paying the supplement. But I don't know about Jamie. I've not yet spent enough time with him even to know if he's the sort of person whose choices would be easy to predict.

Giant spiders are rampaging about on screen.

'I'm going to have to request a hug, Mum,' Sam says.

I stretch out my arm, feel him nestle into the side of my body. I wonder if there are women out there, maybe the same women who love their homes, who are in love with their husbands. I close my eyes and try to transport us both to the grey corner sofa in Jamie's flat. Maybe he's just popped out to buy grapefruits and burrata. It's no good. I can picture myself in the scene but not Sam.

'Why are you crying, Mum? This isn't sad. It's frightening.'

'I'm thinking about what happens later.' I can never grasp who is who in these films, what they are looking for, or why they are fighting. Hopefully this is one where someone gets killed in a battle at the end. 'You know, that sad bit later.'

'Don't anticipate problems, Mum.'

I ruffle his hair. 'You're very wise.'

'Barbara says that's what Ken says.'

'Good for Ken.'

'Barbara also says Doreen has got a Sunday face and a Monday-to-Saturday face. What does that mean?'

'That she puts on a show for church. Makes an effort to be pleasant on a Sunday. But she's different underneath.'

'I don't think she's nicer on Sundays than other days, do you?'

I shake my head. 'Not really, no.'

And I realise that I have allowed myself to have a face for Jamie that is different to the face I wear around Sam. I don't want Sam to get my second-best face. And I hope that a sad bit comes along soon so that I can cry some more.

Jamie calls when Sam is in bed. I feel instantly better at the sound of his voice. He's at the hotel because he was almost there when I texted. He had the seabass with a kale and radish salad, and a side of broccoli. He's not easy to predict food-choice wise, he says, might have gone for red meat on a different day. Never bothers with puddings, unless he's at someone's house when he eats them to be polite. No, he's not going to try the outside bathtub. He's not sure he'd fancy it even in summer. Unless I wanted to, of course.

'Shall I drive down tomorrow? I promise I won't try to shag you over the breakfast bar. I'd just like to see you.'

'But it's miles.' I'm delighted both at the thought of spending time with him and that he wants to make the effort.

'I'm already halfway.'

I go to bed happy and expectant but wake in the night, heart thudding, from a dream where I've murdered someone and must find a church to ask for sanctuary.

I get up and open the curtains. There is no moon so all I can see is the twinkle of mooring lights in the bay. I feel like I'm in one of those books where the narrative splits off in different directions and the reader gets to pursue the consequences of every decision. Choose your own adventure. Stephen used to like them. He'd ask me for advice at every turn. Shall I go left or right at the Crossroads of Terror? Enter the Cave of Devils? Climb up the Mountain of Doom?

That's my dilemma. Stay on the street of respectable married life or veer off onto the boulevard of instant gratification? I know what Stephen would say if I asked him. He made his disapproval very clear the night he saw me get out of Jamie's car.

He'd been to the corner shop to get some ice cream, he said, when I asked why he was out. 'Not that it matters. Where you've been is more to the fucking point.'

We stood under the lamppost on the corner of Magnolia Road as he delivered me a lecture in a series of angry whispers. 'What are you playing at? He's not available, is he? You don't think he's going to change his life to shack up with you and Sam?'

'I know he's not. That's why he's not a risk. It's not a relationship. Just a bit of time off from ordinary life.'

'You don't get to have that, once you've got kids. You don't get that kind of freedom.'

'Does it have to be that way, though?'

'Yes, it fucking does. What would you say to me if I was plums-deep in someone else just because I'd got a bit bored?'

'That's not fair. My life is not like yours. I am so miserable for so much of the time. When I'm with Jamie, I feel alive.'

'Oh, for fuck's sake. It's like something out of Mills and Boon. You need to think about Sam. He matters. You can't just go out for fish and chips and not come back.'

'I would never do that.' I can hear the outrage in my voice.

'You did it tonight! He made pasta for tea, the poor little fucker, and where were you?'

'He won't have missed me. He has a great time with you.'

'Have you gone completely mad? Do you really want me to agree that it doesn't matter that you lied to him?'

I started to cry then.

'You can't do that. You can't leave a child like that. You just can't.'

And I saw Stephen's tears in the glow of the streetlight and wondered how much he was talking about Sam and how much of himself. And I wanted to believe it was all about him, really, because I didn't want to accept that anything he said about Sam might be true.

I pad into Sam's bedroom. His feet are sticking out from under the duvet, so I twitch it to cover them up. I look down at his face, his dear little face. My boy. My son. He doesn't hold my hand in the street anymore and no longer wants to be tucked in. But he still needs me to be his mother.

I go back to sleep. All the possible outcomes are jumbled up in my dreams, presenting themselves as equally possible. Sam flickers in and out of everything. Maybe it is good for him to spend time with Jamie; maybe he will acquire some of his manly presence. *Fooling yourself, fooling yourself*, says my mother. Maybe I can have it all, do it all. I see myself big with child, cradling a baby, and then I'm wrapped in a blue cloak and I am Mary, watching Jesus in the manger. And I am Mary watching her son be crucified. *Holy Mary, mother of God, pray for us sinners now and at the hour of our death.* And my father is there, on his knees, and I want to say to him, *Don't do it, Dad, this doesn't have to be the hour of your death, don't do it*, but I can't speak, I can't say anything, I can't do anything. And I wake up singing 'The Foggy Dew'. Dad used to sing it when he was drunk, standing, with his hand on his heart. *But to and fro in my dreams I go, and I kneel and pray for you.* I lie and stare at the ceiling. No wiser. Except as the light of day creeps around the edges of the curtains, I know with cold certainty that I can't have it all.

Twenty-Eight

I'm with Jamie in his car at Gull Point, watching the rain on the windscreen. Sam is at home, because I have become a woman who leaves her child alone in front of the telly so she can be with her lover.

'You look tired,' Jamie says. He's so beautiful it hurts. His eyes are greyish today, his jumper a deep petrol blue.

'I hardly slept.' My lip wobbles. 'I'm a bit of a mess. Sorry.'

'Hey.' His voice is warm. 'Don't apologise. Tell me what's up.'

'I don't think I can do this. I think I'm—' I feel a tear escape. 'It's huge. How I feel about you. Too big.'

He holds out his hand, and I slip mine into it. I turn to face him. 'You were right, that thing you said about how honesty gets compromised. I was in despair when I had to turn around yesterday. But I was ashamed to admit it.' I want to hold onto his hand but I let it go. 'I'm too into you, that's the truth. And I can't be. You don't want a proper relationship, and even if you did, I've got Sam to think about.'

A tiny bit of me – maybe an enormous bit of me – hopes Jamie might jump in and offer some kind of declaration. But he doesn't. So I press on quickly. 'I think it's best if we don't do this any more. I need to focus on Sam. I've been all over the place since half-term. I think about you too much. I just want to lie around with you. That's the problem. I'm not interested in anything else.'

'I'd like that too.'

I raise my hand, rest it against his cheek. 'It was spectacular, that afternoon. Those few hours. I'll remember it all my life. I'll be on my deathbed dreaming of you kissing up and down my spine.'

I slump back into my own seat. 'I can't be casual about this. I tried. But it's not going to work.'

The windscreen is all steamed up. *That's good*, I think. *No one will be thinking, what is the vicar's wife doing crying in that car with that handsome man.*

'I hope I haven't been a bad thing in your life,' Jamie says, his voice full of concern.

'You've been a good thing in lots of ways,' I say, 'You got rid of the jumble, for one thing. Introduced me to burrata and turmeric lattes. I might try your grapefruit technique, though I doubt my knife is sharp enough.'

'You deserve good tools,' Jamie says.

'Another thing for my little book of Jamie wisdom. Seriously, you've really helped. I don't regret anything.' I sigh, 'Except that it's not allowed. Which means lying. I don't want to lie to Sam.'

It is unfortunate timing, I think, to be experiencing first love while in my forties and married to somebody else.

'We could go back to being friends. I can behave myself. If you don't want me to lure you into bed, I won't do it.'

I doodle a tiny heart in the condensation on the windscreen. 'I will want to, though. You're like a drug. I'll get more and more addicted to you and then be unable to cope with the withdrawal.'

'I can't be more like a fine wine or a chocolate eclair? Too rich for every day but delicious every so often.'

I laugh. 'Like an aged stilton.'

'Or going skydiving?' He reaches over and draws a little parachute next to my heart.

'A champagne cream tea.' I try to draw a scone topped with clotted cream but it looks like a blob. I scribble it out. 'It's no good. I need to go cold turkey on you. For a while, anyway. Maybe in the future you'll come and help Betsy with the lambing, and we'll chat, and my desire to throw myself into your arms will feel like a distant memory.' I doubt this is true. I think I'll always long for him.

He drums his fingers on the steering wheel. 'There's a job I've been offered overseas. I could get out of your way for a few months. If that's what you want.'

'Where is it?'

'If tell you, I'll have to kill you.'

'Very funny. Is it dangerous?' I start crying again.

'Not much more than crossing the road.'

'I can't bear it that you could be hurt or dead and I wouldn't know. What if I heard about it from Barbara? Or Doreen offers you up as a choice bit of gossip? *Did you hear about that friend of Billy Boscawen who got blown up abroad? His dad is buried in our graveyard, you know.*'

I'm sobbing now. Jamie makes a gesture with his arms, and I press myself against his chest. I breathe him in. I want to remember this moment, the smell and the warmth of him, the texture of his jumper against my cheek, how good it feels to have his arms around me.

When I finally stop crying, I ask if I can take a photo of him. Just one. I sound mad, but I no longer care. He knows who I am. He knows how I feel. I'm glad I'm not trying to hide it any more.

'Do you want me to look towards you?'

'Yes.'

There is such warmth in his eyes. I can't bear that either.

'Look away.'

He looks out to where the sea is, though we can't see anything out of the steamed-up windows. I take the photo. And again. And again. Maybe it will pop up on my phone in the future and remind of what I had and what I lost. How will I feel when it does? Resigned, I hope, like it was long ago. A dream or a scene from a film. Something I imagined or that I consumed and forgot about. Not something that remains etched on my heart.

We pull up outside the vicarage, crunching over the gravel, the church bells ringing.

'What will you do now?' I ask. I'm delaying the moment. I know I just need to get out of his car, go back to my own life.

'I'll drive home,' he says. 'Feeling a bit sad.'

'Will you?' I'm glad to know I have meant something to him.

His smile and his voice are so tender. 'I thought we were at the beginning of something. Not the end.'

I have a last look at him. I lean over and put my lips to his cheek. I pause, feeling the warmth of his skin against mine. I want to stay here, joined to him, connected to him. I pull myself away, reach out for the handle. The door opens. I put one foot on the gravel.

'I'm not missing you yet,' I say. It's a line from a novel, but I can't remember which one. In the novel, the other character says, 'You will.'

Jamie says, 'I hope you don't.'

Twenty-Nine

Sam is watching a dragon set fire to a village with its breath.

'Aren't you cold, sweetheart?' I touch his bare foot. It's icy.

I make a couple of hot-water bottles and bring down Sam's duvet and a pair of socks. 'Let's make a cosy nest.'

'Don't we have to go to church?'

'I feel a bit sneezy. Shall we give ourselves a day off? Stay warm?'

'Yes!' He does a fist pump.

I hold out the socks.

'Can you do it, Mum?'

It's been a while. As I ease them on, I wonder how many times I've done this. Now his little baby feet are bigger than mine. Once I did everything for him, but now he can ask for what he needs or wants. This might be the last time ever that I put his socks on.

We snuggle under the duvet. I think of Jamie driving north in the rain. Windscreen wipers at the double. I can picture his hands on the steering wheel. He's taking a bit of my heart. But most of me is here, where I have chosen to be, with my boy. 'Tell me what's going on, Sam. Who is she again?'

'That's Tauriel. She's the captain of the Elven guard. She fell in love with Kili, but he's a dwarf. She saved his life when he was shot with a poisoned arrow. He's about to rescue her, but then he gets killed.'

We watch Kili sacrifice himself for Tauriel. She kisses his dead body, weeping. She says, 'If this is love, I do not want it. Take it from me, please.'

I feel my tears well up again.

Tauriel asks, 'Why does it hurt so much?'

Another elf says, 'Because it was real.'

'That's the king,' Sam says. 'Earlier he told her it wasn't real, that it was all in her head. He didn't want her to be in love with a dwarf. His son Legolas is in love with Tauriel too. But the king thinks she's not good enough for him.'

I lean back on the sofa. I'm so tired. 'That's a lot of love going on.'

'Only in the films,' Sam says. 'No one falls in love in the book.'

'What do they do instead?'

'Adventures, spiders, trolls, orcs, dragons, fighting, treasure. There's plenty to do without love.'

Stephen phones that evening from his car when Sam's in the bath and I'm halfway through the washing-up. He's in the shed, he says. He's been tidying up and he's about to flatten loads of cardboard boxes, if I wonder what the weird noise is.

'Sorry I haven't been in touch,' he says.

'I've been feeling the weight of your disapproval.' I hold the phone with my shoulder so I can carry on. 'I assumed that's what it was, not that you had actually died and Sarah didn't bother to tell me.'

He groans. 'I deserve that. I'm sorry. Sarah gave me a right old bollocking this morning when I told her we hadn't talked since half-term. The words "none of your business" featured strongly, and "You've only got one sister," and "Stop being such a judgemental twat, you judgemental twat."'

'Did Sarah really say "twat"?'

'I'm paraphrasing. Anyway, I *am* sorry and it *is* none of my business.'

'Thank you.' I put the last dish on the draining board. 'It's all over, anyway. Factory settings have been restored.'

'I'm relieved,' Stephen says, smugly.

I pull the plug. 'I don't feel happy about it.'

'Well, you won't, will you? That's what happens when people mess around.'

'Could you be a bit nicer to me?' I dry my hands on a tea towel. 'Dial down the judgemental twattery?'

I hear the clatter of him tramping on cardboard.

'I'm just saying a fact. No such thing as a free lunch. You can't have your cake and eat it. It will all end in tears.'

I throw the tea towel down by the washing machine. I'd quite like to throw a saucepan at Stephen's head. 'Have you turned into Mum?'

'Sorry. I'll shut up. Speaking of that particular devil, Mum sent my birthday present so early I didn't realise what it was and opened it.'

Mum has never sent my present early. Nor is there any variety. I always get a Boots voucher for twenty pounds, which I spend on functional toiletries for Sam and Tim. 'Go on. What is it?'

'A plate she made at her pottery class. Orange. The same colour as your lino. It says, *I'll meet you in the field beyond right and wrong.* What does that even mean?'

'Our curate says that. It's about not getting bogged down in whose fault something is. It's not a very Mum-like sentiment, to be honest.' Mum only ever goes to the field where she knows she is 100 per cent right.

'I don't know where to put it. It's not fired, so we can't get it wet. Sarah says she doesn't want any more of Mum's odd shit up in the house.'

'Why not put it on the wall of your office? You could read it out to complaining customers. Or stick it in the dishwasher by accident. That'll melt it.'

'Poor Mum.'

'Whatever. If you've got sympathy going spare, you could chuck a bit my way.'

'What for?'

It's not likely Sam will overhear, but I don't want to take the risk. I step out of the door and into the dark and cold. 'I'm sad, Stephen. I'm trying to do the right thing, but I'm sad.'

'You're not going to do what that bird does, are you?'

'What?' I reach up and fiddle with one of the pegs on the washing line.

'In that novel Liam bangs on about. The one they're

doing for book club, except it keeps getting shoved on another month because no one can get through it.'

'*Anna Karenina*?'

'That's the fella.'

I wonder why he is referencing Anna Karenina when we have our own home-grown example. Why does he not say, *Don't do what Dad did?* I flick the peg, try to make it whirl round in a circle. 'Of course I won't. I wouldn't do that to Sam.'

As I listen to him jump up and down on the cardboard, I know he is thinking about Dad doing that to us. I wonder how often we are both thinking about him but don't say so. I turn and look at the vicarage, at the spot through the kitchen window where I spend so much time.

'There,' Stephen says, with satisfaction. 'All done. Quite a manly job. Or as manly as I get in this post-industrial age.'

'Well done,' I say, 'And how are you getting on birthday-wise? Not long to go now.'

'I've not been so bad as it gets closer. It'll all be over one way or another.'

I'm too cold. I walk back towards the house. 'Good luck with working out what to do with your plate,' I say, as I go back into the kitchen. 'Looking on the bright side, if you do snuff it before your birthday, it won't be your problem any more, will it?'

He laughs and then we tell each other to fuck off and it feels like we are back on track.

Thirty

Father Robert dies on Monday, and Tim arrives home late that evening after Sam is in bed. He is pale but calm, not trapped in the usual vortex of undone jobs and irritations major and minor. He's carrying a suitcase that looks like a prop from a wartime film, with a long black cloak over his arm.

'Robert gave me his cassock,' Tim says, and I hang it up, trying not to wrinkle my nose or indulge in mean-spirited thoughts about having more of that damp, doggy, fag-ash smell to deal with.

'Hungry?' I ask instead, filling the kettle.

Tim nods and sits at the breakfast bar as I make scrambled eggs to Jamie's recipe, with lots of butter and no milk. I have no chives to chop and scatter. Tim thanks me when I put the plate in front of him, and I wash up the pan as he eats.

'Thank you,' he says again, after the last mouthful. 'That was really good.'

'I'm trying it a different way,' I say. 'Tell me about Father Robert. You're glad you went?'

Tim nods. 'I have never felt so close to God.' He looks at me as though he is asking for permission.

I sit on the other stool. 'I'd love to hear about it,' I say, and it is true.

'He was completely himself still. Frail, with bruises all over his arms and his breathing was laboured but he could talk. I gave him holy communion when I arrived, and we sat in silence together for a while. He said he felt a deep gratitude, to have spent his life in the service of God. And then he talked about his childhood. Being on that naval destroyer in 1945. He was four. He was given a teddy – he thinks by his stepfather, though he's not sure. He remembers his mother saying he had to change his name, that he couldn't be Siegfried any more, and that he mustn't speak German. She said to him, "Robert is an English boy. You need to forget about Siegfried and be Robert."'

'Poor little chap,' I say, thinking of Sam at that age, how scared young Robert must have been.

'His father was in the Wehrmacht. Killed during the war. The stepfather died in a car crash not long after they got to England, so then it was just the two of them.'

I try to imagine what life was like for that woman, all she must have seen during the war: widowed twice, raising a son in a foreign country.

'Then, yesterday morning, he asked me to anoint him. He said he was ready. So I did, and we prayed together. And as his voice faded, I carried on. From then, it was like he was drifting in and out. He said, "Go forth on your journey," a few times, and just after dawn today he said something in German. I didn't understand, but it sounded peaceful. And then he died, as the sun was coming through the window.'

I remember Tim coming home after first meeting Father Robert and saying he was full of God. He looks like that right now, illuminated from the inside.

'Were you up all night, then?' I ask. 'Aren't you tired?'

Tim rubs his forehead. 'I had an armchair. I dozed off every so often. I didn't want to leave him. It felt like a sacred task. To be with him.'

I put my hand over his. I can feel it. I don't know what it is exactly, just that there is a special quality in Tim tonight.

'He wants his real name on his gravestone,' Tim says, 'as well as his adopted name.'

'He wants to be reunited with himself.'

Tim looks at me. 'What?'

'People talk of being reunited with lost loved ones after death. But it was himself he lost on that ship when he was four. That's what he wants. He must have spent his whole life feeling incomplete.'

Tim nods. 'Yes, he said it stuck too well, that instruction to forget about Siegfried. He hardly ever told anyone. There was a girl he liked once, but he could never bring himself to confide in her, and she got engaged to someone else. He felt known by God, he said, but not by his fellow man.'

I am moved — by Father Robert's life and by Tim's witnessing of it, and because Tim and I are having what feels like a real conversation for the first time in years.

'He must have been lonely,' I say, 'but he felt known by you, didn't he?'

'He did. And me by him.'

'And you helped him to a good death.'

Tim fetches the suitcase from the corner and lifts it up. He takes out a small wooden box. 'He wanted me to give him communion from his set. And when we had finished he said, "And now it belongs to you."' Tim runs his fingers over the lid. 'It's made of olive wood. He bought it in the holy land not long after his ordination.' Tim opens it. 'But the chalice and patten are much older. He got them from an antique shop. They're engraved. Look.'

He gently tilts the chalice. It is a thing of beauty, delicate and simple, silver on the outside but with a gold sheen in the cup. There is a date: 1902. And the initials SH.

'His real name was Seigfried Hartman. He said when he found this, it felt like it was meant to be.'

I pat his arm. 'And now he's given it to you. How beautiful.'

'He said it made him happy that these objects would continue to serve God, that I would be their custodian as he had been, as the original SH had been.'

Tim reaches into the suitcase again and takes out a blue Danish butter biscuits tin.

'What's that?'

'Lucky.'

'What?'

'His dog. The stray who turned up at the church. The clever one who could take herself swimming. He called her Lazarus at first, he said, because she had looked so close to death. But once she was well and fed, Lucky suited her more.'

Until she got hit by that car, I think. Though I suppose she had a good bit of life until then.

'That was the main thing he wanted me for,' Tim says. 'More than communion, and prayer, and anointing, and both his names on the gravestone. He charged me with making sure Lucky's ashes are buried with him.'

'Is that allowed?' I ask.

'Not really,' Tim says. 'I mean, it isn't. I could ask the bishop. But he might say no. So I thought I'd just do it.'

I like this new version of Tim, full of meaning and purpose and prepared to break the rules to do the right thing.

'I've been thinking,' he said, 'of what you said. About our life. The way I am with Sam.'

'Don't worry about that now,' I say. And I mean it. I can see God in him; here in this funny, scruffy kitchen, I can see Tim is connected to the divine, whatever that means. I don't want to hook him back down to earth to rake over his shortcomings as a human and a husband.

'I want to,' he says. 'You're right. I don't know how to be a father. I told Robert some things. He said I should tell you. Can I?'

'Of course.'

Tim speaks in a rush, as though if he stops to consider he won't get it all out. 'My father didn't like me much. I don't know why. He hit me all the time. He didn't want my mother to interfere or show me any affection. "You'll spoil him," he'd say. "He's too namby-pamby."

320

She didn't stop him. Maybe she couldn't. She just said I should stay out of his way.'

Tim glances at me, quickly, and I see the shame in his eyes. I put my hand on his arm. It's rigid. His whole body must be braced.

'You're doing really well.' I stroke along his arm. 'Have a couple of breaths.'

He relaxes a little bit. 'Shall I carry on?'

'If you can.'

'He didn't beat me. And it never felt planned. Or even—' He stops. 'He just lashed out at me when he was in a bad mood. Which was often. He sent me flying. I had a black eye a few times. A cut lip. People must have known. I wasn't the sort of boy who was always falling out of trees.'

Tim puts his hand up to the side of his head. 'I've got a scar here. He knocked me against a table. I had to go to hospital for that one. Then they sent me away to school. I don't know if my mother was trying to protect me. Or just wanted me out of the way.' He looks at me. 'I don't hit Sam, do I? I've never hit Sam?'

He sounds like he is asking me rather than telling me.

'No, you haven't. You don't hit him. You are not a man who hits his child.'

He is crying. 'I'm sorry,' he says. 'He hated me crying. He used to say, "If you upset your mother, I'll give you something to cry about."'

I put my hand on his shoulder. 'My mum hated me crying. Told me off for it during Dad's funeral.'

'He did that too. I'd only come back from school the night before. I tried to hug him. I don't know why, because we never touched each other. I must have thought it was what you did when someone died. He sidestepped me and shook my hand. Told me to go to bed. The next morning he burnt the toast. I couldn't eat it, too dry. I could see he thought I was being soft. He said he hoped school had taught me some control. He said, "No one will want to watch you making a spectacle of yourself."'

And I see the boy in Tim then. Not that much older than Sam is now. Scared and sad and lonely and ashamed of all of it. Tim tries to stand, but I stop him, put my arms around him. And I'm not holding the man he is now, but the boy he was who needed some human affection. I stroke his hair as he weeps, thinking of the hidden scar beneath. How sad it is that there could exist in this world a child who only experiences the touch of their parent in violence, and that I could have lived all these years with Tim not knowing this about him. I feel the wet of his tears come through my shirt to my skin.

'Robert said I should tell you. I'm sorry. I should have told you before. When we met. But I didn't know how. And you were so . . . I hadn't thought I'd be able to get married or have a family, and then I met you and I thought I could. But maybe I was wrong. I'm sorry. I don't deserve you. You're a good person.'

And I feel like the world crashes in around my head. It's too late; we're too tired; I shouldn't rock the boat. But I open my mouth anyway. I say it. 'I'm not a good person, Tim.'

And then I tell him why.

Thirty-One

I don't tell him everything, just the bare facts. I say it happened in London at half-term and confess that Caroline doesn't exist. I don't tell him who it was; not for any reasons of my own, but because I don't want to make things awkward for Tim with Billy and Betsy. I tell him it has all stopped and don't pretend I did that for him or for any moral reason but admit I was scared I would get in too deep. 'It was for Sam really. I didn't like lying to Sam, or in front of him. I knew I couldn't have a life he wasn't part of.'

Tim nods. He looks tired, but he's not angry.

'You're taking it very calmly,' I say.

He reaches out his hand, gives me an awkward pat on the shoulder. '*Let he who is without sin cast the first stone.* You must have been unhappy. I'm sorry.'

And I think how strange he is, my husband, such an unusual man. I know what he'd order from a menu, and how he'd respond to a traffic jam, and what he'd do if a parishioner was in crisis. But I could never have anticipated such immediate and generous forgiveness.

We talk late into the night. Tim opens up more about his relationship with his parents, and I see that while I find our family life a bit joyless compared to my childhood, it is paradise in comparison to Tim's. I feel humbled that he has been carrying around all this pain and still putting so much effort into trying to do good in the world. I cry when he says he didn't know any kind of love until he came to God and found calm and safety in prayer. I admit to him that my own faith is tenuous and rocky, that I feel closer to God in the graveyard than in church, when Derek is making nit-picking announcements, or Doreen is testifying or asking people to pray she gets a good parking space at the supermarket. But that I'm not sure I believe at all, really.

Tim apologises for not being more present during Sam's birth and that I have so often felt neglected. When I say how hurt I was when he gave away the yellow pram, he tells me what I didn't want to hear at the time; about the woman he'd given it to, who'd been trafficked from her own country and was pregnant by an unknown father and adrift in a strange land. I shed more tears then, say I'm sorry I couldn't take her story in at the time. That, with almost a decade of hindsight, I'm pleased he gave her the pram, that I chose a father for my child who cares about other women and their children.

'I know I'm not good with Sam,' Tim says, 'but I don't think you want me to be involved with him.'

I take a deep breath. 'What happens, Tim, is you come home too exhausted to make an effort or cope when things don't go to plan. I need you to be loving with him. Don't just issue instructions and critique his behaviour. Be with him.'

'I don't know how.'

I lean forward and cover his hand with mine. 'That's because your dad didn't talk to you. But you can learn. You don't have to be perfect. Tell him why you believe the Bible but not Greek myths. Share your frustrations with him about politics and injustice. He's hungry for it.'

Tim nods.

'And he's got to be allowed to be himself. It's one thing me having to bend myself out of shape to be a Vicar's wife – not that I want to do that anymore – but it's not right to put pressure on Sam.'

He nods again. 'Yes, I see that.'

'He hasn't got a halo and isn't always easy, but he is a miraculous creation. And you are his father. You have everything you need to be a father to him.'

'I will try. I promise. And can I be a husband to you? Or is it too late?' His tone is neutral. He's not pleading, but there is a hint of humble curiosity in his demeanour. He's asking for my opinion, no more, no less.

'Oh, Tim.' I stand up. 'I don't know, is the honest answer. But let's be kind and gentle with each other. We've had a whole marriage's worth of chat in one night. Shall we see how we go?'

Tim stands too and we have a friendly hug, both yawning. I catch sight of our reflection in the window as we sway together, almost too tired to speak.

'I'll tell you what I am sure of,' I say, as I fill the kettle to make our hot-water bottles. 'We made an amazing child together. And it is really good to feel like we are on the same team. And there are worse places to be right now than in the kitchen of the New Vicarage in St Brida.'

Thirty-Two

I've almost finished ironing the altar cloth when Sam comes in from helping Barbara with her gardening jobs. He's rosy-cheeked and smells of fresh autumnal air.

'Where's Dad?'

'A wedding at St Anta.'

Sam gets a Tupperware out of his rucksack. 'Barbara said she's sorry there's only enough for one, but she knows Dad's keen on a crumble.'

He takes a five-pound note from his pocket. 'And she gave me this. I tried to say no. What should I do?'

I look at his sweet, worried face. 'Keep it. I bet she liked giving it to you.'

'That's what she said.'

'It's exciting, then. Your first wages. What did you do?'

As I carefully press the embroidered panel of the altar cloth, Sam explains how he had to throw all the apples behind the compost bins, then rake up the leaves and spread them on top. And be careful not to get stung.

'Barbara said there shouldn't still be wasps in November. It's a sign of the times. And her parents would be turning in their graves if they knew she was composting the windfalls, but the garden's too steep and her knees aren't up to it any more. She used to have a chap who took the apples for cider. But he died.'

'How sad,' I say, as I collapse the ironing board.

'She can't give them away. She says young people don't want to be bothered when you can buy a jar of filling from Iceland for a pound.'

I smile. 'That's true.'

'She's got a freezer full of sliced apples already. That's why she makes all those pies. And she said baking calms her down. So I don't think we can tell her to stop. We'll have to learn to like them.'

We take the altar cloth down to the vestry, then head to the dry cleaner's to drop off Father Robert's cassock so Tim can wear it at the funeral. It's all planned. The bishop is coming to do the eulogy, and there will be what Doreen calls a 'do' in the church hall afterwards.

When Tim went to see the funeral director, Rosie, carrying the butter biscuit tin, she already knew about Lucky and was ready to bend the rules. She'd got very fond of Father Robert over the years, she said; he'd always been supportive of her eco-friendly approach. She'll transfer Lucky into a biodegradable bamboo pouch, then slip her under Father Robert's joined hands.

Tim chose a seagrass coffin for Father Robert's last journey. They come in two shapes. He was about to opt for traditional, but when Rosie described the rounded shape as a bit like a giant Moses basket, he thought of Father Robert wanting to be reunited with his childhood self and plumped for that instead.

Barbara and Doreen have agreed to bury the hatchet out of respect for Father Robert. Derek told Tim they have at least one big argument every year and that no one can ever work out why. Tim thinks it's about the harvest festival, but I'm in Barbara's confidence. She swore me to secrecy, then told me she was fed up with Doreen being such a one for knowing things, and sticking her oar in. She panicked Ken about his nose, telling him his scaly patch was probably cancerous, when it was only a blemish. 'She should have minded her own ruddy business,' Barbara said to me. 'Ken hardly slept for the week before his doctor's appointment. And he's still having nightmares about his nose falling off.'

I expect the hatchet burying will be of short duration as Barbara is still furious and also disapproves that Doreen has dyed her hair turquoise because she fancied a change. Barbara thinks it would have been more respectful to go for a neutral colour for the funeral and has warned me off eating any of the food Doreen provides for the wake. 'I was in bed with a bilious attack for three days last Christmas after eating an M&S coleslaw round at her house. I don't trust her on sell-by dates.'

On our way back from the dry cleaner's, we call in at the bookshop. Sam looks at the Tolkien display in the back, and I browse cookery. I want to extend my repertoire as I'm fed up with mince, but all the books are a bit aspirational and glossy. What I really need is something called *Cheap, easy, non-depressing short recipes that are impossible to fuck up*. Or maybe I shouldn't bother. Sam did a lentil and bacon soup last week that he'd learnt at school, and Barbara is going to teach him to make pasties. Perhaps he'll soon be knocking up tea a couple of nights a week, and we can have toast the rest of the time.

Cheered by this excellent decision to turn my back on cookery, I pick up a promising-looking novel from the front table. I'm reading the back cover when the tall man behind the counter hangs up the phone a little too vigorously and says, 'Thanks for nothing.'

He catches me looking at him and apologises. 'My Christmas temp was supposed to start on Monday, but she's split up with her boyfriend and is moving back to Scotland. Why does she think I care about her love life? That's young people for you.'

'Does it leave you in a hole?' I ask, putting the book down.

'Yes,' he says gloomily. 'We're already one short for the Christmas rush. Maternity leave. Twins due on Boxing Day.'

I feel my heart beat a little faster. 'I don't suppose I could apply, could I?'

The man looks me up and down. 'You don't come across like an axe murderer. Any experience?'

'I've never worked in a shop,' I admit. 'But I'm a librarian.'

330

He doesn't look impressed. 'Not always friendly, are they? Can you smile? That's a great advantage in a retail environment.'

I give him a huge grin.

'And you wouldn't yawn behind the desk, would you? That's my pet hate.'

'Never.' I shake my head energetically and try to look very awake.

'What if you were on your own with a queue and the phone started ringing?'

'I wouldn't pick it up,' I say. 'I'd deal with the people first.'

He seems to like that, but it's hard to tell. He's not following his own guidance about the importance of smiling in a retail environment.

'Would you turn up on time? That's the main thing. Even if people are useless, they need to be on time.'

I decide to take a risk. 'Sounds to me like you've been traumatised by rubbish employees.'

He nods. 'You wouldn't believe what I've had to put up with over the years. I've got a nice bunch now, but it's a big risk taking on someone new.'

'If you take a chance on me,' I say, feeling like I am about to burst into song, 'I promise I'll be enthusiastic, polite, resourceful, punctual, and you'll be really pleased I happened to be here when you got that phone call.'

He almost smiles and tells me his name is Mike. We're shaking hands when Sam comes back down the stairs. I beckon him over. 'This is my son, Sam. He has an encyclopaedic knowledge of *The Hobbit*.' I put my arm around him. 'I'm asking for a job, sweetheart.'

'Here?' His eyes widen. 'That would be great.'

Mike looks down at him. 'Do you think she'll be any good?'

'My mum,' says Sam, 'knows everything about books.'

'And is she good at talking to people?'

'Oh, yes.' He nods. 'Even when she doesn't like them.'

And that seals the deal.

Thirty-Three

We stand by the lychgate, waiting for Father Robert to arrive.

'We've got a lovely day for it,' Barbara says, looking up at the clear-blue sky. 'Cold and crisp.'

'It's a good job,' says Doreen, pulling her coat more closely around her. 'That path down to the church gets slippery in the rain.' She lowers her voice and inclines her head to the group of men standing on the other side. 'And some of the pallbearers aren't as young as they were.'

'None of us are as young as we were,' Tim says, and Doreen and Barbara nod solemnly, as though he has said something wise and spiritual. He does look impressive today. Father Robert's cassock suits him. And smells fresh.

We hear the noise of traffic from beyond the corner.

'This might be it,' Barbara says, and we all look towards the bend in the road, but it's a recycling van. *Don't bin me!* it says in big red letters, next to pictures of an egg carton, a cereal box and a milk bottle.

'Blast,' says Doreen, 'I knew I'd forgotten something. What with all the excitement.'

'Look' – Barbara points – 'the hearse is behind. There's not enough room to overtake.'

'I don't want to get stuck behind a recycling van on my final journey,' Doreen says. 'I don't want to have to wait as it keeps stopping to pick up empty beer bottles and baked bean tins.'

'You won't know about it if you do,' Barbara says.

'I might. I might be looking down on you all.'

Barbara raises an eyebrow at me, and I try to keep a straight face. I'm sure Doreen will love being dead if it means she can get her nose even more thoroughly into everyone else's business.

Tim raises his arm, looking a bit like he is hailing a taxi.

The car pulls up, and the coffin is transferred to the stone platform in the lychgate. The greenish blue of the seagrass is beautiful, and we stand around it, heads bowed, as people have done here for centuries past.

There's a moment, as the pallbearers shift the coffin onto their shoulders, when I think they are going to drop it. But they don't.

'Steady,' Tim says, 'there's no hurry.'

And we move down the path towards the church.

The service goes off well. Tim is perfect, and Bishop David does a splendid job of the eulogy. He talks about Father Robert's life of service, but the most moving part – I am not the only one to cry – is where he describes his early years, and draws a connection between the man who everyone knew and loved and the refugee children of today, who, through no fault of their own, have no homes and can find no safety.

In the church hall afterwards, everyone flocks around Bishop David, pressing him to take more tea or another sausage roll. Barbara is flustered and girlish, holding out her plate of apple pie as though she's offering it to Jesus.

'No, no,' he keeps saying, patting his non-existent belly. 'Very tempting, but Louise has her eye on my blood pressure.'

Mrs Holt is looking glamorous in a silver-and-black leopard-print coat with beautifully manicured hot-pink nails. She says she feels so well that she's decided to give her granddaughter her small inheritance now: 'I don't want her hanging around waiting for me to die.'

Doreen offers us a tray of buttered malt loaf and says her big news is that she's taking on a miniature York-shire terrier called Binky. 'My son got her to save his marriage, but she has fits so can't be left. She'll have to come everywhere with me.' She sounds both gleeful and aggressive. 'Weddings and funerals. I'll have to bring her to church. She literally can't be alone for a second.'

I catch Barbara's eye. We both know Doreen is de-lighted to have an excuse to secure continual pet church for herself and is heading off any potential complaints.

Mrs Holt asks me about the bookshop, and I'm saying how much I love my new job when Doreen interrupts, 'I was in there the other day, and none of the Advent calendars have a religious theme. Not one!'

'You've got to move with the times, Doreen,' Barbara snaps. 'Not be so stuck in your old ways.'

Doreen twitches and takes a bite of malt loaf, leaving tooth marks in the butter.

Barbara continues, 'I must say, I think it's a crying shame there are no Mindful Mondays in December because Bryony is running the Advent course in that time slot. I don't need to "Come to the Manger!" I know all about Advent already.'

'Well,' Doreen says, still chewing, 'I think Advent is much more important than deep breaths into the tummy and all that guff about white light.'

I fear the truce might be about to end, but then we all notice Sam is by the door looking around rather shyly. Tim has spotted him too, and comes across from the other side of the hall.

Mrs Holt tells Sam how handsome and grown-up he looks in his school uniform. Doreen explains about Binky and asks if he might be interested in an occasional dog-walking job, and Barbara says he can't do it on Saturday mornings because he's helping her in the garden.

'He's been very good with the windfalls. I'll do you a bit of baking later,' Barbara says to Sam. 'You like my apple pie, don't you?'

I feel his hand slip into mine and decide that now is not the time for honesty. I would eat Barbara's apple pie every day of my life rather than let on to Doreen that we don't enjoy it.

'We love it,' I say.

'Actually, Barbara,' Tim says, 'can I make a request? I hope you don't think I'm ungrateful. Would you leave the clove out? Reminds me of having toothache when I was a boy.'

'My father used to say sucking on a clove was better than any modern painkiller,' Barbara says, happily. 'But it's not to everyone's taste. I'll try it with a bit of cinnamon instead. Or nutmeg. Pastry all right, is it? I think my Rayburn might be slowing down. Give it a bit extra in the oven if you think it needs it.'

And then she gives us a merry wave and trots off, and Tim takes Sam to meet the bishop.

'The heartburn I had after her mince pies last year,' Doreen grumbles. 'She's not as good at pastry as she thinks she is. And she makes too many. Never trust a mince pie after Boxing Day, I say. They've been hanging around too long.'

Then she asks if I know what's happened to the service booklets for Advent. She's pretty sure they were in a cardboard box in the vicarage. Can she pop round for a look?

'Anything church-related is kept here now,' I say firmly. 'Except Tim, of course.'

Doreen roars as if I have made the funniest joke in the history of the world, and moves on with her malt loaf.

Mrs Holt gives me a conspiratorial smile. 'It's good you've got that job. They'll all take advantage otherwise. Even that husband of yours. He does a good funeral, I must say. Got him in the right grave, too. I've already bought my plot here, you know, so he'll be doing me when the time comes.'

'Not for a while yet, I hope.'

'I've got a few years left in me.' Mrs Holt rests her pink nails on my arm and lowers her voice. 'They thought I'd had a heart attack, but now they say it might have just been blood pressure. A big fuss about nothing. Not that I tell people. I like Father Tim to get the credit for the deathbed miracle.'

I smile. 'That's kind of you.'

'Not really,' she winks. 'I like making them jealous, these boring women. There's nothing they'd all love more than to have the vicar bring them back to life.'

Tim, Sam and I escort Bishop David and Louise back to the car park, but they've been blocked in by a badly parked fish van so we all end up in our kitchen.

As I fill the kettle, Bishop David asks, 'Any chance of a proper drink?'

Tim gives me an anguished look, and I remember Stephen coming around with the remains of his holiday drinks cupboard.

'Gin and tonic?' I suggest. 'Or my brother gave me a bottle of Scotch, if you like a single malt.'

'Why not?' The bishop rubs his hands. 'Just a drop to keep the cold out.'

'I'm driving,' says Louise. 'But I'd love a strong cup of tea.'

As I sort out the drinks, Tim tells Bishop David that he is trying to get the bus stops changed to improve access to the food bank.

'That's a great idea, Dad,' says Sam.

'I agree,' says the bishop. 'What a practical difference to make to people's lives.'

Louise asks Sam how he's getting on at school.

'It's OK,' Sam says, lightly, 'but I'm no good at anything.'

'You will be,' says the bishop. He drops a friendly hand on Sam's shoulder. 'And we all worry we're not good enough, but it's worth remembering that Jesus was a failure in lots of ways. He ended up being crucified and all his friends ran away.'

'That hasn't happened to me yet,' Sam says.

'Tell Bishop David your thoughts about the Garden of Eden, Sam,' Tim says, encouragingly, and I nearly fall over.

'I think it wasn't very nice,' Sam says. 'If you don't want someone to do something bad, you shouldn't make it easy for them to do it.'

'Do you think it was a trick?'

'If God really didn't want Adam and Eve to eat the apple, he should just have hidden the tree at the corner of the garden and not drawn attention to it.'

Louise laughs. 'That's a good point, Sam. Now, speaking of gardens, do you think if we wrap up warm you could show me yours before it gets dark?'

Louise and I put on our coats and go outside. Sam runs off to the camellia, and we stand by the washing line and watch him.

'What a lovely boy. He's a real bundle of energy.'

339

'He struggles to sit still in church.'

'Our son was just the same. Always wandering off. He tipped over an enormous Advent display once because he couldn't resist dipping his fingers in the candle wax.' She sighs. 'He's a paramedic now. I look at him and have no idea where all the time has gone.'

Sam is climbing in the camellia and rocking the branches around.

'I never know if I should let him do that,' I admit.

'Boys are more important than bushes. Let him have a bit of fun. It's hard when everyone thinks your dad is public property and expects you to behave yourself.'

'Thank you,' I say, warmly. 'That's good advice. He said the other day that being a vicar's son is like doing full-time RE out of school.'

Louise smiles, and I think she's considering adding something, but then the kitchen window opens and Tim pokes his head out to say the van has gone, and their exit is now clear.

'You've got a private washing line, anyway,' Louise says. 'That's a boon. In our first parish, I had to hang my smalls on the inside of the whirligig because I didn't want everyone looking at my knickers.'

We wave them off, and as we walk back into the kitchen, Tim tells us that Bishop David doesn't see his priesthood as dispensing wisdom from on high, but about learning to be a better person.

'That sounds less stressful than trying to have all the answers,' I say.

'He said demands on Christian leaders are soul-destroying. It's a constant struggle to keep a sense of joy in his ministry and to stay connected to what matters.'

'You do your best, Dad.' Sam pats Tim on the arm in a gesture that is both awkward and mature.

'I'm sorry if I'm grumpy sometimes.'

'You're not that bad,' Sam says.

Tim continues, 'Bishop David says he's seen it happen again and again in the church, how one person's vocation and commitment can suffocate their family. He says he must always remember he is called to be a husband and father as much as he is to do God's work. And it is doing God's work to accept himself as a deeply flawed human being, even as he seeks the divine.'

Clever old Bish, I think, dispensing advice so effectively that Tim hardly noticed he was getting it.

Later that evening, I'm washing up, Tim is drying, and Sam is peeling a satsuma by the bin.

'You dropped a bit of peel,' says Tim, gesturing to the lino.

'I'm eating an orange of my own accord, Dad,' says Sam. 'I think that's what you should be focusing on.'

I look across at Tim. His expression is hard to read. I wonder if he is thinking of his own father, of the impossibility of ever saying anything like that to him.

Tim laughs.

And Sam picks up the peel and puts it in the bin.

Cornwall, December 2019

Thirty-Four

On Stephen's birthday, he texts me first thing to confirm that he's outlived our father and survived into his forty-fifth year. I'm not surprised, but I do have a little weep as I reply with rows of hearts and party poppers. Then – without thinking about it – I lift my eyes from the phone screen to the heavens and send a little prayer asking that there is ease and comfort in the future for my lovely brother, that he can find a way to wrestle his demons and move more smoothly through his life.

We have breakfast in the kitchen as Sam uses my phone to send Stephen a birthday video. Then Tim announces that he's planning to do Friday fasts all through Advent.

This is the moment. I need to seize it. I take a deep breath. 'I don't think that's a good idea.'

Tim looks surprised. He starts to talk about spiritual preparation and penance and purification, and the horrors of consumer capitalism, but I cut him off. 'Sorry, Tim, I'm sure you're right about all that. But you're too busy in December to not eat properly.'

He says something about personal sacrifice, and I interrupt again. 'You can be as willing as you like, but Sam and I are the ones who'll have to cope when you're in a bad mood because you're hungry as well as exhausted.'

Tim stares at me open-mouthed and I think I'm going to have to invoke Bishop David, but then I see the penny drop.

'I'm called to be a husband and father, too,' he says, like he's reciting a lesson. 'Is that it?'

I nearly try one of Sam's fist pumps. It occurs to me that it might also be better for Tim's ministry to accept every gaudily wrapped chocolate offered in the next few weeks with enthusiastic thanks rather than lecturing the giver on the real meaning of Advent, but I suddenly notice the clock. 'Yikes, I'd better get a move on. I'm working an early shift today to help with the Christmas windows. I don't want to break my promise to Mike to be the most punctual person he's ever employed.'

The window display looks fantastic, and I have lots of enjoyable chats with customers, taking compliments about it – 'I just handed stuff to Mike, really.'

Barbara pops in just before lunchtime and spends ages in the religious section. She wants to read up on Buddhism, she says. And reincarnation. She's already told Ken not to kill the spiders that come up through the plughole, and to stop using the manual mower because it decapitates glow worms. But she's not sure the book is right. She'll think about it.

Then Doreen turns up. 'Say hello to Binky,' she says. She turns around, and I see a little dog behind the see-through panel of her backpack. I can't see much of Binky because of the enormous holly-patterned ribbon giving her a sort of ponytail sticking up on her head.

'What a dear little creature,' I say, and then notice Doreen is sporting a bit of the same ribbon in her hair. It doesn't go brilliantly with the turquoise. Doreen launches into how she's already peeled and par-boiled her potatoes for Christmas Day and put them in the freezer. Her son has invited her for Boxing Day, but she won't stay overnight because she doesn't trust the bedding will be fresh. She could take her own sheet to put over the top but do I think he'll be offended if he finds out?

'Sorry, Doreen,' I say, 'I've got a customer,' and it is highly satisfying to leave her standing there and go to help a woman in a pink bobble hat decide which literary jigsaw would most suit her bookish niece.

After lunch, Derek pops in for a birthday card. He's got a glut of yacons at the allotment. Should he drop a couple in? Easy and versatile. You can slice them in a salad or eat them as a snack. I accept and he tells me he's not looking forward to Christmas. 'My sister-in law is coming, who nobody likes. And my son's adopted daughter has got Alzheimer's.'

'Has she?'

He frowns. 'Maybe not that, but something like that.'

Barbara comes back just before I finish my shift. She's decided to go for it with the Buddhist book. 'If I can get reincarnated, I'd like to come back as a garden bird for the healthy outdoor life.'

I'm not sure it works like that, but I don't say anything.

When I hand over her change, Barbara says she's happy to take back the church laundry, now that I've got this job. If that would suit me.

'That would be magnificent,' I say. And it would. I hate doing that fiddly altar cloth. I come out from behind the counter and walk her to the door. 'Shall I tell you a secret, Barbara? I'm not very good at ironing.'

'You won't be, will you?' Barbara smiles and pats my arm. 'You're an intellectual. Your mind wants to be on higher things.'

'Gosh,' I say. 'I've never been called an intellectual before.'

'That's what Lillian Holt said when she rang me about the laundry. And she's right – you've got enough else on.' Barbara opens the door. 'She offered to do it herself, you know. I couldn't believe it. But I wouldn't trust her not to put the whole lot in with a pair of red knickers. So I said she could leave it to me.'

As I walk home, I call Stephen. He's had a delightful birthday, he says: a day off work and a fancy lunch with Sarah, who gave him a bottle of poo drops. 'How civilised is that? You squirt them down the bog with a little glass dropper. Nice citrusy smell. Now even my shit won't stink.'

I won't tell Tim about them, I think. They might tip him into the same despair for humanity that he experienced when he first learnt about Advent calendars for adults.

'And I'm well chuffed with my wifi-enabled Christmas lights. I can operate them from my phone. No more scrabbling under the tree trying to turn them off at the wall. No more arguments in bed. *Did you turn the tree lights off? Can't remember. Did you? Go and check. It's cold, I don't want to. Well, one of us has to so we don't burn the house down.*'

'Do houses burn down when people leave their tree lights on?'

'Fuck knows. But ours won't. And we planned our New Year's Eve over lunch. We're throwing a dinner party to say goodbye to this greedy, soulless decade. That's one of Liam's things. He's quoting some poet who said it about the thirties. Do you think things can get better?'

'I hope so,' I say, trying to suppress a pang at the thought of Stephen's last dinner party and how much I would like to sit opposite Jamie again. 'We need to find a way to be optimistic, don't we? Especially with kids. It's important to be hopeful about them and the world and the future.'

Stephen makes a noise of assent, though he doesn't sound convinced.

I walk past the entrance to the pier. A busker is murdering 'In the Bleak Midwinter'. 'And how do you feel?'

'Pretty good, actually. Hang on.' I hear the clunk of the French windows, can picture him stepping past the blue sofa and out into the garden. Maybe he's leaning against the shed or standing next to the rose trellis.

'I don't think I'm going to die any more. All that terror has just lifted away.'

His voice sounds lighter than it has for months.

'And I thought about what you said. So I told Sarah everything over lunch. And I'm going to have therapy. Sarah says she'll find me someone. There are different types. You don't just rock up at the mental equivalent of Kwik Fit and ask for your head to be fixed.'

'Good luck. If it works, maybe I'll try it too.'

'There's not much wrong with you, is there?'

I can hear the fear in Stephen's voice. And I feel it in my body. The breathlessness, the churn in my belly. My instinct is to reassure him, but I don't.

'I know how to dodge it,' I say. 'Most of the time. When I'm not crying on the floor. I know how to keep myself upright. But we step around each other too, don't we? On the minefield of our childhood, what happened to Dad, what Dad did. Maybe we don't have to be like that.'

I look out across the harbour at the lights twinkling in the dusk.

'Fair enough,' Stephen says, eventually. 'This is all a bit heavy, isn't it? Shall I chuck in a couple of knob gags for a bit of light relief?'

I laugh.

'Actually, I've got another serious thing to say. I'm

sorry I was shitty about your man. I told Sarah about my apology, and she said it was a non-apology. Was it?'

'Probably. You were right though. It was mad to think I could have a casual fling and that it wouldn't affect my relationship with Sam.'

'Well, I'm properly sorry. You're not too sad?'

I allow it in for a few seconds. The memory of how I felt with Jamie. The sorrow that I can't have him in my life. 'Sometimes. But I know I've done the right thing, so that helps. I try to keep busy and look on the bright side. We've got a delightful new neighbour called Kim. Sam has made great pals with her son, Jake. They hit each other with sticks and discuss whether they'd prefer to be burnt at the stake or hung, drawn and quartered. And I love my job in the bookshop. Mike has already asked me to stay on. They're opening a cafe and events space in the spring.'

'That's right up your street,' Stephen says. 'And how are things with you and Tim?'

'He's been kind and forgiving. Sam doesn't have to come to church anymore but he and Tim talk. The other day I heard Sam say he felt sorry for God, that he had all these awful human beings doing terrible things in his name.'

'He's such a great kid. Hey, you'll never guess who I saw. I was having lunch with a client, and this woman came over and said, "Stephen Barry, as I live and breathe."'

'Who?'

'Kitty Graham.'

I struggle for a moment. 'My old friend Kitty Graham? What's she doing now? Presumably she didn't become prime minister, or I'd have heard about it.'

'Works in HR. Getting divorced for the second time. Says she's done with men, but I'm pretty sure she was giving me the eye.'

'You weren't tempted, I hope?'

'My younger self was saying, "Get in, my son," but I showed her photos of the kids, which is always a good strategy if things get accidentally flirtatious. Any stirrings of lust were quashed by me making her watch a video of Alice playing the saxophone.'

'Did she ask about me?'

'I told her you live in an idyllic seaside setting with a delightful son and a husband who is a good man.'

'I suppose that's all true.'

'And that you minister to the poor and are so beloved in the congregation that they would cough up for a tribute to you if you died.'

'Really?'

'Of course not. But I didn't tell her how cross you get about having to make scones and listen to people bang on about their problems.'

'I do not!'

'I don't blame you. Hang on. Sarah's waving at me. She wants a word.'

I hear the French windows again as Stephen carries me back into the house. I picture Sarah standing at her kitchen island in her stripy apron, surrounded by aubergines and red peppers and jars of sauerkraut.

'I thought you'd like to know that we finally had the *Anna Karenina* book club.' Her voice sounds lighter too, as she tells me that only Sandeep managed to read the whole thing, but none of them could bear the thought of postponing again and having to roll it over to another year.

'Did it help Liam with his novel?'

'We put him off. We all understood Anna preferring Vronsky to the boring knuckle-cracking husband, but none of us got why she had to kill herself when it went wrong. Sandeep said that if Liam wanted to create an homage, he should read *Frenchman's Creek*, where the heroine has a high old time with the sexy pirate and doesn't get punished at all. Then Suzannah asked why he had to base his novel on something else. Could he not make something up from scratch? Then he muttered something about seeking the security blanket of structure and went home.'

'Oh dear,' I say. 'I do feel a bit sorry for him.'

'Juliet's relieved. He's hard to live with when writing a novel.'

I open the church gate and walk up the steps.

'Suzannah's got a new chap. He's a farmer down your way. She was unsure about the lifestyle, but he's keen to commit, so she's bought some wellies and is keeping an open mind.'

'Good for her.' I sit on my bench, wrapping Jamie's scarf a bit more tightly around my neck. 'Stephen says he confessed all to you over lunch. I hope you're not angry I didn't tell you what was going on.'

'Sweetheart,' she cries, and I hear all the warmth and love in her voice. 'Of course you couldn't break his confidence. And he's giving you full credit for having got him through the last few months. Says he has no idea what he'd do without you.'

My eyes fill. My little brother. All through our lives, taking it in turns to lean and be leant upon. 'It's not weird for you?' I ask Sarah. 'That we're so close.'

'It is sometimes a bit odd,' she says slowly, as though she is figuring it out, 'that my best friend is my husband's sister, and that I'm married to the brother of my best friend. But given the vast joy you both bring me, how can I be anything other than grateful?'

It's getting dark as I walk up through the churchyard, past poor long-dead Jane and her husband and all those children. Tim has been so calm and settled lately that it wouldn't surprise me if he stayed here for ever, and ended up buried not far from all the other vicars and Father Robert and Lucky.

I don't know if I'll be sharing Tim's grave. I suspect he'll always think life is a rehearsal space for the kingdom of heaven, and I'll always want life to be the main event, not a trial or a warm-up for something that I don't really believe exists.

We're still in the single beds, and Tim has admitted he'd forgotten to let anyone know about the collapsed ceiling. I'd have been so angry and upset by that a few months ago, but I just thought it was funny. He has reported it now, so at some point it will get fixed, and

I'll have to decide what to do about the fact that I don't want to be in a double bed with anyone but Jamie.

I pause in front of Rosina Lucy, and picture Jamie standing in the sunlight. I don't regret any moment of being with him. Even if I never see him again, I'm glad I experienced it, that feeling of safety and desire and curiosity. I'm glad I know how it can be, between two people, when everything feels right. I have a little peep at his photo every so often and wished him luck when he texted me to say he'd be out of the country for at least six months. Sometimes I wonder where he is and if he thinks of me. It did feel real, whatever it was, and I know he felt it too. I've no idea what happens in the future. Right now that isn't important. My job is to be with Sam. There might come a time when he needs me less and I could choose another life, but I am not – I can't allow myself to be – in a hurry to get there.

So I don't know if I'll always be Tim's wife, or if I'll ever be anything to Jamie. But I will always be Sam's mother. And Stephen's sister. And my dad's daughter. Those relationships do endure, even beyond death. I look down at Rosina and wonder who she loved. They never got a mention on her grave but what led her to want to lie underneath those words? *Brief is life but long is love.*

A robin alights on the headstone.

'Hello,' I say. 'Are you looking for juicy worms?'

He tilts his head at me.

I remember Barbara and her theory of soul carriers. I feel silly but decide to go for it. Maybe that is what faith is, after all. 'Thanks for being my dad,' I say. 'For being so funny and kind.'

And I fill up with the pain of it all: the missing, the wrongness. Always wishing things had been different, this yearning for a life unmarred. And I could collapse into it. But I don't. I don't want to sink. I don't want to be stuck.

'I'm sorry you couldn't stay around,' I whisper. And then I know what to do. I sing, slowly and softly, the second verse of 'Danny Boy', about the grave being warmer and sweeter. And I start on 'The Foggy Dew', but after the first verse I can't remember the words, so I skip to my favourite lines, as I remember him singing them; my dear father, standing, hand over his heart: *But to and fro in my dreams I go, and I kneel and pray for you.* I can't think what comes next. But the last note echoes among the trees, among the graves, between the living and the dead. I hold out my palm towards the robin. He looks at it, considering, then tilts his head and flies off. And I laugh, standing there in the graveyard. I lift my hands to the skies and I laugh.

I find them in the sitting room. Father and son. On the sofa, sharing a packet of jam tarts. Sam in his Hog-warts hoodie, Tim still wearing his dog collar. I can see dwarves feasting on the screen.

I lean over and ruffle Sam's hair, rest my hand for a moment on Tim's shoulder. 'I thought goblins weren't your thing?'

'Sam persuaded me. I'm enjoying it. Gandalf knows what he's talking about. He says our only duty is to decide what to do with the time given to us. I might put that in a sermon.'

Sam elbows him in the ribs. 'You can just watch the film, Dad. Not everything has to be turned into a sermon.'

'That's true,' Tim says. He sounds surprised, as though he has never quite appreciated this before.

I leave them to it. There's an hour until I need to think about feeding us all. I could have a hot bath with my book and an enormous cup of tea. As I fill the kettle, I think that what I most want from this world is to be with my son as he grows into himself. And I have that. Maybe not for ever, but I have it for today.

Cathy Rentzenbrink is the author of the novel *Everyone Is Still Alive* and several acclaimed works of non-fiction including the *Sunday Times* bestseller *The Last Act of Love*.

Credits

Phoenix would like to thank everyone at Orion who worked on the publication of *Ordinary Time*.

Agent
Rachel Mills

Lucy Bilton
Claire Boyle

Editor
Francesca Main

Audio
Paul Stark
Louise Richardson

Copy-editor
Claire Gatzen

Georgina Cutler

Contracts
Dan Herron

Proofreader
Donna Hillyer

Ellie Bowker
Oliver Chacón

Editorial Management
Clarissa Sutherland
Alice Graham
Jane Hughes
Charlie Panayiotou

Design
Nick Shah
Charlotte Abrams-
    Simpson

Joanna Ridley
Helen Ewing

Photo Shoots & Image Research
Natalie Dawkins

Finance
Nick Gibson
Jasdip Nandra
Sue Baker
Tom Costello

Inventory
Jo Jacobs
Dan Stevens

Production
Hannah Cox
Katie Horrocks

Marketing
Ellie Nightingale

Publicity
Aoife Datta

Sales
Catherine Worsley
Victoria Laws
Esther Waters
Tolu Ayo-Ajala
Group Sales teams
across Digital, Field,
International and Non-
Trade

Operations
Group Sales Operations
team

Rights
Rebecca Folland
Tara Hiatt
Ben Fowler
Alice Cottrell
Ruth Blakemore
Marie Henckel